MIDNIGHT MATTRESS

AUSTIN MOONEY

TREPIDATIO
PUBLISHING

"Wax" first published in print in *Year Four* (Black Hare Press, 2022) and online in "Trembling with Fear" (The Horror Tree, 2022).

ISBN: 978-1-68510-132-9 (tpb)
ISBN: 978-1-68510-133-6 (ebook)

First printing edition: August 23, 2024
Printed by Trepidatio Publishing in the United States of America.
Cover Artwork: Don Noble
Edited by Sean Leonard
Proofreading, Cover Layout, & Interior Layout by Scarlett R. Algee

Trepidatio Publishing, an imprint of JournalStone Publishing
511 Deer Lake Drive West
Carbondale, Illinois 62901

Trepidatio books may be ordered through booksellers or by contacting:
or
JournalStone | www.journalstone.com

This book is dedicated to cats and dogs. You're all doing a wonderful job.

Contents

MIDNIGHT MATTRESS

Moss

SUNLIGHT SOAKED THROUGH the fabric of its brilliantly clear liquid body, and the moss ball suspended within it glowed a fantastic hue of lime green that Luke had never seen. He had received a mysterious package in the mail this morning, which contained the smart little clear container filled with water and carrying a soft moss ball about the size of a nickel. There was no return address to be found on the package. It was wrapped in brown paper with a neat tweed string knot on top. The only information accompanying it was a small card describing the moss.

Screaming Moss
Found in the depths of Iceland's most remote lakes,
Screaming Moss is named for its loud lime-green hue and
the "screaming" sound it produces when it dries out.
Keep in fresh water and clean container daily.

Luke assumed it must have been a gift from one of his friends. He had gone to the Saturday Market with a modest group of them the previous weekend. Local artists, food vendors, gardeners, and craftsmen from the surrounding area come together in a small clearing by Lake Donovan every Saturday to sell their wares. It has primarily become a place for locals to take visiting family from out of town to give them a taste of the city, but some discoveries surprise even the oldest frequenters. On this particular afternoon, Luke saw a new booth selling moss balls.

His friends were surprised when he earnestly commented that he would like to purchase a moss ball. They scrunched their faces and looked at him, confused. They asked him why he would want something so useless.

"It's not useless," he replied. "It's like a pet."

The group's movement kept him from exploring the booth further than a passing glance and a light remark. The man maintaining the temporary storefront was mostly hidden, sitting behind his neatly uniform displays. The top of his head was all they could see. Curly gray hair stretched toward the sky. He appeared to be looking down at his lap, and Luke got the disturbing feeling that he could hear them discussing his passion. They swiftly moved away from the booth and joined the wandering crowd, the moss balls quietly dissolving behind them.

Luke thought it was lovely of his friends to send him something so thoughtful for no reason other than his expressed interest in it. He would need to find out who had sent it and return the favor somehow, but for now, he needed to find a place to display his newest friend. It deserved prominence in his home.

The container made an excellent decoration on his desk. Clean, modern, and containing a living organism, it was a perfect new addition to the shrine of personal objects that kept Luke calm during his working hours. It quickly became his most prized possession, and he loved it as though it were a proper pet. However, the day after he received it, he realized how strictly the instructions for cleaning the container were meant to be followed.

Black slime and waste lined the container in a thin glossy film. The moss ball was rotting away its already crowded habitat and suffocating itself with its own refuse. Luke gasped upon seeing it and took it into the kitchen. He removed the container's lid and poured the ball into his hand. The fuzz tickled his palm. He placed it on a plate and began scrubbing the container with soap and hot water, assuming the ball would be fine for the moment it took him to complete his chore. He did not consider putting it into another container of water. He let it sit, drying on the plate. What harm could a couple minutes bring?

The moss ball began to change shape, vibrating with a lime-green color that was becoming more intense, draped in the fading sheen of its drying skin. At first, it appeared to be shriveling. Then the wrinkles found definition. The features of a face, an older man's face, formed across the fuzzy surface of the moss ball as its hot emerald glow became harder and harder to bear with naked eyes. Once the exclamation of its color reached a fever pitch and the face fully formed, its features shook with intent and involuntary spasms. Then the screaming began.

A blaring, sharp, agonizingly evil and terribly distressing expulsion of energy in the form of a scream filled the room and knocked Luke backward. Sonic boom. Its mouth appeared to be open, but whether the screaming had waited for that detail to begin wreaking havoc was unclear. Did the moss ball need its mouth to scream? How could it make a sound like that?

Luke's mind clumsily rattled and raced for a solution. He quickly filled a cup with water and dropped the moss ball, with the explosive flush of energy still venting out of it, inside. The screaming ended as it gently sank to the bottom. The face faded away, and the color returned to its typical hue. The wrinkles smoothed out. It was a standard moss ball again.

He wasn't worried about his neighbors' reactions to the noise. They wouldn't react even if it was a person. He shuddered to imagine this situation occurring during one of the many days his landlord shut off the water in his apartment complex for one reason or another without warning. After taking a moment to catch his breath and lower his heart rate, Luke telephoned a friend who was with him on that Saturday afternoon at the market.

"What's up?" Sarah answered.

"Hey," Luke said before taking a moment to touch his ear and lament the damage done to his hearing. "Did you send me a moss ball in the mail?"

"No," Sarah laughed. "Do you want me to?"

"I got one yesterday, and I don't know where it came from. I didn't order it, and there's no return address, but it's addressed to me. So I thought maybe because we saw that moss ball stand at Saturday Market, and I said I liked moss, you guys sent me a moss ball."

"Oh, that would have been nice. I wish I had done that. Sorry."

"Do you know who did?"

"Nobody said anything to me about it, but we were with Keith and Jesse the whole day. I don't know how they could have done it without you knowing unless they went to the seller's website or something. Have you asked them?"

"Not yet, but I don't feel like they did it either," Luke said.

"That would be uncharacteristically thoughtful of them," Sarah said with an audible grin.

"It's so weird."

"Maybe the guy running the stand heard your interest, figured out where you lived, and sent it to you."

"Why would he do that?"

"I don't know. He sells moss at Saturday Market. He's probably weird. I don't know. I'm just trying to come up with ideas."

"Will you come with me to the market again tomorrow? I want to see if the vendor is there, and I can ask him about it. It's a pretty crazy moss. It's from Iceland."

"Whoa, that sounds cool. Yeah, I'm free. I can meet you."

"Ten? I'll buy coffee."

"Perfect."

Luke called the others. Keith and Jesse had the same response as Sarah. They all said they would meet him at Saturday Market the following day to speak with the moss salesman. After he got off his final call, Luke dipped the clean container into the cup. He scooped up the moss ball, making sure not to let it leave the water, and returned it to his desk.

The following morning, Luke woke to the sound of screaming.

Tides of wailing rattled the walls of Luke's apartment as he threw himself out of bed and sprinted to his desk. He had forgotten to secure the lid back over the container. The water had evaporated overnight, and now the moss ball was fully exposed. In its death throes, it screeched louder than before. Its vibrancy began to fade, and it started shifting from lime-green to dark green to brown. As its color faded, its screaming got louder.

Luke picked up the container and ran it over to his kitchen sink. He turned the faucet, but nothing came out. The distinct low fizzle of empty pipes attempting to suck up absent water pierced through the moss ball's cries. The water had been shut off. Then, in the chaos of his mind, Luke acted on the first of two impulses that would surprise him that day. He took a knife out of his kitchen drawer and cut the moss ball in half.

Of course, any notion of this thing being his pet was no longer of concern to him. He did not care for it. It was madness to impose such a responsibility onto someone. The two halves formed into two faces. Both screaming. Both getting louder. He pulled a box of matches out of the drawer, lit one, and set them on fire. The screaming stopped. Everything stopped. Silence. Luke felt the cool, wet presence of blood flowing down the left and right sides of his neck. His fingers followed the paths up to his ears. His eardrums had burst.

He could still feel the screaming, perhaps louder than before, but he could not hear it. The blast of energy rattled through his abdomen. Sensations wrapped into each other, and sounds became feelings. He could feel it. Deep inside. It made him sick. His stomach turned rotten. Even deaf, he could not escape. The moss balls had burned to black ash, but they were still screaming. The ash was screaming.

Luke wiped the ash back into its container and fastened the lid over it to stifle its cry. He needed to remove all remnants of the cursed orb from his home. He put it in his trunk, wiped the blood from his neck, and drove to Lake Donovan.

It was a quarter after nine, and Saturday Market vendors had just finished setting up their stands. The sun was rising over the water, and the weather was expected to cooperate. It was, for everyone else, shaping up to be a perfect Saturday.

Luke parked and got out of his car with the container. He knew people were wondering about the screaming. He knew they were looking at him carrying his moss ball container full of ash. For a moment, he was happy he could not hear anything. He didn't want to hear anyone try to stop him.

He approached the water's edge and looked down. There wasn't a beach to speak of. Luke was standing on an elevated platform, roughly twenty feet above the water's surface. The water went down another forty feet below that. It got deep and dark very quickly. He took the container out of his pocket and removed the lid before dropping it into the water. The moment it touched the surface, the pain in his gut went away, and he felt immense relief. Stress from the sonic attack that had been waged against him dissipated. He was safe.

However, soon that feeling was replaced by another. He felt the ghostly presence of someone behind him. He could tell who it was. It was the same feeling he had last week when he thought the moss seller could hear him. It was him. He was standing behind Luke.

As a hand touched Luke's shoulder, he acted on the second of two impulses that surprised him that day. He pulled the hand forward and threw the person behind him into the water below. A small, old man's body slapped against the water and slowly sank. His curly hair grasped toward the surface like a crowd of little arms, all crawling against the pull of the deep. His face turned toward the surface, and Luke could see it was the same face that had formed in the moss. It was his face.

The ash of the former moss ball still near the surface clung to his limp body as he sank. It began to spread out and grow. Dark sludge wrapped him in a slimy cocoon. It turned from black to brown to bright green. His body was bringing the moss back to life, and the moss was feeding off his body. It was thriving around him. Before disappearing into the darkness, Luke saw the true size of this new moss ball, and the pain returned to his stomach.

Another hand touched his shoulder.

Luke turned around and saw Sarah. She was speaking, but he could not hear her. His strength gave out, and he abruptly sat on the ground. Sarah asked him a couple unanswered questions before making him stand back up and guiding him to her car.

While she drove him to the hospital, he looked out the window. He watched the lake pass by and wondered if they would pull the old man's body out. Would they know the enormous moss ball was him? He wondered if they would have to drain the lake to find him. What an incredible sound that would be.

Fried Tarantulas

JACKIE WONDERED HOW fried tarantulas could be so popular. In a town square on the island of Kehtompr, off the coast of Cambodia, near the rim of the Gulf of Thailand, the streets were flooded with vendors selling all the delicious food a traveler with a healthy appetite could desire. The most popular among them, particularly around breakfast and lunch, was a woman named Pisey, who sold fried tarantulas.

Pisey was hauntingly beautiful and seemingly beloved by the local population. Her long, skinny limbs and stringy black hair bent in the air to cradle her presence in a mystifying aura, beckoning those around her. While other vendors frequently had to move through the crowd to attract attention, Pisey stood perfectly still and attracted everyone to her.

After three days in town, Jackie was beginning to come around to the idea of eating spiders. Pisey had offered her a free sample each morning and afternoon as she walked through the area. Jackie had recently graduated from college in the United States with a major in Asian studies and wanted to take some time off before grad school to explore and immerse herself in the culture she had been studying. She had a decent handle on the local language and a hunger to experience their famous cuisine. However, she wasn't sure if she could fully commit to every custom.

She planned to spend three days in Cambodia before heading north through Thailand, Laos, and Vietnam to get to China. When she arrived in Cambodia, she heard so many people tell stories about Kehtompr, and she found herself flushed with a pull to experience its charm. Although it was a small, relatively poor town, it was rich in culture and taste. The fact that everything would be so cheap was another attractive feature for Jackie, who was still, despite her travels being funded by her lovely parents, living a poor college student life. The detour would put her behind schedule, but she felt compelled to visit the small island. Everyone said it held the best shopping and food in southern Asia.

Once she arrived and found her hostel, she spent each day exploring, eating wonderful dishes, and purchasing breathtaking jewelry unlike any she could find at home in the Midwest. The first day she walked past Pisey, she was struck by the spider seller's figure. Her skinny lankiness, although not conventionally alluring, was so profoundly mystifying and unique that she became confusingly attractive. Pisey held a fried tarantula up to Jackie's face and startled her out of her daze.

"Free sample?" Pisey asked with a shimmering smile.

"No, thank you," Jackie replied shakily. "But thank you, though."

Jackie's decline was quickly interrupted by a group of young men behind her who were hungry for Pisey's tarantulas. She moved to a different, less crowded eating area and sat down for a lunch of expertly prepared beef and sautéed vegetables.

On the second day, Jackie desperately wanted to meet Pisey's gaze but didn't want to be offered another sample. She diverted her eyes, consumed by the urge to peek at the woman's gaunt comeliness once more. Again, the vendor stuck a fried tarantula in Jackie's face, stopping her in her tracks. The spiders weren't alive, but it was hard to know that when they suddenly appeared in front of her mouth.

"Free sample?" Pisey asked again with her dazzling smile. The sun radiated off her face, lending a dramatic layer of shadows underneath her brow that increased the darkness of her already wholly black eyes. Her eyes were mostly, if not all, pupils, and they quivered in anticipation.

"No, thank you."

A child jumped into the air, grabbed the tarantula, and bit it in half, spilling its eggs onto the ground. His mother scolded him for wasting the eggs and then bought 12 more spiders. She held them in her hands and passed them out to the children around her. Her son couldn't have been happier to devour his second tarantula.

On the third day, her last day before leaving the island and heading north to China, Jackie decided to eat one. Why was she here if not to partake in the local customs? Everyone loved the fried tarantulas, and Pisey seemed like a lovely woman. Jackie was ashamed of herself for fearing something clearly so ordinary. She knew she would regret it if she did not at least try one.

"Free sample?" Pisey asked, beaming at Jackie as she walked by.

"Can you tell me more about them? The spiders?" Jackie asked.

"Fresh tarantulas caught this morning. My husband Kosal catches them in the woods near town every day and prepares them for me to sell. He defangs them and cooks them in oil with his special blend of spices. Any poison that might be in them gets entirely cooked out, and we're left with only the delicious white meat inside. They are rinsed and fried while they're still alive. The squeal that comes from frying their little furry bodies makes our neighbors super hungry. Some people come running as soon as they hear it."

The tarantula in Pisey's hand had its legs lifelessly folded around her fingers. Small bits of shiny ivory meat ruptured and oozed from the tips and joints of its legs. Its abdomen crunched between her index finger and thumb. She plunged it into her mouth and ripped off its head, crunching its eyes around with an expression of pure bliss.

"See here?" Pisey showed the inside of the tarantula to Jackie. "This one is full of eggs. The ones with eggs are a special bonus. They're the best part. Good for your vision."

Pisey devoured the rest of the spider and savored it in a performance of heightened pleasure. She reached for another.

"Now you try," Pisey insisted, handing the new one to Jackie.

"Okay," Jackie agreed begrudgingly. She took the tarantula in her hand. Its abdomen felt warm and heavy between her fingers. The fur on its legs felt coarse and wild, prickling and defacing her fingerprints. She brought the spider to her mouth, and then she saw it.

The tarantula still had its fangs.

It awoke from its stasis, apparently having not been fully killed during the cooking process, if it was ever cooked. This horrific oversight left the tarantula alive, fanged, and angry. It closed the gap between Jackie's hand and face before she could react, and it bit her bottom lip.

Jackie tried to scream, but nothing came. Her lips swelled, and her throat tightened. The tarantula had released poison into her system. Her body stiffened while Pisey's smile grew, appearing to wrap around her head in a fog of fading consciousness. As Jackie fell to the ground, paralyzed, a pair of strong arms—a man—caught her. She looked down to see a tattoo of a spider on his left forearm. Pisey resumed selling her tarantulas to the hungry audience behind Jackie as the man dragged her away from the vendor stand. Her vision blurred, and the light went out.

***

When Jackie awoke, she was tied to a wooden chair in a small, dimly lit shack. A kitchenette with a cutting board and a filthy stovetop was tucked away in the corner. The dirt floor was littered with boxes, and gray plastic bins filled the entire shack in stacks that reached the ceiling.

The door opened, and the man with the spider tattoo walked in with another bin. He was bald, lean, and stood about six feet tall. His forearms and hands were swamped in veins and muscular, presumably from catching and cooking tarantulas all day. Jackie closed her eyes and pretended to be unconscious. Soon, however, she felt a light tug on her pant leg. The tug got heavier, taking on the general shape and weight of a baseball. A sticky baseball that was slowly rolling up her shin.

She opened her eyes and saw it. A tarantula was crawling up her leg toward her knee. Jackie instinctively released a small cry and shook her leg until she kicked it onto the floor a few feet away.

"Whoa," the man yelled without taking his eyes off his work to look at her. "Easy with that. I've got to make a living, you know."

"Who are you?" Jackie asked.

"I'm Kosal. Remember when you met Pisey? The lady who sells the spiders. Pisey is my wife."

"Why am I here?"

"You could have died." Kosal laughed as he set the bin on the counter and wiped his hands on his raggedy flannel shirt. "Sorry about that. Sometimes these guys slip through my fingers, and I don't get them defanged or cooked all the way through. Huge oversight on my part. That hasn't happened in forever, so I'm super sorry about that. I gave you some medicine. You should be all good soon."

"Why am I tied to a chair?"

"Sometimes the medicine makes people thrash around once they're unlocked from the paralysis. You didn't thrash around, though. You did great."

Jackie studied Kosal as he grabbed the tarantula off the ground with his index finger and thumb in a way that made it physically impossible for the revolting creature to attack him. He took out a pocketknife, and with a single movement, like removing a bottle cap from a bottle, he cut the tarantula's fangs off and threw its body into one of the boxes.

"Haven't washed these yet. See?" he said as he smiled and tilted the box with his foot to reveal its contents to Jackie. Inside were no less than two hundred live tarantulas, crawling over each other and intertwining their bodies like horrifically knotted, frayed, and exquisitely vile graying black hair. Jackie gasped. Kosal looked at them with pride. "I caught all of these about an hour ago. I need to cook up a batch before the lunch rush. Excuse me."

Kosal walked into the kitchenette and lit the stove. A massive flame hugged the bottom of an enormous cooking bowl. He poured a deep pool of oil, topped it with a colorful rain of spices, and waited for it to boil.

"Can you untie me now?" Jackie said. "I think I'm okay to be on my own. I can probably stand up."

Kosal quietly watched the oil. Small bubbles started forming against the blistering metal.

"Kosal?" said Jackie.

"No," Kosal said.

"What?" Jackie asked politely.

"You're from the U.S., right? Although the fang was an honest mistake on my part, I'm sure Pisey was aware of the spider she grabbed. You're going to have to contact your family and tell them to send us money. Do you know what a ransom is? It's a really simple process. We're going to hold onto you until your family, or your government, or whoever gives us money to release you. We'll keep you safe until then. I mean, you'll be fine as long as they agree to pay. If they don't, then we'll have to feed you to our spiders. What else would we do, you know? We wouldn't really have a choice at that point. It's crazy to watch. Enough of them working together can devour an entire person. Especially a young woman."

Now both were quiet for a moment. Kosal's voice indicated to Jackie that he was not only calm, but he had most likely done this before. She waited for him to laugh. The oil began to boil, pop, and sizzle, and Kosal picked up the bin. He dumped the slowly twisting, hairy, crawling mass of shockingly long kicking legs, life draining out of their extremities toward the ceiling, into the cooking bowl with a molten splash. The whistling. The squealing of a thousand furry bellies and sharp eyes cooking. It was too awful to bear. Jackie shut her eyes so hard that tears formed, and her hearing dulled.

After a few minutes, the screeching died down, and the spiders were ready to be served. Kosal took one out of the cooking bowl with tongs and walked over to Jackie.

"We're not going to starve you or anything. You can eat all the fried tarantulas you want while we wait. A lot of people would honestly kill to be in your position. It doesn't matter to me. Each of these boxes is full of spiders. I'm catching them faster than we can sell them and, lady, let me tell you, we're selling them pretty fast."

"Why do you need to kidnap me if you already make so much money selling them?"

"I don't want to sell fried tarantulas my whole life." Kosal laughed a loud boom. "Because, I mean, yeah, we sell a lot, but they're spiders, you know what I mean? We're never going to get rich doing that. If we get a ransom for a young American girl, though, then we'd be set for life. Now, open up. I know you never really got to try one. I picked one with eggs for you."

Kosal held the fried tarantula up to Jackie's mouth. Steam rose off it like its soul was escaping through each opening, bursting with hot white spider meat. It was at the very least a relief to see that this one had been thoroughly cooked. She looked into its scorched expression, and her stomach folded in on itself.

"I'm not hungry right now," she said.

Kosal shoved the spider into Jackie's mouth and pushed her head back, knocking her chair backward onto the floor. Her full weight slammed against the dirt and launched the spider into the back of her mouth. She choked on its crunchy body until it broke into enough pieces to scrape down her throat. Hundreds of small, putrid eggs oozed out of its hot egg sac and coated Jackie's tongue. She choked it down purely by the force of gravity. Her choice to swallow was a last resort against asphyxiating on a fried tarantula. She gagged and heaved.

"It's good, right?" Kosal smiled. He set Jackie's chair back upright. "We found your phone on you. You can either tell us the password to open it or communicate the ransom message yourself. It's charging outside right now. I had to connect it to the power generator out there. It was practically on low battery mode, by the way. You need to be better about keeping your phone charged. Especially in areas like this. You can do it now or whenever you feel like you're finished eating. Like I said, there's plenty."

That's when Jackie saw Kosal's defanging knife sitting on the counter.

"Okay," Jackie said. "Get my phone. I'll unlock it for you."

"Hey, that was easy," Kosal said. "Be right back. Don't move."

Kosal left the room. Jackie softly scooted her chair toward the counter, pushing by bins full of undulating clouds of kicking spider legs. She noticed one bin was full of tarantulas that had yet to be defanged. It was marked *Fang-in*, but the writing was considerably faded.

Once she reached the counter, she used her face to move the knife onto the floor. Then she grabbed it with her feet and stretched it underneath the chair and around to her hands, which were bound behind her back, maintaining a stiff core to offset her odd weight balance. She started cutting.

The rope didn't cut like a normal rope. It was like cutting through hair or thick woven strands of spider webbing. Jackie kept her mind off that detail and focused on her freedom.

"What the hell are you doing?" Kosal said as he reentered the room. He put the phone in his pocket and hurried toward Jackie.

Just before he reached out to grab her, Jackie wiggled one hand free, clutched his hand, leaned out of the way, and used Kosal's momentum to throw him into the bin brimming with fang-in tarantulas.

It was disturbingly quiet. A queasy hush. The clicking of tarantula fangs and flurry of movement within the bin was the only audible release from the tension. Kosal's silent screams and body were immediately overcome with poison. He was completely paralyzed, and the creatures were beginning to carry out whatever it was a group of them did to a person. Jackie had no intention of sticking around to witness it. She finished untying herself and stood up.

"Oh my god," she said, realizing the task that lay before her. She used the knife to knock tarantulas away from Kosal's pocket long enough to reach in and retrieve her phone. For a moment, she felt grateful to Kosal for charging it. However, the moment faded as groups of fang-in tarantulas used Kosal's body to escape the bin and rush out onto the shack floor.

The tarantulas cooking on the stove behind her burned, smoked, and snapped. The kinetic energy in the cooking bowl was growing and reaching a point of entropy, morphing into chaos that began spreading throughout the room. Oil exploded high enough to hit the ceiling. Drops of scalding spiced oil splashed onto Jackie, searing her forearms, while little pieces of fried tarantula shot in each direction. A wave of oil splashed out of the cooking bowl and onto the fire below it, gushing flaming liquid onto every flammable surface around it.

Soon the kitchenette was entirely on fire. Murky smoke filled the room, and any tarantulas that were alive furiously scurried around in their bins. Jackie grabbed one that still had its fangs with her thumb and index finger like she had seen Kosal do and ran outside as the flames engulfed the structure behind her.

Wretched wailing. The screeching. An agonizing crescendo of burning spiders flushed toward the sky as the windows and roof burst like boiling skin, releasing billowing smoke towers and the smell of meat into the air. Hordes of tarantulas, some lit on fire and some lucky enough to escape with their lives, scattered out the door and into the forest. Soon the cries of cooking spiders mixed with another scream. A woman's scream.

Pisey appeared in front of Jackie after she got a few feet outside. She must have been coming back to re-up her supply. She wailed in terror as she watched her husband and all their work burn away. Jackie did not hesitate.

She threw the tarantula in her hand at Pisey's face. Its fangs burrowed into Pisey's lip, and her cries died away. Her face swelled, and she fell to the ground as the tarantula scurried away into the woods.

Jackie stood outside the burning shack beside Pisey's paralyzed body. Her hair lay limp, and her lanky limbs shrank even skinnier and folded inward. Her spine rigidly retreated and curled as the life left her body. Jackie could hear yelling coming from town. People would show up soon to see what happened and extinguish the fire.

Jackie kicked Pisey's body into the flames of the burning building and shut the door. The whistling and crackling of her body mixed with the charring tarantulas and put Jackie strangely at ease. What happened to her would never happen again.

She walked back toward town and passed the crowd rushing to the fire. She told them there was a kitchen fire, and Pisey and Kosal had been paralyzed by spiders before they could get out. Everyone she told was devastated. They put out the fire, but the shack was already a hollow onyx shell. Thousands of toasted tarantula corpses and pounds of spider hair ash blanketed Pisey and Kosal. The town's top fried tarantula vendors, the renowned gastronomical pride and joy of the area, had died.

***

Jackie arrived at her hostel and connected to the Wi-Fi to call her mom.

"Hey, honey. How's Cambodia?" her mother asked.

"It's great. I went to this little island, and you'll never guess what I ate," Jackie said.

"Oh my god, I hope it wasn't anything gross."

"I ate a fried tarantula."

Jackie's mother laughed.

"You're so brave. I couldn't do that. Yuck," her mother said.

"They're not bad once you get used to them. They put spices on it and stuff, so it's actually pretty good. I'll fry up some of the ones around your place once I come home."

"Please don't. I'm glad you're having fun. Enjoy the rest of your trip, and I can't wait to see you when you come home. Love you."

"I love you too," Jackie said.

After the call with her mother ended, Jackie got on a boat back to Cambodia and resumed her trip north, right on schedule.

One Night at Connor Inn

ABOUT A HALF-DAY'S trek up the side of Mt. Connor, a shimmering recreational climber's dream in the Pacific Northwest, there sat a cozy, modest inn for weary hikers. Connor Inn was run by a middle-aged married couple, Claudia and Leo, who lived on the property. They had gotten enough money together years ago to purchase the building, which was previously abandoned, and turn it into a small but profitable inn.

Being the only accommodation in the area, every traveler who did not wish to sleep in a tent or on the ground made reservations. They had agreements with the guided tour companies in the area to shelter passing groups of tourists. The temperature was mild throughout most of the year at their elevation. Even tonight, the air was invitingly cool and still. It was a peaceful life.

Supplies were usually brought to the mountain base, and either Leo or Claudia would retrieve them. The only road to the inn was treacherous, and most larger trucks could not traverse its shaky ground. Still, the couple had become well-versed in driving their small pickup around the unforgiving landscape and were happy to complete the journey for their suppliers. The recurring trip had become an exciting escape for Leo, who loved having an excuse to spend time doing anything outside of the inn. Claudia enjoyed reading during her off-time, but the duties of her job had been keeping her from it recently.

Because they were so busy tending to guest quarters and whatever else needed to be done, the couple began hiring a rotating cast of temporary employees who would stay with them to help. They were usually comprised of backpackers and foreign travelers who wished to exchange labor for room and board. Some stayed so long that Leo and Claudia considered paying them, but everyone left eventually, which significantly contributed to the wonder of life on the mountain. Even though Claudia and Leo remained in the same spot, no two days were ever the same, and the characters they met were plenty, rich, and sundry. On this night, however, the windows of help had failed to overlap, and once their last employee departed, the couple was left to tend to the inn on their own for the next month.

They had spent the first few years running the inn alone, so they felt confident in their ability to keep things working smoothly. They had seen ten years of issues, but they had also become accustomed to assistance. The operation had grown considerably since taking on more hands. With the increased labor force, they were able to build additional guest quarters on the grounds, and they were feeling its weight.

With only the two of them, most of the guest accommodations reserved for the evening, and a shipment of supplies scheduled to be delivered during an otherwise ungodly hour later that night, their workload was heavier than it had been in the past. But they weren't worried. They would get through it like they always did.

Experienced mountaineers, leisurely camping parties, and a guided hiking group of tourists mingled and shared drinks throughout the inn's common area, where light food and beverages were available for purchase. It was Halloween, and Claudia had adorned the room with decorations. Some of the guests were wearing masks they had brought in their packs or funny little accessories that Claudia had laid out on the tables.

She loved all holidays, regardless of religion, and took pride in creating a warm environment to reflect that for her visitors. She had a closet devoted to decorations for each of the major holiday themes. Plastic spiders and pumpkins, witch dolls, and bowls of free candy sat on every table. Everything was self-serve. Various machines produced savory snacks, instant meals, alcohol, everyday toiletries, revitalizing vitamin mixtures for exhausted travelers, and many other familiar comforts and necessities at very reasonable prices. Although she loved hosting the guests, automating these processes was Claudia's idea. It left her time to work on other things. She still didn't have time to read though.

In earlier years, one of them would actually hang out in the common area to serve guests during specific hours in the evenings. Refilling the machines every couple weeks proved a much more efficient process. However, she did miss connecting with her customers. If they had enough staff one day, they might open a proper bar or kitchen, but it was a less pressing matter for now.

The evening began to wind down, and guests retired to their rooms, exhausted from the day's travels. Candy wrappers and empty bottles of pumpkin ale and cider sat in satisfied piles in their designated trash cans and recycling bins. Claudia took her position at the front desk greeting area, anticipating Leo's drive to the mountain base. She would be managing the building alone until he returned and would need to be available for anyone to reach her.

One of the many beautiful aspects of running an inn on the side of a mountain is that the guests are never too rambunctious at night. They're always so tired from simply getting there that they'd drink one beer and almost immediately fall asleep. Most travelers are merely happy to see a bed and comforts of any kind. They applauded the endearing display of holiday merriment and proceeded to feel right at home. It was rare to hear complaints.

Claudia picked up a book as Leo's taillights disappeared down the dirt road and into the edgeless shadows of a moonless night. They had a lovely little library of fiction for guests to leaf through. Ashamed of being unable to find time to read in a woodland paradise that was entirely soaked with it, Claudia was eager to jump into a new adventure.

In the early days, she kept the bookshelf stocked with new books as she burned through them, but she hadn't even cracked open most of the titles that now lined the shelf. She was grateful to be tethered to the desk and forced to stimulate her brain. The innkeeper picked up a collection of spooky short stories, but only got through half of the first tale when a group of new guests arrived.

Four children stood in front of the inn. Their silhouettes startled Claudia when she looked up and noticed them separate from the shadows. She thought she had felt a presence, but she wasn't expecting to see four small bodies standing on the other side of the glass door. The tallest boy opened it, and they walked into the light.

Two boys and two girls appeared in the entryway, wearing pajamas. The tallest boy looked to be a teenager, maybe fifteen or sixteen years old. Claudia studied them for a moment. The other children were under ten years old. The smaller boy was the youngest looking. The two girls seemed to be about the same age, only slightly older than him. The tall boy leaned on him as they walked behind the girls toward Claudia.

"Can we have a room, please?" one of the girls asked.

"Uh, hi," Claudia said, stunned. "Where are your parents?"

"I don't know," the girl replied. "We need a room."

"Please, we need a room," the younger boy said. "It's dark outside."

"What are you doing on a mountain wearing pajamas in the middle of the night?" Claudia asked. "It's chilly and so late. Way past my bedtime even. Your parents must be close by and terrified. Are they looking for a room? Is that how you found this place? Did they call ahead?"

"I don't know," the girl repeated. The girl next to her started to cry.

"Please don't cry. It's okay. We'll find your parents. Where do you all live?"

"I'm sorry," the older boy said. "We got separated from our parents, and we need a room for the night. It's too dark to keep looking for them. This is my little brother, and that's my little sister and her friend. We can't keep looking for them in the dark. I'm sorry."

Claudia noticed that his leg was injured. It was bleeding.

"Is your leg okay?" she asked.

"I got hurt outside. It's so dark. I fell. I'm sorry."

"Do you have a room for us?" the little sister asked. Her friend sobbed louder.

"Sure, let's get you in a room," she said, and the sister's friend stopped crying. "We have a special one that has two bunk beds. Does that sound fun? Then we'll help you find your parents."

"Thank you so much," the older boy said.

"We don't have any money," said the younger boy.

"That's okay. Don't worry about it," said Claudia. "It's on the house tonight. You just have to promise me that you'll sleep tight and be all warm and comfy-cozy after you help me eat some of this candy. I bet you poor kids wish you were out wearing costumes and trick or treating."

She flashed a cheesy grin at the children and looked deeply into their eyes with tutelary affection. They smiled and nodded. They didn't return the warmth, but they were probably just scared. She would make their stay as painless as possible and figure out a way to get them back to their parents, and she couldn't have been happier to do it.

After serving them refreshments and giving a bandage to the older boy, who stubbornly insisted on cleaning the wound himself even though he flicked dots of blood on everything around the front desk that she would then have to clean up, Claudia showed them to their room. She asked if they could tell her their names, but they were shy. They said they were scared to say their names to adults, so Claudia didn't press them any further. She wouldn't need to know their names to confirm four missing kids.

Once the children's lights were turned off and the door closed and locked, Claudia called the police. The dispatcher informed her that he had not received any reports of missing children. Moreover, he knew Claudia and Leo to be good people. Claudia promised that the kids were safe, and he knew they were.

"Let them sleep for now," the dispatcher said in a reassuring tone. "I can get someone up there by dawn, and we'll start looking for their parents if they don't show up before then. I'm sure they're close by."

"Thank you," she said, and hung up the phone.

Then, before she could even reach for her book again, her fantasy dissolved around further interruption. Rain formed in the clouds overhead, and a light drizzle rolled down the windows, morphing the dark forest outside into dreadful shapes. Claudia worried about Leo driving on that awful road in a storm.

She sensed another presence, looked out the glass door, and was startled not out of fear but joy. A man and woman in hiking gear were standing outside. They were damp with rain, and their silhouettes looked much more menacing than the relief that their arrival meant, but they had to be the parents. They entered.

The woman looked horrified, and the man distraught. She opened her mouth, it appeared, to shout when Claudia cut her off.

"Looking for your kids?"

"Yes," the woman exhaled. "Are they here?"

"Yep." Claudia smiled. "They came in a little bit ago. I knew you couldn't be far behind. I cleaned them up, served them some yummy food and drinks, a little bit of candy—I promise not too much; it is Halloween, after all—and I put them in one of the bunk rooms. They're safe."

"Thank you so much," said the man.

"Thank god for you," the woman said. "Where are they?"

"I'll show you." Claudia grabbed her key and proudly marched them down the hall.

"We're camping nearby," said the man, "We wanted the kids to camp with real tents and to tell them scary stories around a bonfire but still be nearby your business for safety. I think the kids got frightened or tired of camping and wanted to come inside. We're so sorry for all this."

"No problem at all," Claudia said. "They're delightful. Smart, too. They wouldn't even tell me their names."

When they arrived at the door, Claudia knocked as a final courtesy to her guests.

"Children," she called, smiling back at the couple. "Your parents have arrived."

"Keep them away from us. They're not our parents," the younger boy cried out. "They kidnapped us."

The couple looked shocked. Their eyes widened.

"Samuel," the woman said. "It's us. It's Mommy and Daddy."

"You aren't our parents," the boy, Samuel, yelled.

"Go away," his sister screamed.

"This is ridiculous," the man said as he reached for the door handle, finding it locked. "Open the door, please. We need to talk to them."

Claudia heard the sister's friend begin to cry again.

"Please don't open the door!" Samuel shouted. "I don't want to go back."

"Miss," the man said stiffly, "please unlock the door."

Claudia stood between the couple and the door. The key sat tightly in her grip. Why would the children lie? The couple's story made sense, but if they had kidnapped the kids, their story would need to make sense. She wouldn't be able to live with herself if the kids were telling the truth and she gave them back to their captors.

"How many kids did you say you have?" Claudia asked.

"We have two kids," said the woman.

"These aren't yours, then, because there are more than two of them."

"They brought their friends with them," the woman said. "They each got to bring a friend. There are four kids."

"They told me that three of them were siblings, and one of them was a friend."

"You either misunderstood or they were being unclear," the woman said flatly. "Now, please open the door so I can see my children."

Claudia stood still.

"I think we should wait until the police get here to do anything further."

"Open the door," said the man.

"Stop holding our children hostage," the woman spat. The couple closed on Claudia. The man grabbed her shoulders, and the woman tried to capture the key from her hands. They struggled for a few seconds in the hallway until the heavy sound of a .22 caliber rifle case being laid on a wooden counter echoed off the walls. Claudia's husband Leo had returned.

"What's going on?" he asked.

The couple released Claudia, and she ran over to Leo's side. Claudia recounted the events as they had unfolded. From time to time, throughout the tale, a yawning traveler would poke their head out of a nearby doorway to see what the commotion was about, only to quickly retreat into their room. Finally, when Claudia had finished summarizing the evening, she asked how Leo's trip went.

"Had to turn back early when it started to rain. Didn't want to get caught in it. The supply truck is going to come back in the morning. You said the cops were coming around then?"

"Yes," said Claudia.

"Then I think we should all sit tight until morning."

Leo guided the couple back into the main room, where the four of them sat, eating candy and watching each other for hours. Claudia wanted to read, but she could not fight the temptation to sleep during their quiet staring contest. Soon, she fell into a dream, and in her dream, she sat at the table reading alone.

***

When the police arrived, Leo woke Claudia, who told them everything and took them to the children's room. She knocked. Silence. She unlocked the door, and Leo jumped, startled by his wife's panicked gasp at the terrible scene within.

Samuel and the two girls were bound and gagged on the floor between each other's bunks. They were crying, and they had soiled themselves. The room was cold, with the window wide open. A pathetic, depressing smell. Once they were released, they cried out for their parents. The couple hurried into the room, and the children rushed into their arms. The parents, crying, hugged and kissed the boy and his sister. They hugged the sister's friend to calm her down and noticed a thin red line of dried blood on her neck.

"Where is the older boy?" Claudia asked.

"He left," said the sister. "He said he was going to kill us. He had a knife. He was holding it to her throat. He was going to kill us, but when he heard the police were coming, he tied us up and crawled out the window."

"Logan did that?" the father asked as he turned to his son. "But he's your friend."

"It wasn't Logan," said Samuel. "It was somebody else. He looked like a boy, but he wasn't. He was a man. He came into our tent. Logan tried to fight him. I don't know where Logan is. I don't know. He took him somewhere. Then he took us. He said he would kill us. I'm sorry."

Leo and the police ran outside. They found a boy, Logan, a few hundred meters away, bound and gagged under a tree. Any evidence of his kidnapper had been thoroughly washed away by the rain. He was hypothermic and had been partially eaten by the bedtime terrors of the forest floor, but he was alive. Traumatized, but alive. Police reported the suspect missing. Waking travelers heard the commotion, and soon every mountaineer staying at Connor Inn joined the hunt.

After searching for hours, Leo left to meet with the supplier while the rest of the search party continued their efforts, and Claudia returned to the inn to sit at her desk to recover for a moment. She unwrapped a chocolate bar, prepared a mug of coffee, picked up her book, and flipped to the page where she had left off earlier that evening.

To her dismay, a spot of the kidnapper's blood had stained the pages when she gave him bandages. She stared at the red streak and felt a pit in her stomach grow out of the horrid shape it carved into the page. She thought about the rain running down the window. She thought about how much she loved Leo.

Claudia handed the book to an officer assigned to stay with the family. They had been searching the room for clues that could reveal the man's identity beyond their descriptions of him. The officer took the book to be DNA tested. Claudia sighed and looked out the window at the sun now proudly shining through the trees, mist rising through the canopies, and she laughed at the profound sadness she felt, knowing she would have to finish that story another time.

Washing Machine

WE NOTICED A smell coming from our clothes two weeks after moving into our new apartment. It was my first time living with a significant other, and it was already plagued by an overwhelming rotting stench that triggered a deep, primal urge to avoid whatever was causing it. Neither of us was particularly dirty, but we stank at work, and our towels reeked. No matter how much we washed them, that terrible smell would not come out.

My boyfriend and I became acquainted with the deathly odor the first time we washed our clothes in the communal washing machine located in our apartment complex's basement. The device itself did not smell particularly offensive. Nothing more than old detergent. One washer and dryer set was somehow supposed to accommodate the thirty people living in this building. We asked our neighbors, but most of them used a laundry service. They thought the machine was "gross."

One woman, who had lived in the apartment below ours for over a decade, said she still used it, but she stopped speaking to us when I asked if it made her clothes stink. She snapped the door shut and would not answer our knocking.

The light that normally emitted beneath the door frame remained unlit after that day, and silence encased her gloomy door. She not only stopped speaking to us, she avoided us completely. Every now and then, I thought I heard soft weeping through our living room floor, but it could have been her television.

The last time I tried to clean our clothes in the washing machine, I saw something that I could not explain to my boyfriend. It was midday, but the washroom didn't have windows, so it might as well have been night in there. Even during the brightest sun, that dingy, damp basement washroom existed in total darkness.

I should have left when the motion lights didn't turn on. I've never been in that room when they stopped working before. I should have just called maintenance immediately. But I needed to wash my clothes. My phone's display lit my path through the pitch-black concrete hallway.

After loading the machine and turning it on, I waited for a minute to watch it, my phone light reflecting off the clear door. I wanted to make sure it was working. Soapy water filled the machine's door window. Slowly, the water turned from clear, to pink, to deep red. It swirled faster. Thick, frothy crimson coursed through our shirts and pants, pulsing thick stains. A whirlpool of foamy blood. Then, what looked like an infant's crying face splattered against the window.

I screeched and opened the door to pull out my clothes and save the child. Bubbles and wet garments spilled onto the washroom's dusty floor. There was no blood, no baby, but the stench was unbearable. I gagged and dry-heaved, covering my mouth with my shirt. My hands were wet from the putrid water, which soaked through my shirt and clung to my nose. I couldn't escape the smell.

I vomited down my chest and over the front of my pants, choking and holding my breath between each retch. Finally, my nose was so full of puke and bile and my stomach so empty that I breathed through my acid-lined mouth enough to take my clothes upstairs and hang them in the bathroom to dry next to an open window.

I sprayed the clothes with my boyfriend's cologne, but it only added to the vile fetor. It ruined the scent of my boyfriend. When he returned home, I told him that the machines were broken and we needed to start using a laundry service. He would also need to buy different cologne. He understood.

After that day, the woman below us disappeared. We never knew if she had been forced to leave or left on her own, but one day, suddenly, she was gone, and her apartment was rented to another couple.

The woman of the couple was a few months pregnant, and she told us they had already started using the washing machine. It was working just fine for them. Their clothes always smelled so wonderful.

Papermaker

FOR MY TWENTY-SEVENTH birthday, my mother mailed me a paper-making kit. The box indicated that it was made for ages eight and above, but it was clearly not for people my age. Her note reminded me of the importance of preserving and nurturing my inner child and exploring creatively stimulating toys as a form of meditation. I begrudgingly obliged.

I took the plastic press plate and pulp tray out of their bright primary-colored box and began mixing the paper pulp with water in a beaker. It swirled and bubbled like lumpy pancake batter. The kit came with dye to stain the pages with blotched expressions, but I wanted to make my first sheet of paper as white as possible. I laid the wet pulp out on a screen covering a foam sheet and began to press it through, bleeding the excess water onto a drip tray.

As the sheet took form in the wake of the rolling press, I noticed colors begin to seep out of it. My attempt to maintain the cleanliness and purity of the paper was already falling apart as soon as it began. Once the pasty mush was flattened into a single shape, it turned yellow and then green.

I felt ashamed, angry with myself that I couldn't even make a child's toy work correctly. Embarrassing tears began forming near the corners of my eyes, threatening to fall onto the paper and burn holes through its weak fibers. As I got halfway through rolling it out, a drawing began to emerge, and I blinked the tears back into my head.

A pair of legs in olive pants peeked out from under the roller. I stopped rolling, choking the newly forming sheet just before it was halfway through finalizing its structure. I assumed the tool kit must be dirty, causing it to mark up the paper in an oddly familiar, although random, way. There was no way of cleaning it without ruining the paper at this point if it was dirty, so I decided I would need to finish this piece and try again. I continued rolling it out, and soon, I unveiled a drawing of my father.

I gasped. My mother must have done something to the papermaker to create this effect. It made no sense. How could it roll out a drawing of him? If the issue was the cleanliness of the roller, there was no way that it could haphazardly roll out such a precise picture of my father, smiling, waving, alive. Only bits of white pulp clung to its edges.

I hung the paper up to dry and tried a few more sheets, but it didn't happen again. They were all white. Clean. Perfect. When it finished drying, I framed it to soothe its cracking, chalky edges, curling and grasping for moisture. A few days later, my mom called and asked how the papermaker was working.

"I love it," I said.

"I knew you would," she said.

"Did you do something to it?"

"What do you mean? Is it broken?" she asked, concerned.

"No," I sighed. "It's perfect. Love you."

"I love you too."

The Folding Man

LOW HOWLING RATTLED the wall that Abby shared with her neighbor, Louis. Enough to break her concentration. Abby was an avid runner doing some light stretching before venturing out into the city for a few miles. She had only just begun her trance, closed her eyes, and let her forehead rest on her kneecap to complete a head-to-knee stretch, warming and smoothing the muscles of her strong legs, falling silently into that serene mental state that fueled her jogs, when his cries shook her loose and commanded her attention.

Louis had lived in the building for over ten years, three of which had been spent next to Abby. He was a generation older than her, and he frequently complained about their other neighbors and the previous occupants of her apartment. His gripes were typically trivial, and she had gathered over time that they were nothing more than conversation fodder. Louis had lived alone for so long that he found it difficult to connect with others without searching for a common enemy.

The screaming became more pronounced as Abby stood up and moved toward her door. It was clearly the result of great physical pain. She stood quietly by her door, ear aimed at the hallway, waiting for a sign to interject. It wasn't unlike Louis, who worked from home, to angrily carry out a domestic task by letting everyone in the building know his discomfort, but this time was different. He sounded like he needed help. Then, he called out for it.

Abby opened her door, her running shoes already equipped, and hurried to Louis' door.

"Louis," she said. "Are you okay?"

"Abby," he said, his voice muffled. "Please come inside. I need help. I don't know how it happened."

Abby tried to open his door but found it tightly sealed. The doorknob defiantly held its place in her hand.

"It's locked," she said.

"Oh god," Louis cried. His voice was muffled by more than just the wooden door between them. Something sounded like it was covering his face. A rolling storm of uncoordinated crashing and pained moaning from inside Louis' apartment shuddered the hallway around Abby. She heard him drag and shuffle his weight toward her. The lock clicked, and she opened the door.

Although the scene within that humble apartment contained familiar images, their presentation was bizarre and terribly foreign enough to shock Abby. She gasped and let go of the door, which then closed itself in her face. She promptly opened it again, desperately wishing to consume more visual information, and fully entered the apartment.

Louis was bending his body at the waist so that his forehead was touching his knees. His face was obscured, pointing behind him through his legs. His hips looked overexerted and knotted, and the young woman winced at the sight of them. He was breathing heavily and wobbling back and forth.

"What's going on?" She regained her breath.

"I'm folding up," Louis said. "I'm folding all the way up. I can't bend back. I can't. My skull is going to fuse to my knees. I knew this would happen. I saw it, a story about this on the news. This guy, his spine went all nuts, and he folded in half, and his face fused with his knees, and his mom had to take care of him for decades until he got surgery. I don't have a mom to take care of me, Abby. I can't."

Louis' stiff and teetering legs finally lost balance, and Abby caught him before he fell forward, which would have caused immeasurable agony. She gently laid him in a sitting position with his face pointed toward the floor in a knee-to-head stretch.

"You can't sit up?"

"It took all my strength to even stand myself up so I could waddle over to the door. No. I can't straighten my back. I'm folding. Oh god, Abby, I'm folding."

Abby knew better than to attempt fixing whatever was happening with his spine. She might make it worse. Briefly, she imagined everything he was saying to be in his mind. Perhaps he had become paranoid after seeing the rare condition on the news, and he brought it upon himself in some kind of psychosomatic response. However, his panic convinced her that he had no control over his body or, at the very least, his mind wouldn't allow it.

"Should I call an ambulance?"

"I did, and they didn't believe me. Can you believe that?" he said. "What the hell do we even have ambulances for if they don't do anything? So they just pick up who they want to help now? Wish someone would have told me that."

"They're not coming?"

"They'll probably come. I don't know. I hung up when they didn't believe me because they were pissing me off."

"Did they say they were coming?"

"I gave them my address."

"Okay, I'll wait with you until the ambulance gets here. Is there anything I can do? Can I get you anything?" she asked.

"Yeah, hand me the mirror on the table."

Abby took a small handheld mirror from the counter and handed it down to Louis. He positioned it beneath his legs and angled it so that he could make eye contact with her, and she was able to see his face. She could only see his eyes. His forehead was obscured, pressed against his knee as though it were gripped to it by a cult of ghosts.

"Hey, there he is." She smiled.

"Abby, I'm so sorry I brought you into this. I know the reason I got the condition is because I heard about it, and that's probably how it'll spread to you too. When we go to the hospital, you should have them check you out. I don't even know what they could do, but you'll get it like I did. I know you will. You must get on top of it quickly. You've seen it. Oh no, you love to run. God, you were about to run. I'm so sorry. I've ruined it for you."

"It's okay, Louis. I'm okay. Let's just worry about you."

"I need you to bring me something else," he said.

"What is it?"

Louis closed his eyes and gulped deeply. He took a few shallow breaths and appeared to decide against whatever it was he was going to say. His inner argument fluttered behind his eyes. He looked down at the floor in front of him and then darted his eyes toward the mirror and reflected them at Abby with shrill brilliance.

"Grab the hammer that's in my toolbox in the hallway closet, then grab the kitchen knife in the knife block on the counter. Bring them over to me."

Abby ran to the hallway closet, which sat across from Louis' office. Once she found the hammer and turned to re-enter the kitchen, she noticed his computer through a slightly cracked door. On its screen brightly beamed an article focusing on the tragedy of a "folding man" who had developed a rare disorder that caused his body to fold in on itself. Near the bottom of the screen were photos of many different people who suffered from the condition. It seemed to have affected the entire town where the original case appeared.

"Abby," Louis called. She straightened up, left the office door, and returned to the kitchen, where she grabbed the knife Louis had requested.

"What do you need to do?" she asked.

"It's what you need to do," he said.

She paused.

"What?"

"I can't do it myself. My skull is fusing to my knee bone. By the time the ambulance gets here, it'll be too far gone. It's just getting harder and harder to break them apart with each passing minute. Soon, the bond will be so strong they'll have to remove an entire section of my skull. I'll have brain damage. They might have to amputate my leg. If you can pry them apart right now before they set, I might be able to continue getting up and down these goddamn stairs in this god-forsaken building. I need you to put the tip of that knife blade on the spot where my skull is fusing to my knee and hit it with the hammer."

She took a moment to process this information. The knife and hammer felt heavy in her hands. Abby had never counted herself as someone who could perform such a gruesome act. To clobber an old knife through her neighbor's bones. Her jog would evaporate behind her and feel untraceable for the next few days.

"I don't know if I can do that," she said.

"I can't do it. You must. Otherwise, they'll never separate me. They'll never unfold me."

"Okay." She paused and breathed, allowing a brief meditation to cool her nerves. "Guide me through it."

Louis directed Abby with the tenderness and understanding of someone trusting their life to a stranger. He desperately wanted her to succeed in her task, and the only way to truly encourage her was to show her that he would forgive her even if she happened to mistakenly drive the knife through his brain. Throngs of steel could push through his melting, pulsing mind, and it would be a relief from the terror of this folding.

The modest blade's tip clumsily settled upon the very center of the connection between Louis' forehead and kneecap. She held the handle square and loaded her grip on the hammer behind it. Both sat quietly to ready their minds for the unveiling of their fate and come to peace with each conceivable outcome. Louis closed his eyes.

"Do it."

Abby intended to strike the handle with much more force than what transpired, but she lost her spirit when the moment came. Instead of a clean break, the knife became lodged between Louis' face and leg. It sat there, stuck, blood softly beginning to trickle along its edge, and he opened his eyes. Then he screamed.

He yelled at her to strike him again, but she froze. Her mind pleaded with her to run away, to escape back down the hall and take shelter safely in her apartment. Her flight response had been initiated, and she was working against every fiber of her instinctual programming to flee. What was she doing? She wasn't a doctor. She shouldn't be hammering a knife into a man's head. She couldn't do it. While she mulled over her misfortune, Louis' cries intensified, and again, she was pulled from her trance into a clear decision. She pulled back the hammer and struck the kitchen knife as hard as her strength would allow.

A pop, and Louis turned his head, laughing.

"You did it!" He smiled.

A hole bursting with exposed skull rained blood over his eyes. A patch of flesh that had formed between the opposing sections of body ripped away, and fresh air leaked into Louis' tissue. He cackled until the red mess had completely covered his mouth. Abby searched the kitchen drawers for fresh towels. Only a short moment in doing this chore felt like an eternity, and she excitedly turned back to her poor neighbor once it was completed. However, Abby was met with a horrifying vision that left those clean towels on the floor beside her feet.

Louis retched, gargled, moaned, and released a resounding screech. His bones gnarled, twisted, and cracked. Like twigs breaking in the hands of a child, his body folded again. He had become like a piece of paper now, creased in half twice. The middle of his spine and his thighs split and whipped around in another 180-degree fold. Hot blood gushed from his face like pressure escaping a deflating air mattress or a balloon full of watercolors placed beneath a guillotine. They both screamed, and through the williwaw of their gory turmoil emerged the light song of the door buzzer. The ambulance had arrived.

There was no time for the medical professionals who ultimately saved Louis to move with uncertainty, or they would have been standing in that apartment for hours. Although none of them had seen this condition before, some of them had heard about it, and their decision to stay and help was weighed very carefully against those stories.

Fortunately, nobody seemed concerned about why Abby was clenching a bloody hammer and standing over a knife, because she would have needed to explain herself, which she was incapable of doing. Instead, Louis explained as much as he could before his energy level reflected the amount of blood he had lost. Soon the ambulance was gone, and Abby was back in her apartment, washing the crusty dark red off her hands.

Louis underwent a series of complex and painful surgeries. Essentially, doctors had to break most of his bones to set them back correctly. His entire body, broken. Luckily, he had made it to the emergency room in time. He would recount later that the doctors told him if they had waited any longer, his head would have permanently fused to his knee, and they would have been unable to disconnect it without causing considerable brain damage.

Another patient in the hospital had developed an identical host of symptoms while being monitored for an unrelated medical condition and passed away without ever knowing exactly what was happening to them. Health staff on site were able to make observations during the chaos that assisted in Louis' rapid recovery when he arrived only moments later. Two in one night. They couldn't believe it.

Despite being in physical rehab over the following weeks, Louis would send messages to Abby asking how she was feeling, and she would politely reply, "Worry about yourself."

She put her phone down and resumed stretching for her run. The sun and nirvana of chemicals coursing through her body would soon be giving her a momentary reprieve from the stress of her recent existence. She bent forward and held her breath as she brushed her nose against the stubble of her leg hair in a head-to-knee stretch.

Wax

EVERY PAIR OF earbuds I have ever owned has been destroyed by earwax. I thought it was a common problem. I only buy cheap earbuds because about a month after taking them home, the mesh screen over the sound holes sinks into a coating of my red, orange, and black head sludge. Swirling goop of autumn shimmer. It permeates every possible opening and completely muffles the sound, encasing it forever in a grave of my body's excess slime. A smooth, greasy film of waste pulsing to the music.

I bought bigger headphones to go over my ears, but they were expensive, and I worried about them getting lost, broken, or stolen while I went about my routine in the city. I wear glasses, and those headphones press my ears against them too painfully to experience daily. So I resigned to the fact that I would have to keep buying cheap earbuds and using them until they filled with my horrid wax.

One day, after speaking with a few friends about the problem and realizing that none of them shared it, I decided to visit a doctor that could clean my ears. I told her about my problem over the phone, and before I could finish speaking, she scheduled an appointment for me later that afternoon.

When I entered her office, she was wearing a protective jumpsuit, like a hazmat suit, and she asked me to sit down. A slick maroon apron, made of a material I had never seen, lay neatly folded inside a sealed plastic bag on the chair. The doctor gestured toward it.

"Should I just put this on over my clothes?" I asked. She nodded, and I removed the apron from its packaging, sliding it over my shirt. It was light and difficult to hold, like it was designed to reject even the stickiest mess. It felt like a liquid between my fingers.

"How much are you producing?" she asked.

"Earwax?"

"Yes." Her eyes were unblinking and severe behind her face shield.

"A normal amount, I feel like. It just keeps ruining my headphones. I need a cleaning or something."

"It's not a normal amount."

The doctor turned my head with her hand and looked in my left ear with a flashlight. She recoiled but quickly composed herself, closing her eyes to steady her breath.

"Everything okay?" I asked.

"I'm going to start cleaning now," she said. "Please stay still."

She brought an enormous gun-shaped tool up to my ear, its full details obscured in my peripheral vision, and counted backward from three. When she reached zero, my mind went white.

A rush of warm liquid, growing hotter from the friction of its push, flooded my head as pounds of sludgy earwax plopped onto my shoulder and slid down my apron onto the cold vinyl tile floor. It felt like an animal had been dislodged from my brain. I could hear everything so clearly. I had no idea of the dull reality I had slowly grown accustomed to. In the air of my newfound aural vibrancy, I winced at the shrill squeal coming from the floor next to me.

The doctor quickly and carefully collected the muck into a cooler and wrote the date on a piece of masking tape stuck to its lid. She looked at me and sighed through her smile.

"Little guy made a home in your head," she said.

I looked down at the cooler. It was shaking.

Aunt Meredith

IT HAD BEEN months since Rebecca had seen her Aunt Meredith. Once a valuable lifeline in the city, Meredith was now an upsetting and bizarre subject for her niece. Her drinking problem, although often in order—and she was a tremendous person when it was—had claimed her yet again. This time, however, her behavior had become less predictable, and the subjects she chose to discuss during her blackouts were deeply troubling.

Rebecca desperately did not want to spend twenty dollars taking a car across the neighborhood to eat a confusing dinner with a drunk woman in her fifties, just to be sent home with grocery sacks full of Tupperware and glass jars containing leftovers that were over-seasoned and unappetizing when they were fresh. Meredith had been texting and calling her non-stop lately, and the sense of duty Rebecca felt toward her family bubbled over with guilt as she ignored each notification.

The last time her aunt invited her over for dinner, she arrived to find the door leading outside had been left wide open, and the woman was screaming that her cat had escaped. The apartment was a mess, and an empty bottle of absinthe sat on the kitchen counter. Rebecca had never known anyone who preferred drinking absinthe, aside from men her age who were trying too hard. Meredith's explanation was a chaotic tidal wave of disconnected soundbites, and the bathroom fumed a putrid odor.

She claimed not to know how her cat Yogi, a one-year-old black Domestic Shorthair, could have gotten out. Nothing made sense to her. Nothing she said made sense. The words dripping and foaming underneath her wild eyes filled Rebecca with equal parts anger and sadness as she searched for Yogi in the alleyway next to her apartment building. Everything Rebecca said to her aunt twisted into utter nonsense as soon as it passed through her ears. The only thing keeping her from going home was her concern for the poor creature doomed to be controlled by this horrid woman.

Eventually they found Yogi in one of her kitchen cabinets, sitting, staring, calm.

"This is, it's Yog. I knew he was, fat idiot," Meredith spat as she bent over, laughing at the discovery before glaring through Rebecca with her glossy, unfocused eyes and muttering more indecipherable folly.

"I'm glad Yogi is okay, but you need to look around your apartment more thoroughly before you start freaking out. That scared the hell out of me," Rebecca said.

"Have you seen my living room?"

"Yes, I've been to your apartment many times."

"Let's go look at the living room. I want you to see it. I don't think you've seen it before," Meredith gurgled before hurrying to the bathroom, tripping on the lower corner of the door frame, landing on her bloated stomach and vomiting an ugly dark green puddle on the white tile floor. She then proceeded to fall asleep, face down in the shocking mixture, dreamily exhaling through the muck and sucking the nauseating cocktail up into her nose.

After Rebecca dragged Meredith to bed so that she would not drown in the waste of her own guts, she looked at the living room and confirmed it was the same living room as it had always been. The young woman put fresh food in Yogi's bowl, changed his water, and closed the door behind her, vowing never to return.

***

The Campbell family, in which Meredith shared lineage with Rebecca's father, Hank, had a difficult past with alcoholism. The generational trauma of its influence echoed through each family member, with the loudest corner reverberating its power in unholy concert within Meredith's blood. Rebecca had no problem with others drinking, but she avoided it for this reason. Hank had managed to raise his own family and lead a productive life despite the disadvantage he naturally possessed against fighting off the seductive call of inebriation, and he inspired his daughter to do the same. He used his helplessness against it as a source of strength to fend it off. That energy then compounded in a heavy shadow over Meredith, and she became the mouthpiece through which this trait would cry its final death throes.

"Tnt?" The text from Rebecca's aunt was read aloud in her headphones.

The young woman had reached her cold shoulder limit and felt unable to continue putting off her aunt's depressing attempts to reconnect. The whole thing made her so agonizingly sad. Meredith could be such a lovely woman without the drink, and Rebecca wished again to have a family member in the city that she could rely on. Her parents lived a few hours outside of the city, and both still worked at their jobs, which made it more difficult to orchestrate get-togethers with them. Meredith was only a few blocks away, recently unemployed due to an embarrassing incident at her office, of which Rebecca had not been fully given the details, and she wanted gravely to see her only niece.

Then, Rebecca's phone rang, as it had so many times before over the last few months, and she decided to finally answer it.

"Hey, Aunt Meri," she said in her "little girl" voice that she used to put members of her family who still considered her "the young one" in a good mood. "What's up?"

"I've cooked everything. It's done. It's, hello? Where are you?" Meredith responded in a critical tone as though they had made plans the day before.

"What are you talking about?"

"The dinner? Hello? I've already cooked it, it's, are you coming over or not? Because I have too much food now, and Yogi is going insane. He's bitten me and scratched me over and over again. I'm bleeding. I don't know what to do about it. It's giving me headaches. I feel sick, and I think it's because of his spit. It's getting into my cuts. Will you just come over now, please, before it gets cold? Thanks."

Rebecca's phone screen lit up as Meredith ended the call, and she returned it to her pocket. She paused for a moment. Would she really bend to the psychotic demands of a delusional drunk? It felt rude to phrase it that way, but she didn't know how else to phrase it. Although Meredith did not sound drunk yet, she had more than likely already consumed a few drinks and would be well on her way to her preferred state by the time her niece arrived. One cannot simply cook dinner and expect everyone in their life to drop everything and come running. The selfish lies this woman told herself and abused Rebecca with. She was supposed to be the adult. Rebecca should have been the one who felt compelled to drink too much, act undesirably, and rebel against the well-wishes of her family. She contemplated the cruel role reversal she was forced to endure in the company of her aunt as she put on her shoes and called a car to take her to Meredith's apartment.

When she arrived, the door leading outside was shut, and everything appeared to be running as smoothly as in any other home. It was a promising vision from the street. She climbed the stairs on the side of the building and knocked on the door that entered her aunt's kitchen.

The door swung open, almost hitting Rebecca as her aunt, feral-eyed and intensely lucid, ran out to embrace her. Her cat, Yogi, quietly sat and watched them from the doorway. As Meredith led them inside, Yogi cried out a rancid meow and sprinted underneath a brown leather couch in the living room.

"He's been doing that. Idiot," Meredith said. "Look at what he did to me."

She pulled her sleeves up to reveal a gnarled mess of craters, scars, and other terrors of war, burying both of her arms in pure infection. Festering wounds leaked red in various contaminated shades as she attempted to continue their small talk.

"Yogi did that?" Rebecca gasped.

"It's giving me migraines," she said. "Cats can do that, you know? Their spit has poison in it that can give you headaches when they bite you. I don't know why he doesn't love me. All he does is bite me and scratch me. It completely destroyed my appetite. I was worried I'd have to eat alone if you forgot to show up, because I wouldn't have been able to do that."

"You should get a trainer," Rebecca said flatly, already exhausted by her aunt's toxic energy and inability to take the proper steps toward solving her problems. "Just get someone to come in here and give some insight."

"I don't want a stranger in my place."

Meredith walked over to a cabinet that sat above the stovetop, where a large pot of chili bubbled away, and she opened it to reveal a half-empty beer bottle. She took a sip of it and returned it to the cabinet. She was hiding it, although not very well, in a clear display of alcoholic logic with which Rebecca had grown quite familiar. The never-ending secrets.

"What are you drinking?" Rebecca asked in a kind tone, free of judgment. She wanted to at least connect with her on that. If she was going to drink, then it shouldn't be viewed as a dirty thing for her to cover up, even if she was doing a poor job of it.

"Nothing," she said.

"I literally just saw you open the cabinet and take a sip of beer."

The faded memory of a warm expression Meredith had been trying to rekindle with her niece leaked down into her jaw, leaving a colorless mass of empty skin and eyes peering out at Rebecca. Her mouth shrank into a small, thin line. Her eyebrows stiffened, and her eyelids formed grotesque slits, casting light in their shapes through the infinite darkness behind her face.

"You can't see anything," she whispered.

Startled, Rebecca attempted to lighten the mood.

"Can I have a drink? I was hoping I could drink with you."

"No. Drinking is bad. You shouldn't drink," Meredith said, widening her eyes and allowing light to reenter her skin. "I think it's time to eat. I've got chili on the stove. It's just an internet recipe. I hope that's okay."

"You should bring Yogi his food before we eat," Rebecca said, hoping to get a moment alone in the kitchen. "He's part of the dinner party! I just don't want you to forget."

"I'm telling you. He'll bite me. It's the only thing he does when he isn't sitting there, plotting an apartment takeover. I should be the center of his universe, but he bites me."

"He won't just be your cat because you tell him to be. You have to build trust."

Meredith released a scorching, pained cry. Her throat crackled and snapped as she pushed Rebecca back with the power of this visceral, sonic retaliation.

"You know your father used to call me 'the blind idiot' when I would drink? Even when it was just a little bit. Just a single beer. He was so mean to me. I don't even drink that much. He was such an asshole."

"I didn't know that," said Rebecca.

"It's true."

"I'm sorry he said that."

"Forget it," Meredith huffed. "Here, kitty. Kitty. Kitty. Kitty. Kitty. Kitty. Kitty. Kitty."

She crept with the food bowl in her hand into the living room to find her petrified cat. Rebecca quietly opened the cabinet and turned the beer bottle's label to examine it.

The Cold One
It's out of this world!

Rebecca had never seen a beer named The Cold One before, which was surprising because the name felt so obvious to her. The stores where she shopped didn't carry it, but she suspected her aunt most likely possessed a peculiar taste that she could only satiate at specialty alcohol stores. The label was matte black and full of white stars drawn to look like beer bottles, with *The Cold One* flying through space, refreshingly chilled by the undying cool of that outer realm. It was a cute and simple label, the kind that conveniently left off the part about alcohol content. She read that it was brewed with Galaxy hops, which further pushed the branding. Nothing beyond the beer's absence from major grocery stores felt peculiar.

She poured a few drops into the sink to see it without the obstruction of brown glass. A daunting emerald potion lined the sink and slowly slunk down the drain. Effervescence sizzled on the stainless steel. A green beer. Rebecca couldn't believe that this sort of thing regularly existed outside of St. Patrick's Day. Since that holiday had passed about a month prior, she wondered if it was perhaps a discounted batch that Meredith had been lucky enough to happen upon. There was, of course, the alternative.

During the struggle with alcoholism that Meredith experienced throughout Rebecca's life, she had followed a certain pattern of behavior when people paid closer attention to her drinking. She would chug a beer and then fill the bottle with liquor and a little tonic water so that everyone would think that she was still drinking low-alcohol beer when, in reality, she was drinking a flask of lightly carbonated absinthe or whatever else she could get her hands on. Meredith had an affinity for absinthe, among other spirits.

Rebecca set the bottle against her lips and tilted it back, expecting to find that anise-laced, licorice, fennel, mind-numbingly revolting taste that she had come to expect from, in her opinion, the world's most disappointing liquor. But instead, she couldn't taste anything. She ceased experiencing her senses. Her world collapsed into a crepuscule beach, ushering new shapes and commanding their destruction within the same measureless cosmogonic breath. Her hands faded into gloom. Her legs fell into dusk, and her chest sank into a murky bath below the surface of the Earth, passing through to the other side and out of the planet's orbit. She exhaled through her obliterated husk and forgave her embarrassing figure as it thrashed and convulsed in the eerie echoes of time and space.

Before her lay a horrible extraterrestrial chamber without the safety of man-made walls, overwhelmed by inter-dimensional fantasies. High winds slithered through a static constellation outlining a woodwind instrument that crashed a pounding, repetitive swoon over the prestige of intellectual frontier ahead of her. Vertigo washed over her as she considered the balmy emptiness of her former life. She spun in limbo as she was tortured by visions of each of her family members walking up to her celestial corpse, waving goodbye, and walking back across the stars toward Heaven while she lay stuck in some rural area of the solar system, trapped for all eternity. Her mind reeled and pleaded with a God she knew nothing about until this moment. Rebecca held her mouth open to scream, but nothing came. Chaos consumed her soul.

Then, she woke up in the back of a car.

Music coming through the speakers perfectly layered over the concussive flute commanding her recent nightmare and softly straightened out into a pleasant radio hit. The dimly lit sedan, playing ataractic worship music, had been called to pick Rebecca up at her aunt's house. She did not know how or when she got into the car, but approximately thirty minutes after arriving at her aunt's apartment, she was already on her way home with a lap full of Tupperware and glass jars containing leftover chili wrapped in a plastic grocery bag. Rebecca looked at her phone, but did not see a ride being carried out on any of her transportation apps.

"Hey, I'm sorry," she managed, shaking the silence from her mouth. "Uhm, are you, er, how did you pick me up?"

"I picked you up because a woman named Meredith paid me to," the driver said. "You know Meredith, right?"

"Yes."

"Well, you have to thank her. She said you were pretty toasted. You were barely even awake when you got in the car. I asked her. I said, if I got to carry your niece up to her door, just know that it's going to cost you, and she said, alright. If you puke back there, it's a hundred bucks. You and I are both lucky you woke up. I would have left you on the curb in front of your place."

Rebecca winced at the assault of the driver's voice. She had not gotten drunk, but she had been drugged. Whatever that beer was, it was like nothing she had ever experienced. How could her aunt drink something like that and remain conscious? When Rebecca arrived home, she threw the grocery sacks full of chili into her refrigerator, fell into a deep, dreamless sleep, and did not wake for many hours.

When she returned to life the next morning, her head felt foggy and distant but not painful. The hangover she expected to be suspended over her was surprisingly clean and flexible. She could move with relative ease. However, she felt an excruciating hunger throng through her body as she stumbled into the kitchen and eviscerated the leftovers that had been stowed away the previous evening.

Cold, wet meat slopped and slid down her tongue and into her stomach in a euphoric celebration of life. Her shirt eagerly collected the stains of her primal feast. Her eyes dilated, and she fell into the peace of the kill, bloodied across her teeth. Once the chili was consumed with almost tasteless agility, her mind fully returned and she felt revitalized. Then she turned to her computer and began researching possible brewers of The Cold One.

The internet revealed very little to her beyond the fact that beers are often referred to as "cold ones." It seemed that whoever was brewing this beer was a small enough operation that they didn't have a presence online yet. Was such a thing even possible these days? Worried about this inadmissible detail, she did the unthinkable and texted her aunt.

Initiating a text conversation with Meredith had been a difficult habit for Rebecca to break once their relationship leaned from positive to negative influence. Still, she did it for her own good many weeks ago, and she did not revel in returning to it. She texted Meredith, apologizing for her behavior and begging to know what that beer was, truthfully confessing that she had taken a sip of it. She couldn't imagine her aunt being upset with her for taking a sip of her drink. She had been taking sips of her aunt's drinks since she was young. Although, when she was young, Meredith had her alcohol consumption under control, and her drinks were usually nothing more than sweet tea and lemonade. Why should it be different now? Now that she could participate in the world of adults.

Meredith did not respond. The silence grew in orbit as Rebecca marinated and boiled in the wake of her unanswered message. How dare her aunt refuse to respond after all the late nights she kept that hot light emitting from Rebecca's phone? The last few months were nothing more than wind tunnels, bouncing the depraved chant of blisteringly drunk and "unattractive" moments. Rebecca had been expected to catch and nurture her aunt every time she rode the cheap amusement of her fall from grace. She grew weary from her position in this melodramatic horror. She called her. Nothing. The young woman drank a glass of cool tap water, put on her shoes, and called a car to take her to her aunt's apartment.

When she arrived, she found the door leading from the kitchen to the old wooden stairs that flowed down into the alleyway was standing wide open. Again. Rebecca vented an annoyed breath of frustration through her nose, expecting that she would soon find her aunt either passed out or frighteningly awake and looking for Yogi, who was probably hiding somewhere safer than by her side.

As she climbed the stairs, she worried that perhaps her aunt had suffered a terrible accident. In Rebecca's mind, a vision of that gory wreckage covering her arms flashed and melted as her terribly saggy, wrinkled skin was pulled to the floor by the immense gravity radiating from the energy in her home. The pool of her existence had become so deep and treacherous that it was threatening the life of its host.

Maybe Meredith wouldn't be there at all. Maybe she left town completely in a fevered, irrational dash, hopefully leaving her cat behind so that it may have a chance at surviving the impact of her madness. Perhaps Rebecca had left the door open when she adjourned the previous evening, and it was never closed. Of course, she couldn't remember.

Rebecca crossed the doorway threshold into her aunt's apartment and gasped.

The hardwood floor was coated in a sticky, ill-green film that cracked apart from Rebecca's shoes with each step as she made her way inside. She nervously contemplated whether the stickiness would entirely capture her stance if she held still for too long. Empty bottles of The Cold One rolled around on the numerous bends, lumps, and knots in the floorboards. There had to have been close to fifty beer bottles toppled over and discarded around the kitchen. She must have gone through two whole cases of that damned ale this morning. Or was this mess from last night? She couldn't tell.

She called out her aunt's name, and to her surprise, she answered.

"I'm in the living room," Meredith serenely uttered down the hallway.

Rebecca walked past the bathroom, its door tightly shut, and rounded the corner into the living room. The couch had been pushed against the wall to make room for Meredith to lie down. A small river of blood was draining toward the doorway. She was lying on her back as a hot red lake formed around her, but she appeared calm. As Rebecca got closer, she realized that Yogi was sitting on Meredith's chest and seemed to be licking her face. Upon further inspection, she realized that the cat was biting and removing chunks of her aunt's face, and her aunt was smiling.

"Yogi!" Rebecca cried. "Get off!"

Rebecca rushed over and grabbed the cat, but Meredith reached out, clenched her arm, and stopped her.

"It's okay," she said. "I want him to do it."

Meredith's nose had been torn off. A boiling pond of deep crimson collected in the middle of her ravaged visage and streaked down her cheekbones. Holes in her cheeks revealed the inner workings of her clenched jaw and aching teeth patterned with stains from the concoction she craved.

"Aunt Meredith, your nose. Oh my god. Do you not feel it? I'm calling an ambulance."

"Don't," she said. "They won't understand. I need you to understand."

"Understand what?"

"It's right here. I've taken it in, and I will soon become it. This is the final step. It told me. It's happening. I've been chosen to be the next God of creation at the center of the universe."

"Who told you that?"

She smiled. Her eyes were soupy with a mixture of tears and blood, wetting her unfocused gaze that peered beyond her niece's concerned face, glittery with terror. "There's one bottle left. Drink it, and you'll see what I see."

Meredith formed her hand into a guide and pointed toward a single glass bottle sitting defiantly on the floor near her with its cap still securely fastened. A low hum vibrated beneath its label and spread like a gas, filling the space between it and its target.

Rebecca, at first, felt overwhelmingly compelled to drink it. She opened it. Then she recalled the strength of her father, walked over to the kitchen sink, and began pouring it down the drain.

Her aunt was immediately behind her, and she snatched the bottle from her hands. How had she stood and pursued her so quickly? Rebecca had little time to contemplate likely scenarios that allowed Meredith to be that fast. Instead, she was now confronted by anger fuming out of her aunt, and the scene ahead of her, draped in demonic shadows, reminded her of the vision she had on the stairs before she entered.

Blood, snot, tears, slivers of skin, and spit pushed against each other, formed and separated across Meredith's tattered face. Inky spots of drool pushed through the holes in her rosy cheeks, and her nose dumped a thick burgundy broth that slumped its way down her mouth and chin before splashing onto the floorboards below. A steady stream of lime-green and pink mucus lubricated her lips. Her eyes hung sourly. She held the bottle in her right hand and clenched Rebecca's jaw with the dirty fingers in her left.

"Witness it," Meredith said as she punched the glass bottleneck through her niece's teeth, breaking the top front two in half upon entry. As the incisor fragments swirled and mixed with the intruding flood of muddy green beer now barreling down Rebecca's throat, the young woman made eye contact with her aunt. The apartment walls fell away, and she began stretching far out into the looming great beyond.

Suddenly, Rebecca was limitless and free, open in space, treading revolutions near the center of her solar system. Stars and planets aligned as sunlight burst forth from her, and the light coming toward her from other stars evaded obstacles to meet her wandering gaze. She somehow lay warmly in the embrace of frigid space, light-years away from any decently inhabitable conditions created by the thoughtful cradle of a planet roughly three orbits away from its heat source.

Turning and fidgeting to find Earth or any other familiar face in this bewildering arena, Rebecca finally rested her sights on a distant figure.

Meredith was floating about one hundred yards away from her. A soft hum grew in the distance. Then Rebecca realized what was behind Meredith.

The crashing sea of time and space growing and folding smaller and bigger behind her was soon revealed to be alive and exhibiting accelerated entropy. What Rebecca had recognized as further emptiness was, in the current reality, an enormous creature, snarling, twisting, and emotionless in its untestable knowledge of nothing and everything. From it, an illusion of creation hung over their heads as all matter was born and destroyed with pure neutrality. The greased, creasing, wriggling creature formed a nose that planted itself on an even larger image of Meredith's tortured, nebulous face, now suffering in the form of a constellation. Then she released a deep, shuddering moan, and the stars fell from the sky. Sound ceased, the world went Stygian, and Rebecca fell from grace.

***

When she awoke, Rebecca was propped upright on a hospital bed, wearing a paper gown and listening to the gentle grind of friendly voices projecting from the television monitor mounted into the dusty drywall across the room. An adorable "mew" shot forth from her left. She saw Yogi lying with his front paws folded into his chest in a black animal carrier. He blended in perfectly with the shadows beneath its matching finish. Only his watchful eyes emerged from it, and she felt soothed. The world felt stable again. Shortly after she regained consciousness, a man entered the room.

"Hey, you're awake," he said. "How are you feeling?"

"Great," Rebecca lied. She rubbed her tongue against the jagged break where her two upper front teeth had busted and considered how best to accommodate the injury in her speech. The discomfort of it didn't necessarily hurt, but it felt like it should. A light lisp followed her every word. "Where am I?"

"The hospital," he laughed.

"Which one?" she asked, agitated by his cheery demeanor that falsely implied that Rebecca's reality was somehow still held undamaged in the wake of her experience.

"Don't worry. The doctors will come in shortly and fill you in on everything," he said. His outfit communicated that he was neither medical staff nor a police officer. He was just someone in her room.

"Who are you?"

"I was on duty when we picked you up. I'm just making sure you're okay. We responded to a domestic disturbance called in by one of your aunt's neighbors. We found loads of blood where you were passed out, but your aunt wasn't around. You wouldn't have any idea where she is, would you?"

"No," Rebecca said.

"Didn't think so. Do you know why she was bleeding?"

"She accidentally cut herself. She was drunk."

"Yeah, your aunt definitely liked to drink." The man smiled. "We've been called to her house a few times, but not for anything quite like this. You don't have any idea where she is?"

Rebecca sat quietly and stared ahead at the glowing television for a moment. She could have told them everything, the entire truth as she remembered it, but they wouldn't understand. How could they? Unless they knew about this drink. Maybe he did. Was it possible they had seen this behavior in someone else infected by its influence? Had they been watching Aunt Meredith because of this? Maybe they knew something about it that could put her at ease.

"Have you heard of The Cold One?" Rebecca asked.

The man's face fell into a sober seriousness, and he leaned in.

"What is The Cold One?" he asked, all humor erased from his expression. "You have to tell me."

"Ask me later," she said, exhaling from an anxious reserve of breath that was the only thing sustaining her rise. "I'm tired."

"I will," he said, imprinting one more hard look into her mind. "We'll talk more when you're feeling better."

The man walked over to Yogi's carrier and picked him up.

"That's my aunt's cat," Rebecca said in a daze. Either they had given her drugs without her permission, or she was still under the influence of whatever it was that successfully infiltrated her aunt's apartment. Whatever was happening, her life felt extremely heavy and inflexible, but her devotion and love for Yogi remained.

"We're going to take him to the animal care area so he'll be safe," he said, and she believed him. "You can take him with you when you're well enough to leave. You should call your parents."

Rebecca looked inside the carrier to get one last glimpse of the closest living creature she had to family in that moment. The cat's pupils burst open wide, glinted, then narrowed into slits like protective windows for castle archers. He exhausted his breath in a rattling purr that overtook the carrier and, subsequently, the handle leading to the man's hand tasked with supporting the creature's weight. The whole figure shook.

Submerged in the cat's eye, Rebecca saw her Aunt Meredith whistling and floating through a bottomless meadow of stars. Small grew large. Space expanded, stretched, and dragged its wretched bones farther away from the dead center of the galaxy as she screamed her evidence of life to the furthest reaches of her new power. She now stood, enormous, unwavering in the action of valleys across planets and stars, each shuddering with its own personality to lend into service of this new God. The blind twisted mesh of unorganized flesh and rot fumed an excruciating spell of fetid odor and repellent sensation. This new mass, drunk with power, hollowly sang along with the surrounding growl of the great beyond, scraping along the unknowable edges of our timeline. Her bloodline was trapped in that hunk of hanging gas and explosive matter that, at one point, only existed for Rebecca in the form of science fiction, and from it ushered the makings of the future.

Rebecca reached her hand out to the carrier and whispered her wish to hold the cat. The man refused, claiming to be working in the better interest of the creature, and told her that room service would be in soon to tend to her needs. He asked her if she was hungry. She agreed.

"What would you like to eat?" he asked. "They can get you pretty much anything. Within reason."

"Chili," she said.

The man nodded. Yogi unfolded his left front paw to reveal an almost insignificant spot of leftover blood. He licked it away from the fibers of his proud coat and folded his paw back underneath his body. Then he scratched his ear, and the man carried him out of the room.

Jackalope

I ARRIVED AT Denver's house around 7:00 p.m. I remember looking at the clock because I thought it was too dark outside for this time of year. We worked together at a bar, and he invited me to hang out for a drink at his place after one of my early shifts. He said he had something to show me.

Denver lived alone in a small rental property he'd recently moved to, a few miles from the bar. It stood on a quiet street at the edge of town. It was a small town, but Denver didn't even like *that* much light and sound. He always said he could get more bang for his buck living farther away from everyone. Silence and freedom were worth the drive.

When I entered his home, the first thing I saw was an animal head on the wall, frozen in a false expression. It was an impossible creature. A rabbit's head with pronghorn antlers protruding out of it.

"I see you noticed it already," Denver laughed as he put his hand on my shoulder.

"Where'd you get that?" I asked.

"Oh, I went jackalope hunting not too long ago and shot it myself," he said. "Just finished the taxidermy. Looks great, doesn't it?"

Convincing people that jackalopes are real is a tradition in certain areas around here. As I reached out to touch the point of contact between the antlers and the rabbit's head, a wave of horror washed over me, and I felt the overwhelming urge to leave.

"Jackalopes aren't real," I said, "but nice try. Where did you get it?"

"I told you. I killed it."

He walked to the kitchen and brought back two open beers. He handed me one, but I didn't feel like drinking anymore. I placed it down on an old, chipped wooden table and sat on a dirty couch, which served as the only other piece of furniture in the room. Copper stains warped and stretched along its arms.

"Let's toast to the jackalope," Denver said, raising his beer can.

"I think jackalope taxidermy is gross, Denver. People kill rabbits, antelope, and deer just to stitch them together for decoration. Don't you think that's weird?"

Denver's eyes fell, and he turned annoyed.

"You don't think I could kill that thing myself?"

"It's not real. It's just morbid taxidermy art."

Denver slammed his beer can on the table. White foam shot out of it and grazed blond droplets against the ceiling. I realized that he had drunk quite a few beers before I arrived, and he was visibly drunk now. He composed himself and laughed.

"Come on, let's go into the other room. We can watch some TV or something. Don't forget your beer."

He walked to a door behind where I was seated. I stood up, leaving my beer behind, and followed him. I didn't want to be rude, but I was desperately thinking of a reason to disappear.

"Is that all you wanted to show me?" I asked, hoping our business was finished.

The door opened, and the harsh sting of putrid death slashed its way through my senses. Denver turned on an overhead light to reveal a small windowless room with a drain in the middle of the floor. A table stood above the drain, coated in bloodstains once thick red rivers running down its legs. Then I saw what was on the table.

Denver laughed as I ran out of his house. I got in my car as fast as my body would allow and sped away down the dirt road, a storm of ground debris flailing behind me. Adrenaline pounded my brain against my skull. Then I heard three gunshots ring out behind me.

When I arrived at the police station, I found a bullet hole in my trunk and one in my license plate. I told them what happened, but when officers went to his house to check on him, he greeted them with open arms. There was nothing they could do. Nothing they would do. They simply told me he was one of the town's many respected jackalope hunters and laughed.

I quit my job at the bar and moved to the nearest city to look for work. The lack of nature puts me at ease. The noise helps me sleep. The safety of being surrounded by people is worth the chaos. But every now and then, I look out at the park across the street, into the darkness of the heavy tree clusters, and think about the jackalope.

Fuzz

NAMING ANIMALS HAS always come easily to me. I grew up with a mess of outdoor and indoor friends, and they all had names. Inspiration usually strikes the moment I meet one. But the most recent cat we adopted was different.

A year ago, my partner and I adopted our first cat together, Cashew, an orange tabby, and we thought it was time to get another one. He needed a friend, and we had more love to give. When we brought the new girl home, a white Domestic Shorthair, I couldn't figure out what to name her, and she did not get along with Cashew.

Eventually, I fell on the name Fuzz because she was constantly shedding enormous white fuzzballs all over the apartment. I didn't like the name much, or the trait, but it stuck.

One evening, while I was preparing dinner alone in the kitchen, Cashew released a brassy, fat, guttural growl that I had never heard from him or any other cat before outside our open bedroom door. He had been growling at Fuzz regularly since we brought her home, but this growl was much more urgent than the others. I walked to the bedroom.

The floor was covered in thick patches of white fur, more than I had ever seen. Fuzz sat on the ground, surrounded by pounds of her hair, inches deep. It was everywhere. It felt impossible. There was no way a cat that small could shed all this fur in such a short timeframe. The air was a blizzard of thick bodily fabric suspended in escape. Cashew growled in the doorway again, gagged, threw up a massive white furball, and continued growling.

Soon, the hair began to swirl around Fuzz. A delicate, fuzzy cyclone consumed the room in a white cloud. I couldn't breathe. I couldn't speak. I could only watch. My eyes itched and burned, and I snapped out of my stunned amazement, grabbed Cashew, and closed the door.

High-pitched whining pierced the air and rattled the doorframe. The knob shook in my hand. Cashew growled deeper, each growl more primally alarming than the last, and batted at the door with his paw. Suddenly, the noise stopped. Everything was still.

I opened the door.

Hundreds of cats, all identical to Fuzz, were now roaming around the room and climbing on top of each other. Loose fur littered the floor and hung lightly suspended in the air. They all began hissing and pushing their way out into the living room. They bit at my ankles. I screamed. A group munched and scratched at my feet. They reared up and bit my knees. One jumped off a dresser and slashed my face. Another clawed at my shins and drew pools of blood that drenched my shredded clothing.

Cashew growled, hissed, and fought to get out of my arms, but I couldn't let him go. I was sure they would kill him. I kicked thirty or forty Fuzzes out of my way while they feverishly hunted for fresh flesh to rip apart and meat to consume. They were hungry. I put Cashew in his carrier and left the apartment, locking them inside.

When I called my partner, he told me that he received a message from the adoption center claiming Fuzz had been scheduled to be euthanized before we picked her up and that she would need to be put down. They weren't supposed to give her to us. She suffered from an incurable condition that made her a danger to herself and others, but they wouldn't go into further detail. He was angry. He wanted to know how the shelter could make such a disgraceful mistake. He said we would fight it. Fuzz was a part of our family now.

I told him what happened.

We agreed to let animal control officials from the adoption center come over that night. They were outfitted in heavy protective suits and commanded that we stay out of the apartment until they contacted us. After I cleaned my wounds, we spent the night in a hotel.

When we returned the next day, the apartment was clean. There was no trace of the night before. I released Cashew from his carrier, and he ran around happier than I had ever seen him. He sprinted into the bedroom and immediately cozied up in bed. I lay next to him. The apartment was ours again.

A small piece of white fuzz fell from the ceiling and landed on my shoulder. Cashew growled, but I petted him and assured him that everything was okay. Fuzz was gone. The team just missed a spot. I picked up the small clump of hair and saved it in a wooden box as a keepsake. Cashew stared at the box until he fell asleep.

***

That night, I opened the box in a moment of weakness. I missed my cat. I screamed. White fuzz overflowed out of it, and pounds of hair fell onto the ground. Cashew snapped awake and hissed. He hurried over to the fuzz, now the weight of a new cat, and started eating it. He lapped up every scrap of it. Every piece was swallowed. His belly filled and stretched with hair while I watched in petrified disbelief.

Once he finished, he painfully waddled over to the fireplace and proceeded to vomit all of it onto a pile of ash. Heaps of dripping wet white fur clumps dusted with black coal and laced with bile coated the fireplace bricks. He looked at me and then back at the fireplace.

I doused the fur in lighter fluid and set the blaze.

After that day, we decided that Cashew would be our only pet. But once a day, I dream about getting him a sister or a brother to play with. I see hundreds of them. I see them so clearly in my mind, and I have names for all of them.

Slug House

HEAVY, LAZY, WET, hardly a sound at all, Robin heard something moving in the hallway outside her bedroom. The night before, she noticed it much fainter and farther away, but she fell asleep. It hadn't frightened her then.

Now, rhythmic cracking and gnashing lightly floated above the deeper, unending slurping that aurally slipped through the cracks around her door. She had moved into this duplex only two days earlier, but she knew this sound was not normal. It had gotten worse. Louder oozing, bubbling sludge in her mind, the ghastly racket echoed like a horrific ocean of blood and guts quivering inside a skinless body, desperately working to cover its holes. It was a festering sound. An awful sound.

On the afternoon that Robin moved in, she noticed a small garden in the back yard. She assumed it belonged to her neighbor until he walked by.

"Hey," he said, "I'm Parker. I live in the duplex connected to yours. You're the new person who lives here, right?"

"Yes. I'm Robin. Pleased to meet you."

"Awesome. Well, welcome. In case you didn't already know, the people who lived here before you loved gardening. That garden and pretty much the whole back yard are yours. I don't use it, so go nuts."

"Great." She looked at the garden. Dehydrated tomatoes ached in the hot sun, and weeds choked the rest of the bed. She hadn't gardened much in her past, but it had always been of interest to her. The slight advantage she was given by the previous tenants was unfortunately overshadowed by the gloomy state of it.

"Nice meeting you too," he waved. Parker entered his side of the duplex through a sliding glass door as Robin waded out into the backyard grass to meet her new land. It crunched and curled softly beneath her bare toes as she found a trail to the garden.

The plants were pathetically unkempt, having missed the touch of their previous caretakers for what must have been weeks. Maybe months. But they were still alive. They were deathly parched, and their desperate plea for love sowed an unexpectedly accelerated feeling of devotion deep in her heart. Robin watered them enough to satiate their thirst using a nearby faucet, but would need to return to them later. She worried about them, but settling into her new home was the most critical task ahead of her. Once she finished, she would restore the garden to the efficient little world it begged to be.

A snail sat on a leaf to her left and looked up at her in between bites of it. The soft crunch relaxed Robin. Although she was still unsure about her new home, this moment felt nice. She had chosen a good spot for herself. She looked at the leaf, and the snail was gone. Silently, a thin pool of mucus faded in the sun's heat with the memory of its existence, and Robin went back inside.

***

During her first night, she heard the noise. It was faint and far. The wet smudging, topped with rhythmic crunching and crackling, fit together like moldy tiramisu. The following morning, she saw Parker getting into his car to go to work.

"Hey, Parker, can I ask you something?"

"Sorry, did you hear me using the bathroom last night?" he asked.

Robin stopped.

"What? No, I don't think so," she said, surprised.

"I'm just kidding," Parker laughed. "What's up?"

"Uhm, I heard like a wet, weird, I don't know, crunching last night. It sounded like something was moving around, maybe outside. Have you heard anything weird like that?"

"You know what it might be? It could be snails and slugs."

"Snails and slugs?"

"The people who lived here before you, well, they loved having snails and slugs in the garden. They seemed to think the more, the better, so they dumped a ton of them back there. Don't get me wrong, they help make good soil and everything, but they can also kill the plants. I mean, it's possible to have too many of anything. They were obsessed with that garden though. Maybe a little too obsessed with the 'slugs' aspect of it. It's hot out, so most of them are hiding, but there are a ton of them. You can hear them munching on stuff. Especially at night. People say they move silently, but I swear I can hear them slithering around sometimes."

"I think that's what I heard," she said, remembering the snail from the previous day. "It's kind of nice, the little munchies, but it's kind of gross too."

"Uh, yeah. You can see why I don't go in the back yard much," Parker said.

"Thanks for clearing that up. I won't keep you."

"No problem. I was for real kidding before too, by the way. I'm sorry. That was gross. I'm super quiet when I use the bathroom. I promise."

She laughed and gave Parker a thumbs-up, turning her face in an expression that communicated her disinterest in further details. He smiled and drove to work while Robin finished unpacking the rest of her belongings and decorated her new home.

On the second night, it no longer sounded like a group of slugs. It sounded bigger. The undulating weighted sludging topped with light crunching turned over like a massive compost pile in Robin's mind. This stark contrast in auditory sensations filled her with pure, primal dread. Whatever it was, it was in the hallway outside her room, it was massive, and it was slithering closer to her.

Robin kept a small souvenir baseball bat near her nightstand for protection. Her father had gotten it for her at a Chicago Cubs game when she was in college. She didn't possess any allegiance to any specific sports team or sport, but it made her feel safe to have it nearby, although she had never used it as a weapon before and wasn't entirely sure she would use it effectively if such action became necessary. It barely had enough weight to do any real damage to a person larger than her, but it was something. She grabbed it, held it above her head, and opened the door.

Light from her bedroom gleamed off a gigantic puddle of the thick, snotty mess now coating the floor in front of her door. It ran the length of her hallway. Thick, clear mucus soaked into the wood and rugs. There was no way of knowing which direction it all led. It had become one enormous directionless mass.

Robin put on her boots before walking through the hallway and down the stairs. Every surface in her home was encased in the slick, greasy film. The air felt humid. Her feet sank into the snotty pools and got more difficult to lift with each step. Finally, she reached the front door of her home. Three snails were slowly scootching out as if they had been asked to leave. Robin laid her bat horizontally and crushed them in unison. Gooey concert. She walked to the kitchen and pulled a two-pound salt container from the pantry. Rage filled her chest, and her instinct to protect her new home cemented her sense of belonging. A moment later, she was in the back yard, killing every snail and slug she could find.

She dug them up, picked them off plants, and grabbed them off trees. She chucked them in a pile, salted them, and struck the pile with her bat.

Again and again. Snotty, vibrant colors. A chummy bloodbath. Snail bits soared past her red eyes. Like a small, drowned carcass, the superorganism of gritty wet lumps mutedly absorbed each blow with a cold thud. She wanted to hear each of them scream.

After she had killed the last one, all the remaining energy in her body evaporated. She walked back inside, locked the door, and fell prisoner to ten hours of dreamless sleep. She would clean the mucus in the morning.

When she awoke the following day, the ghostly mucus trails were gone. Robin found Parker in the back yard, fixating on her massacre. He seemed upset. The line between sadness and anger blurred across his face.

"I had to kill them. They were coming into my house in massive hordes. My place was disgusting last night," she said.

"Hey," Parker turned his head and smiled, "I get it. They're gross."

He walked back into his half of the duplex and slowly slid the door closed, clasping it shut with a tiresome, long click. Robin sat in the dirt by her garden, smelling the scorching snail carcasses and watching Parker's sliding glass door until darkness fell. No movement occurred inside his home, and no lights were ever turned on. He was simply gone. As the sun sank, charcoal clouds breathed easily through his windows, weaving the night seamlessly through his half of their building.

That evening, Robin did not hear a sound until her bedroom door opened.

The soft uniformity of silence was broken by the creek of her bedroom door hinges. Then, heavy, slow, wet, hardly a sound at all, Robin heard something move past her doorway, across the floor of her bedroom, and underneath her bed. It was that thing, whatever it was. It couldn't have been another horde of slugs. She killed them all.

She breathlessly grabbed the bat from her nightstand and crept toward the foot of her mattress. Peeking over the edge, she could see a fresh, clear slime trail leading to the small, terribly dark corner beneath her. Slowly, she bent and lowered her head to look underneath the bed.

On the farthest edge of the murky world underneath Robin's bed, Parker, completely nude, covered in lube and petroleum jelly, lay crying and shaking and asking for her forgiveness.

Robin screamed.

She grabbed her phone and ran outside. The police were called, and Parker was arrested. Officers searched the home and found that the two duplexes were connected by an attic. He had used an entrance to the attic in his upstairs bathroom to move between the homes undetected, coating himself with lube and pretending to be a slug in a mysterious fantasy that he would not explain. He only cried. They never understood why. They only knew that it had happened and that his home was brimming with hundreds more of those nauseating creatures.

When Robin returned home the following morning, she made her way around the crew that was removing the mess from both sides of the duplex. It was the hottest day of the year so far, and the smell was awful, but it was quiet, and she couldn't wait to begin work on her new garden.

Midnight Mattress

ROBERT DRIED THE brown water from his hands with a brown paper towel and reached for the breakroom door handle. He breathed deeply. His first week of training at Midnight Mattress, a 24-hour mattress store about a mile walk from his apartment, had gone smoothly up until tonight. Halloween. The owner and manager, Linda, had scheduled him during the busiest night of the year. Robert asked why Halloween was their busiest night, but she wouldn't give him an answer. She only laughed.

***

In most places, a 24-hour mattress store is difficult to come by. It's a confusing business model that has worked out surprisingly well for Midnight Mattress. Robert didn't mind the hours. He liked working the night shift. He had just moved to Chicago without a job already secured, and Midnight Mattress was the first place to respond to his application. Linda explained it to him on his first day.

"Why would a mattress store close at night if people sleep at night?" she asked.

"Because…" Robert paused, "they're asleep?"

"That's when people need beds the most," Linda exclaimed with her index finger pointing in the air. "That's why we stay open all night. So when people are at their most desperate for a comfy spot to rest their head, they'll always be able to come to us."

Wouldn't people be out going to parties or asking for candy? Why would someone want to spend time trying out various firm settings and spending hundreds of dollars on a bed from a showroom? Who would be trying to figure out whether they're going to transport the bed themselves or pay for it to be delivered to their house at midnight on Halloween? On Robert's second night, Linda almost told him.

"Inventory," she said. "The other employees take the night off because they don't want to do inventory. Newest person usually has to do it. I have to be here to make sure it gets done. Don't forget to bring something to eat. You won't have time to leave the store to get anything. It's just going to be you and me taking care of customers while we simultaneously do inventory."

"Inventory of what?" Robert asked. "The beds?"

"Everything," Linda said. Then she continued training him to talk to customers and locate price tags at each mattress's upper left corner. She showed him how to pretend to be surprised by how inexpensive the bed is and smile back at the customer after looking at the tag. She would not divulge any further.

Linda was a fit early-fifties, five feet and seven inches. Her energy and attitude made her seem even younger and larger. She had shoulder-length salt and pepper hair that was tied back with a yellow bandana. Robert only ever saw her in her work uniform, the standard purple collared t-shirt and black pants, but he imagined she dressed pretty cool outside of work. He had seen the leather jacket in her locker.

When Robert arrived around eleven in the evening to begin his Halloween shift, he sensed a more chaotic energy than usual from his boss. The holiday spirit was concentrated into a single pumpkin decoration, about six inches tall, hanging from the front door window. Otherwise, the store was the same. A mattress store.

He quickly stashed his backpack in one of the flimsy breakroom lockers and returned to the floor. She was pacing around the showroom, talking to herself and using a clipboard to scribble on a piece of paper.

"Oh, thank god you're here," she said. "Are you late? No. Never mind. Right on time. I don't even know what time it is. Beautiful. Love it. Okay, I've begun the inventory. Now, things are going to get super busy within the next hour, and I need you to be ready. Do you have to use the restroom or anything? You brought something to eat later, right?"

"No, I'm good. And yes, I did," Robert said. "Do you want me to start counting? Should I grab another clipboard?"

"I'll take care of writing stuff down. You just tend to customers when they come in."

"Oh, actually," Robert stammered, "I forgot. I brought a sandwich for my break, and I need to put it in the refrigerator. It's in my backpack in my locker. I'll be right back. I'm just going to take care of that quick."

"Okay. Please yell my name if you need help with anything."

Robert wondered why he would need her help putting his sandwich in the refrigerator. She must be overwhelmed, and it was causing her to speak strangely. He opened the door to the breakroom and walked to the unlocked locker, barely holding itself closed, that held his backpack.

After moving his sandwich into the refrigerator and closing the door, he noticed the tip of something sticking out from underneath it. The object was onyx, profoundly darker than the area surrounding it, and shiny. The exposed part of its tail glinted the overhead light into Robert's eyes at a much higher intensity. Everything around it drowned in that light. Robert couldn't believe something so dark could be that bright. He couldn't tell what it was, but he knew it shouldn't be there. This was the breakroom. Robert bent down, grabbed it, and pulled.

Then, suddenly, a screech pierced his ears and rattled his senses. He fell backward into the lunch table. The creature tucked itself farther underneath the fridge.

Robert opened a cabinet below the sink and found a menagerie of chemicals and cleaning paraphernalia. He grabbed a cleaning spray bottle and trash bags. He unfurled a trash bag and placed the mouth of it at the base of the refrigerator. Then he tucked the nozzle of the cleaning spray underneath a corner of the fridge and sprayed while he rocked the machine from side to side. He hoped that whatever it was would attempt to escape into the trash bag. He didn't want to kill it. He just wanted it out of the breakroom.

Without a moment to react, the creature darted into the trash bag with enough force to yank it out of Robert's hands. It blindly ran around the room, knocking over chairs and denting lockers, the bag wildly crinkling around its body, thrashing with weight and speed that stole Robert's breath.

He tried to grab the bag, but the creature jerked free each time he thought it was secure. The thin plastic easily ripped apart in Robert's fingers. Little holes emerged in it around the front of the creature. It was like a small, muscular person was running around inside the garbage. Then it hit a stack of lockers hard enough to make them come crashing down on top of it. After that, everything was still.

Dark brown liquid leaked out of the bag. A little at first, but soon it flowed out as if it was being fed by a broken gasoline hose. Gallons of dark brown bubbly muck gushed out of the bag and coated the floor of the break room. It stained Robert's shoes and drenched his backpack, which had been tossed out of its locker during the commotion. He grabbed his bag, bathing his fingers in the sludge, and then Linda entered.

"Oh crap," Linda said. "He's early."

"Who is?" Robert said, running water from the sink over his backpack. The horrid mess slowly rolled off like molasses, leaving thick stains in its wake.

"Okay, look, I'm sorry to tell you this now, but this is part of why tonight is our busiest night."

"What is?"

"There are, I guess you could call them creatures, in the beds, and they come out at midnight on Halloween."

"What?"

"See, this is why I didn't want to tell you before. It's hard to explain, and people always freak out. Can you just try to understand? Please? I've had to fire so many people," Linda said. "You know how people always talk about monsters being under the bed?"

"I do," Robert said slowly.

"Well, they're all wrong. The monsters are *inside* the beds."

"What are you talking about?"

"Why do you think we have such good deals?" Linda raised her voice slightly. "None of these beds have had the monsters taken out of them. Saves us a lot of money, but then we also need to have someone here to make sure they don't mess up the whole store on Halloween. That's when they come out of the beds on their own and wreak havoc. But then they go back in the beds after a little bit. The beds are fine. Great beds. Most people never notice them. We used to only be open during the day, and we would have someone stay overnight on Halloween, but then they sold a few beds during the overnight shift one year, and we were like, wow, maybe we should start selling beds at night all year round. Totally just kind of stumbled into that idea. It's been working out great. It's just tough on Halloween, you know, because they come out, and then we have to make sure they don't kill anybody or do anything crazy. I don't want to close the store if we could still make money. But I also don't want people to see these things. To be honest, I'd love to get rid of any of them that we can while they're out. Don't kill yourself doing it, though. That reminds me, make sure you take your break tonight. When things get overwhelming, I find that eating something always makes me feel better. Couple chomps of that sandwich should do you good. Hey, you good?"

Robert threw up in the sink.

"It smells so awful," he choked.

"Oh yeah," Linda laughed. "I forget. I'm used to it. It's gross when they gush out like that. We have a lot of deodorizing things out in the store, so you don't even notice it out there. Plus, we're not going to kill one out there. Okay? Don't do that. I didn't think one of them would get in here. They're not supposed to come out until midnight. I'm not mad at you for killing it, by the way, but please try not to kill them inside. Otherwise, this happens. We can clean this up later. Just be careful."

"There are more?" Robert asked.

"Yeah. They're in all the beds."

"And you still sell the beds?"

"I mean, yeah, and you will too, in no time. I promise. You'll get the hang of it."

Robert grabbed his sandwich out of the refrigerator with his cleanest hand, put it back in his backpack, and slung the wet bag over his shoulders.

"I'm not leaving my stuff in here," he said. He washed his hands three times and rinsed out his mouth. He looked out the employee lounge window at all the beds in the showroom—roughly one hundred—and imagined the creatures stirring inside of them. He imagined the entire showroom coated in the dark brown sludge. Robert dried the brown water from his hands with a brown paper towel, reached for the breakroom door handle, and breathed deeply.

"Hey, buddy, don't worry," Linda reassured him. "I do this every year."

They entered the showroom. Artificial lavender scent floated through the air. For now, it was a normal 24-hour mattress store.

A customer entered: a middle-aged man wearing khakis and a tucked-in light blue collared shirt. He looked like he was either working late or wearing the costume of someone who was working late.

"Hi, how can I help you?" Robert asked, glancing at the clock. Although at least one of the creatures had emerged earlier than anticipated, they still had ten minutes.

"Oh good, you sell beds here." He smiled, pausing to wrinkle his face at the sight of Robert's backpack but choosing not to mention it. "My wife and I just moved into our new house nearby, and we don't have a bed yet. We thought we would sleep on the floor for one night, but I remembered you guys are open, which is awesome, and I said I might as well drive over here and buy a bed tonight rather than wait until tomorrow."

"An excellent choice, sir," Robert raised his voice, his nerves taking control as he gestured to the rows of beds behind him. He felt like he was becoming Linda, and he cringed deep in the back of his brain. "What sort of mattress do you have in mind? We have every kind. Do any of these catch your eye?"

"We want king-sized, definitely. Nothing with springs. Something that has an equal balance of softness and firmness. I don't know. A bed. Do you have anything like that?"

"Right this way."

Robert led the customer to the closest king-sized bed and considered that the size of the bed may affect the size or number of creatures within it. The man sat down.

"Ouch." The man quickly stood up. "This one has springs. No, no. What about this one?"

The man walked to a bed a few rows away and sat on it. "This is great. Wow. How much is this one?"

"I don't know. Hey, Linda. How much is this bed?" Robert yelled.

"Look at the price tag, Robert," Linda shouted back from the opposite end of the store.

"Right." He felt around for the price tag, located at the top left corner of every mattress. When he found it, however, its shape was different than the others. Something had ripped most of it off. In his distress, he clenched the remainder of the tag and ripped it off completely.

"Does that mean it's free?" the customer laughed. When Robert turned to smile at him like he had been taught, the man's expression froze.

The customer was lying fully stretched out on the bed. He moved his mouth to scream, but nothing came. A red cloud started expanding throughout the fabric of the mattress beneath him. His back was leaking blood at an astonishing rate. It flowed from him like brown water from a trash bag. Robert grabbed his shoulders and tried to sit him up, but he could not lift him. Something was holding him down. A crooked oval of urination soaked his khakis. Then, it let go.

The customer sat upright. His back had been gnawed, sliced, sucked on, and drained of blood. The gnarly meat of his back was wet with the creature's saliva. The skin was removed entirely from his shoulder blades. His spine was exposed. A red slab slowly oozed over his waistband. He screamed.

"What the fuck?" he shouted.

A small hole pooled with blood in the middle of the bed behind him.

"Do you want to see any of our other options?" Robert asked.

The customer stood up and collapsed in pain. Every movement, he was strapped to a bed of nails. His exposed nerves cried in agony. Out of the little hole in the mattress, the creature flashed its face.

Linda appeared from behind the two men with a double garbage bag, a bag put inside another bag to increase its strength, and pulled the creature out of the bed. It was a storm cloud in her hand. The tip of a dark tail poked out from the opening of the bag as she held it up.

"Hi, so sorry, a wild animal got into the store," Linda said, the bag thrashing around in the air next to her, pulling her back and forth. "It has been captured and is no longer a threat to you. Robert, go ahead and make sure this gentleman receives 66.6% off the price of any of our beds for his trouble. Happy Halloween, sir. And my deepest apologies again."

"I need to go to the hospital," he said through pained gasps.

"Sure, sure," Linda said as she nodded and walked the rustling sack outside. She lugged the bagged monster over to her car and locked it in the trunk. She reentered, her car rattling behind her, just as Robert finished speaking to the 911 dispatcher.

"An ambulance will be here soon," Robert said.

"Why did you call an ambulance?" Linda asked.

"Because he needs one?" Robert said, confused by her question. "I told them a wild animal attacked him. Like you said. They asked what kind of animal, and I hung up."

"Don't call an ambulance. Now the cops are going to show up. We'll get shut down if they show up during our busiest night of the year. This place looks awful."

"He needs an ambulance." Robert gestured to the bleeding man lying face down on the floor beside him.

"We might as well burn this place down, because that's what the cops are going to do," fumed Linda. "I know you're new, but oh my god. You messed up so bad. I'm sorry, but like, I can't hide how displeased I am with you right now. I'm pissed, Robert. To be honest. I am. I have to fire you over this."

"I'm not going to let him just lay here and bleed. This place *should* get shut down. This is insane."

Linda lunged at Robert and wrapped a garbage bag tightly around his face. He began to lose consciousness. Then, he heard monsters screech, Linda scream, and the world turned off just as the clock struck midnight.

***

Robert woke up in a hospital bed. A nurse was opening the blinds. Sunlight danced on the cool blue and coral-colored vinyl floor.

"Hey, good morning," the nurse, a plump man with an out-of-focus face and a calming voice, said. "I'm Stephen."

"What happened?" Robert asked.

"You were attacked. The police found you at the mattress store. It sounded like it must have been nasty. They couldn't tell us much about it."

"What did they say?"

"I'm sorry to tell you this, but Linda passed away at the scene. We're not sure who or what did it, but they were unable to revive her. I'm so sorry."

"She tried to kill me."

"Really? Oh. You need to tell the police that. We thought you three were all attacked by the same thing."

"You found the other guy? Is he okay?"

"Yes, Daniel, the other gentleman, is alive. He isn't *okay*, necessarily, but he's recovering. He won't speak to anyone about what happened. His wife is trying to get him to talk to the police now. He's in shock. Whatever happened must have been extremely traumatic. Do you remember anything?"

"There are monsters in the mattress store."

"Monsters?"

"In the beds. There are monsters. They come out on Halloween. That's why it's their busiest night of the year." Robert paused and looked down at his hospital bed, horrified. "Is this mattress safe? Has it had its monster removed?"

Stephen looked at Robert with soft, concerned eyes.

"You should rest now. You've been through a lot. We can talk all about it when you're feeling better. How does that sound? Don't worry. We brought your backpack too. It's right over here."

Stephen pointed to Robert's bag on the floor next to his bed, still coated in brown stains. Robert bent over, opened it, and took out his sandwich.

"I'll feel better after I eat something," he said.

"Hey, that sounds good to me. Hit the button next to your bed if you need anything else, and I'll be here right away."

The nurse smiled and left the room. As the door closed, Robert saw Stephen's smile fall serious while he spoke to a police officer in the hall. They looked in at him. Robert unwrapped his sandwich and took a bite, running his free hand up and down the bed.

Whacking Willy

THERE ARE MANY reasons why a child may be forbidden from going out at night. Even in the small Midwestern community of Casper, Iowa, away from the crime and violence of major cities, the prevailing belief among residents is that nothing good happens after midnight. Some children might be forbidden from going out at night because they're in trouble, and some because they're being kept out of trouble. Either way, there's a certain kind of trouble that can only be found once the sun goes down.

Michael had just turned fourteen years old and successfully attained his learner's permit, which enabled him to drive a vehicle while accompanied by an adult possessing a valid driver's license. This new sense of freedom lifted his spirits in a way nothing ever had in his budding life. He couldn't stand being at home, although he lived fairly comfortably with his loving parents. He wanted to travel. He wanted adventure.

One Friday night, Michael's friend Carter slept over at his house. After a few hours of playing video games, eating pizza, and pretending to get drunk on caffeine-free Diet Pepsis, the night began to wind down. Michael's parents wished them goodnight, reminding them of their agreement, which allowed the boys to choose when they went to sleep as long as they remained in the house and quiet.

Michael and Carter put on a convincing performance, climbing into their sleeping bags. They maintained that they were already feeling the pull of sleep and would probably only have enough energy to watch a movie for a little while. They lowered the volume on the television and lay quietly until about midnight, when they were sure Michael's parents were soundly dreaming behind a thick bedroom door upstairs.

"Where should we go?" Carter asked, finally feeling comfortable enough to whisper.

"Let's go see if Whacking Willy is real," said Michael.

On the edge of town, near where the road gets fast and buildings become fewer and farther between, there is a light brown house nestled neatly into an unassuming cul-de-sac. A woman runs a daycare on the first floor of the house during the day. People say her father, William, lives upstairs. The legend goes that if someone drives to the house at night, parks in the driveway, flashes their headlights, drives away, and then returns to the driveway, Willy will be looking down at their car from one of the second-floor windows. If the visitors flash their lights again, William will come outside. And if they turn their car off, he'll put on a show.

Whacking Willy was an urban legend around their school. A few classmates claimed to have successfully spotted him, but their stories were impossible to prove. He was almost always described as a short, slim and toned, scraggly older fellow with long, curly gray hair and an unkempt gray beard. After the night of Michael and Carter's sleepover, parents and older folks around town would describe him as looking like Charles Manson, although most kids didn't know who that was.

One girl said Whacking Willy sat next to her in the back seat of her cousin's car and told them his entire life story. She said he told them he was a sex worker in Europe for many years. He said he went to jail in France for beating someone to death with a bat that he still kept next to his bed, although Michael never believed that detail. He moved to the U.S. when he got out to live with his daughter. When kids asked her what his "show" was, she said that he stood in front of the car, bathed in headlights, and masturbated.

That part always made kids laugh. It sounded made up, but it was the one part of the story that was consistent throughout each eyewitness account. His backstory would morph into more egregious and graphic tales, but it always ended the same way. Sometimes, he offered to do more explicit things, but nobody accepted. So, he stood in front of curious teenagers' cars and made himself orgasm on the pavement for their amusement. If he had done something more than that, it had not been reported by the victim. Somehow, the daycare in his home stayed in business.

Surely the police knew about Willy by now, Michael thought. Children assured themselves that there was no way something like that could keep happening without adults in the neighborhood finding out. No way his daughter could continue running a daycare out of the same building. Of course, none of them had ever told an adult. And naturally, Michael and Carter needed to find out if it was true.

They snuck out the basement window on the opposite side of the house, away from Michael's parents' bedroom, and tiptoed to the street where the ten-year-old forest-green Toyota Camry that would fully become Michael's on his sixteenth birthday was parked. After what felt like the brightest cabin lights on Earth turned off and what sounded like the loudest engine created by man ignited, they drove away from the safety of Michael's sleepy home as quickly as the rules of the road would allow and set off on their adventure.

The drive was in no way a joyride. Michael was a talented driver, and he regarded traffic laws with the respect of someone who had recently been forced to commit all of them to memory. He drove by a police vehicle drenched in the exposure of a well-lit intersection without a second thought. Carter's heart jumped into his mouth when he saw the cop, knowing their night would end the moment a police officer asked to see Michael's identification. However, Michael was driving with purpose and knew that they were clean. The officer had no reason to pull them over. He loved feeling the road moving beneath his tires, knowing that he was in control of the future. The adrenaline coursing through them increased along with the distance they put between themselves and Michael's house.

Then they saw it.

On the southern edge of town, where the road gets fast and buildings become fewer and farther between, an unassuming cul-de-sac opened its arms to them.

Michael was happy to turn onto a residential street. Although he had taken to driving quite well, he was still nervous about traveling anywhere over fifty miles per hour. That street got to sixty in some parts and felt too advanced. He had never driven that fast before. Michael was beginning to worry that he might get pulled over for driving too slowly.

As the boys crept down the cul-de-sac, they looked for a two-story light brown house. This neighborhood was dark, cast in shadows from a combination of too few streetlights and too many trees, and all the homes appeared to have a similar murky colorlessness to them. Then, at the back of the cul-de-sac, nestled between two larger homes, sat a two-story house with a wide variety of cheap, revoltingly filthy, and sometimes broken children's toys littering the front yard. As the headlights touched them, they all appeared to be coated in a dried drool film.

"The daughter runs a daycare," Michael said. "That has to be the place."

Once they parked in the driveway, the headlights revealed the house to be a sickly light brown color. The muteness of the brown did not fade under better lighting. It appeared dusty and frozen in time, desperately in need of some touching up. Michael waited for a moment, flicked his headlights, and put the car in reverse.

The directions for triggering an interaction with Whacking Willy were somewhat vague. They weren't sure how far away they should drive or how long they should wait before returning to the driveway. They drove to the end of the cul-de-sac, near the exit which led them back toward town, and turned around at the intersection.

Carter swore he saw a naked old man standing in the window on the second floor as they approached the house for the second time, but before they could get into the driveway, the red and blue strobe of a police cruiser blinded Michael from his rearview mirror. He pulled over.

"Oh my god. We're so fucked," said Carter.

"Let's just tell the officer the truth," said Michael. "Maybe he'll let us go because there's a pervert living over there. That's worse than what we're doing, right?"

The police officer cautiously approached the window before realizing its passengers were two teenage boys, barely old enough to be sitting in the front seat, wearing sober, horrified expressions.

"What are you boys doing out past curfew?" the officer asked.

"We were just driving around. We're bored," Michael said, trying to lie but really only able to accomplish a half-truth.

"You pulled an illegal U-turn at that intersection. License and registration, please."

"Sure, uhm, which one is registration? What is registration?" Michael gasped, now drowning in nerves.

"It's usually in the glove box," the officer replied coolly.

Carter popped open the glove box, found what his best guess told him was the registration, and handed it to Michael, who then gave it along with his learner's permit to the officer.

"I'm sorry," Michael said.

"This is a learner's permit," the officer said.

"I know. I'm sorry. We're not supposed to be out."

"What are you two doing out here? Looks like your address is only a few miles away."

"I mean, you know why we're here, right?" Michael said, taking an enormous pause, assuming the cops had to know about the house. Why else would he be all the way out here?

"What do you mean?"

"Well, I mean, you know about this house, right?"

"Which house?"

"That one," Carter said, pointing at the light brown house near the back of the cul-de-sac. The officer looked but didn't seem to understand its significance.

"What's at that house?" he asked.

"Well, we heard that if you come here at night and flash your headlights, then drive around, and then come back and flash your headlights again, an old man comes out and jacks off in front of you," Michael said, the honesty in his voice striking the officer with a combination of surprised humor and extreme concern.

"Why would you want to see that?" the officer asked.

Michael and Carter had not considered such a question until that moment. The answer had always seemed obvious to them.

"Because it's weird? I don't know," Michael said.

The officer looked at the documents in his hands, then back at the daycare in front of them just in time to see one of the curtains in a window on the top floor gently sway back to a resting position. A chill ran under his uniform.

"Okay," the officer said, "I'm going to give you a warning, but I want you to drive straight home. Don't stop anywhere. I patrol all night, so I'll know if you're still out. Don't drive around or take a long way home. Go straight home and stay there. Do you understand me?"

"Yes, sir, of course," Michael and Carter each repeated multiple times in various ways, speaking over each other and mixing each other's words.

The officer handed the license and registration back to Michael, and he handed them to Carter, who put them back into the glove box. They turned around and drove away from the flashing lights, unceremoniously topping out at sixty-five miles per hour for Michael's first time after they reached the main street. They went straight home without uttering a word.

When they arrived back at Michael's house, they parked the car in the same spot on the street where they had found it and turned it off. They got out, closed the doors behind them softly, and snuck back into the house through the basement window. The boys got back into their sleeping bags. Although they had not gotten the night they wanted, they were safe, and their thirst for adventure was satiated. They closed their eyes and convinced themselves they would be able to sleep for the next few hours until sunlight poked through the basement windows.

During breakfast, Michael's parents seemed to know something was up, but they didn't pry. They believed it was good for their son and his friends to have some secrets. Whatever mischief they had gotten into was probably beneficial to their development. They assumed it couldn't have been anything worse than staying up too late to watch R-rated movies or sneak some of their alcohol. They never considered what could have happened, or what did.

Michael's father was watching the news in the kitchen and making a second helping of pancakes for everyone. He called Michael's mother over to show her what was happening on the television. She stood by him and put a hand over her mouth as a local breaking news story continued to unfold on the screen. They were both pale with worry.

"That's so awful," she said.

"I can't believe something like that could happen in this town. A psycho like that living just a few miles away," Michael's father said.

"That poor police officer. I bet we know his family. It's just terrible," she said, a look of devastation dragging her face to the floor.

On the television, Michael saw that unassuming light brown house from the previous evening. A line of police tape blocked off the property as paramedics and officers went about their jobs, flushing in and out of the front door. Broken toys from the front yard were photographed. Garbage bags were being cautiously carried out of the house. A messy oval of blood stained the driveway pavement.

"What happened?" Michael asked. Michael's mother turned the television off and started playing relaxing pop music through their stereo.

"Nothing you two need to worry about," she said, transforming her despair into a radiant smile. "Did you have fun last night?"

"So much fun, thank you," Carter said.

"Good. Tell your mother you're welcome here anytime. We love having you."

"I will."

Michael's mother smiled, and they finished eating their pancakes.

Toothpicks

PICNICS ARE DIFFICULT to organize in the city. The unyielding compromise of space and comfort that poisons every natural space in Chicago was doing its best to ruin the day for three women who decided to enjoy the newly emerging sun. Spring had officially begun the weekend before, and Mara, Ariana, and Eve were eager to return to the parks near their homes. The trees were budding, and green regurgitation was oozing from the reviving grass on the ground. Birds sang as the temperature reached its highest peak since fall. It was the perfect day for a picnic.

They stopped at three different parks before admitting that finding an oasis for their blankets and items of leisure would be nearly impossible. The overwhelming gross of human flesh pushed together in each recreation area, attempting hundreds of relaxing afternoons and achieving none of them, pulsed in one hazy cloud of sweat and breath. Wavy body heat misted the air, filling the space between them and causing Mara to gag. The women retreated to the nearest sidewalk and gasped at the fresh motor exhaust coming from a busy intersection.

"There's a high school by my place, and it has a field. So let's just do it there," Mara said to her friends once they had distanced themselves from the crowd. She scraped at her tongue with all her teeth and spit the remaining moisture coating her mouth on the pavement.

"Is that weird for us to do? Hang out at a high school?" asked Ariana. "We're in our thirties now, Mara. We can't just drink on a soccer field."

"I think it sounds fun," said Eve, taking a drag of her vape pen.

"Let's check it out. They don't have school today, so we should be good. The worst thing that can happen is someone might tell us to leave. And then we'll just leave," said Mara.

Ariana begrudgingly agreed, and the women returned to Mara's neighborhood. Two blocks away from her apartment building sat a small high school. Connected to it, amassing one square block, was an all-purpose sports field. They laid out a red flannel blanket, weighed it down on each corner with their shoes, and began setting out their picnic.

Camembert cheese, firmly chilled, with a gorgeous French baguette and an assortment of mouthwatering jams. Wine, prosciutto, olives, salami, chocolate, and more cheeses glimmered at the core of the blanket while the women chatted about their recent lives, snacked, and passed around Eve's vape pen. Music flowed lovingly from a small teal Bluetooth speaker and cocooned the women in the prize of their immaculately peaceful afternoon.

Suddenly a young man, high school age, appeared in front of them.

"What are you doing here?" he asked. The boy was short and lanky, which seemed an odd combination. He looked like a tall person that had been shrunken down. Long, dirty blond hair covered his eyes, and his pale white skin screamed under the sun in the shadowless field.

Ariana choked on her bread, startled. She coughed the soggy bits of baguette and red jam onto the blanket in front of her. It hypnotized her, seeing through its pulpy crimson hue to the deeper, darker red flannel on which it now soaked. She transfixed upon it. All the different, infinite worlds of red. Mara, however, was not in the mood to have anyone crash their party.

"We're having a picnic," she said. "What are you doing here?"

"Don't you think it's kind of weird to hang out at a high school?"

Eve noticed that the boy seemed to be speaking without moving his mouth. His face sat still like a ventriloquist without his dummy through every word. She couldn't believe her eyes, but none of her friends reacted to it. Mara was standing up to talk to the boy, and Ariana remained hypnotized by the spot of jam just beneath her shins as she sat cross-legged and facing away from the confrontation.

"Do you want to hang out with us?" Mara asked. "Because we've got room."

Mara understood that the fastest way to get rid of high school boys was to embrace them and then continue talking about your adult problems. She would go back to telling her friends about her job, and he would soon disappear.

"Honey," a cooing, otherworldly, maternal voice called from somewhere beyond the school grounds. Buttery silk, the voice calmed and warmed the cold front brought on by the boy. None of the women could pinpoint where it came from. "Come here. Leave those girls alone."

The boy turned and promptly sprinted behind the school. As soon as he left their field of vision, a woman was standing behind them.

"Sorry about my son." She smiled.

Mara and Eve yelped and turned around, embarrassed. Ariana's body was positioned toward her, but she continued to stare at the fuzzy, sugary, goo-soaked fabric before her.

"It's all good," said Mara, exhaling the residue of her cry. "You startled us."

The woman was tall and beautiful. She had dirty blonde hair, like her son, and wore black jeans and a black crewneck with the high school logo on it. The cartoon demon mascot reflected her smile. Her face was milky white, her eyes were cold teal, and her features were perfectly symmetrical and powerfully feminine. She was holding a large Tupperware container against her tight stomach.

This was a well-off neighborhood. Mara rented her humble apartment, but the average house cost over a million dollars. She thought this woman was probably one of the area moms with loads of money and a flawlessly photographed family. Everyone was quietly surprised that there wasn't a dog in a purse slung over her shoulder. Then she did the unthinkable. She sat down.

"Do you girls want to try some of my scotcharoos?" she asked, smiling, her perfectly straight ivory teeth glinting in the sun. "They're really good, but be warned, they're super sticky and ooey-gooey."

Mara and Eve were in uncomfortable awe of her casual forwardness, but they did not want to be told to leave. They obliged her bizarre offer and accepted the scotcharoos, although they did not have to be convinced much beyond being shown the delectable treats. The thick peanut butter and crispy rice base smothered in chocolate glowed in the sunlight and called to their watering tastebuds. The wine and vaporized cannabis had fully stimulated their desire for indulgences. Mara grabbed the biggest one she could see.

"Ariana, do you want one?" Mara asked.

Ariana broke her gaze and looked up at the woman.

"No."

The woman laughed.

"I understand. They're not good for you at all. Terrible for your teeth. Rot them right out. And you girls have such beautiful teeth. Look at you. Tell you what. I'll leave the rest of these here, and you can enjoy them. I've got to catch my son," she said, placing the Tupperware on the blanket. "I can get it later, so don't worry about it. You ladies have a nice afternoon. Sorry again about him, oh my gosh."

She laughed as she walked out of sight behind the school where the boy had escaped. Mara took a bite of her scotcharoo.

"Whoa, this is so good," she mumbled through the sticky mess.

Eve picked up a piece and bit into it as the chocolate layer chipped and rolled down her hands, immediately beginning its luscious melting phase.

Knee-trembling flavor washed over her consciousness and gave her sublime clarity. Her existence became obvious, and her reason for living was simply to enjoy the taste of this magnificent treat. The decadence of their earlier fare paled in comparison to the sensation she was experiencing. However, the pure stickiness of the treat soon began to pose a problem more significant than the pleasure of its taste.

The two girls chewed, but could not work the gunky peanut butter and chocolate apart into small enough pieces to swallow. Their mouths were stuck. Sealed. The range of motion in their jaws decreased with each passing mastication. They used their fingers to pry the treats out of their mouths, but they couldn't dig them out. Their fingers got lost in it.

They moaned through the gooey mass, now entirely blocking their trembling gobs. The wails vibrated through their throats and from behind the thick muck walls. Only the woman from which the scream came could hear it rattling through her own skull. Then, quite suddenly, the boy's mother returned.

"How are they?" she asked.

The girls communicated their problem through a display of it. They pointed to their mouths as they struggled to plead for help.

"Oh, well, that's alright. I thought that might happen," she said, pulling a small Ziploc bag out of her pocket. "Use these toothpicks. They're specifically made for this purpose. They'll get everything out."

From the bag came three small blue wooden toothpicks. Although the ladies felt confident the wood would snap inside their mouths, possibly creating irretrievable and painful debris, they each took one. Mara and Eve began picking at their teeth. Ariana, having never tasted the cursed treat, discreetly dropped her toothpick to the ground. Soon she could hear her friends screaming clearly. This time, it was not blocked by thick sludge, but bubbling through thin sheets of goopy liquid. Then she saw it.

Globs of scotcharoo mixed with teeth of every size and shape flowed out of their mouths until their sorrowful gaping maws were left entirely toothless. Blood freely followed close behind, down their chins and spat upon the picnic remnants beneath them.

Ariana looked to where the woman once stood, only to see the empty, windless field. She looked back at the pile of food and blood to locate her friends' teeth, but they had disappeared as well. As her friends gargled and cried, she helped them up, led them to the car, and drove to the nearest hospital.

***

Medical staff in the emergency room were able to stop the bleeding, but when they asked what happened, the women were unable to give an answer that seemed possible. Ariana was relied upon to vocalize the details of the afternoon. The medical staff asked why they didn't stop picking at their teeth once the first one fell out, but Mara and Eve hadn't felt the first one fall out. They were all, all of a sudden, just out. Then they were gone.

"Your teeth are probably still on the ground somewhere. Unless that woman took them," said one staff member. "Boy, that would be weird."

Mara and Eve would need to undergo surgery to implant permanent dentures. For now, however, they were safe and recovering. Therapy for their trauma would also be necessary, but that could perhaps take longer for them to get to than surgery. They weren't even entirely sure what had happened. Eve thought about the boy speaking without moving his mouth, and she cried. A nurse offered her pain medicine, pills that clinked around in her hand like loose teeth, but she refused. She could only cry. She needed to cry.

Ariana confirmed her friends were taken care of, got back in her car, and returned to the high school to collect their belongings. Once she was standing over that spot of faded grass, bent beneath the weight of their lovely day and freckled with blood and food waste, she searched for the teeth.

To her right, on the other side of the field, a slight sound of cracking twigs dirtied the clean spring air. The boy was watching her. She started walking toward him, and he ran. So she ran.

She followed him to a small, run-down, off-white house, caked with dirt and age, with teal shutters on a bare concrete foundation just outside the field's fence. She hadn't remembered ever seeing this house before, although she hadn't paid much attention to her surroundings when she came to this part of the neighborhood. Rust poked through long stretches of the gutters, and ancient paint chips littered the pavement in front of it. Broken rocks and bits of metal chain filled in for any resemblance of a yard that may have existed at the feet of its cracked screen door. The screen door stood slightly open.

Ariana walked up to it, kicked aside the chipped bits of driveway, and knocked. Nothing. She opened the door slightly and peeked her head in to call out, but before she could utter a word, her breath stopped, her mouth hung agape, and she stared.

Inside the tattered, unfurnished living room, the boy stood. He was facing away from Ariana and holding his face in his hands, crying. It wasn't clear exactly how or for how long, but his body shifted from one form to another. Before her eyes, he became the woman. He grew and pushed his limbs to unconscionable lengths compared to his original form. Cracking and snarling rumbled from deep in his bones. In her bones. Only the woman was no longer that put-together mother that had dropped off a Tupperware of scotcharoos mere hours before. Instead, she was a wretched, withered, skin-cracked, crooked-spined, wart-covered witch with a nose dangling like a dead rat's tail, and her sobbing turned to cackling. Her screeching laughter shook the building. A single filthy bottle rolled off the counter and shattered on the ground. Broken glass hurled itself at Ariana's shins. She shrieked, and the woman turned.

"I told them they were sticky," she howled. "Poor girls. They had such lovely teeth."

She pulled a handful of teeth out of her pocket, tossed them into her mouth, swished them around and chewed on them before swallowing with a low, aching gulp.

"Are you sure you don't want one?" she smiled. Her teeth were putrid green and brown, with streaks of blood running over orange plaque that climbed down their sharp edges. Black mold oozed through the spaces between each cavity. "I like to suck on them."

Ariana's face had lost color, and her voice failed her. She backed out of the home and ran. The woman's laughter rattled the world around her as she attempted to maintain her balance in a place that now felt wobbly and lopsided. Her instincts took over her conscious mind, and she didn't stop running until she regained awareness next to her car. She locked herself inside and called the police.

One excruciating hour later, the police arrived. They didn't believe her story, but they were at least kind enough to humor her. She walked them to the area where she remembered seeing the house, but it was gone. Nothing but a concrete lot with a basketball hoop remained.

An officer whose children attended the high school assured her that children played there and that a house had not occupied that spot since the school was built. She walked them to the patch of sick grass where her friends had been picnicking, hoping to find any evidence of what had happened. Then it showed itself to her. The blue wooden toothpick that she had dropped.

"This is one of the toothpicks," she told them, holding it up. "It tore my friends' teeth out."

"You're saying this toothpick tore your friends' teeth out?" the head officer echoed.

"Yes," Ariana said flatly.

"Let me see it."

Ariana handed him the toothpick, and he examined it. He rolled it in his hands and looked at it closely in the dying light of the setting sun before opening his mouth and picking at his teeth.

She screamed. She couldn't believe his bullheaded misjudgment as she ran over to pull the sinister blue instrument out of his mushy, coffee-bathed hole, but the other two officers held her back.

"Oh my god," he said.

Everyone turned to look at the officer, the other officers now nervous.

"That has been bothering the hell out of me," he said. The officer spat a small piece of brown food on the ground. "Was eating peanuts earlier, and that has been stuck in my teeth for like two hours. Thanks for the toothpick. Didn't make my teeth fall out though. Luckily."

The officer dropped the toothpick on the ground and asked Ariana if she wanted a ride to the hospital so that they could question her friends about what had happened. They didn't trust her to be driving in what they referred to as her "emotional state."

As she closed the door to the passenger seat of the police cruiser, she looked out the window at the scene in the yellowish-green field. It was as if none of it had even happened. She wondered if her friends would even be at the hospital when they got there. Had they even lost their teeth? She looked back at the school and, for a moment, caught a glimpse of a young man with dirty blond hair, similarly sized to the boy but taller, briefly glancing in her direction before biting into something and disappearing behind the school.

The Tree Keeper

TADASHI RESIGNED FROM an esteemed position at a major manufacturing company the morning after his first visit to Mimi's Tachinomiya. It was a new standing bar that had recently opened outside the train stop near his home in Tokyo. The first few days it was open, he passed it without regard. However, on this evening, he felt the need to unwind with a drink.

Standing bars are relatively small and cater to those who wish to drink alone amongst other solitary travelers. Tadashi tucked himself away into the far corner of the bar, down the narrow hallway that made up the patron area. He wished to savor his beer with only his thoughts and reflections on his life. His work had been mentally and emotionally draining lately, especially today, and he needed to come to peace with it before returning home.

After no more than a half-sip of his lager, a tall, wispy man entered the otherwise unoccupied bar and stood next to him. He was no ordinarily large man. He was head and shoulders taller than Tadashi and the bartender, and he was rail thin. What meat that was left on his arms clung to his bones and threatened to fall off. His skeleton glided beneath his sun-damaged skin. His stringy, filthy brown hair obscured his eyes, and a bushy beard wildly pushed its way out of his face in every direction. His clothes were filthy, flaking off dried mud, and his face was darkened with soil and sunburn. He crowded Tadashi, and the salaryman began to feel annoyed.

"How are you doing?" the man asked. Tadashi could not believe the impolite impulse that caused him to speak to him, let alone ask such a question.

"Good," Tadashi said, diverting his eyes toward the bar and communicating with his body that he did not wish to speak or get bumped by anyone standing too close.

"My name is Itsuki. I've never seen you here before. I come in here all the time. Hey, Mimi!" Itsuki bowed to the bartender, who delivered a drink to his hand and bowed back.

"Welcome back, Itsuki." Mimi smiled. "How was work?"

"Today was awful. Sorry, I didn't get your name. What's your name?" he asked Tadashi.

"Tadashi," he replied before taking a large gulp of his lager, hoping to have it finished within the next couple sips so that he may remove himself from Itsuki's presence.

"Well, Tadashi, I'm a tree keeper," Itsuki said as he leaned in closer, his breath making it clear that he had begun drinking earlier that evening, "and I don't know if you know this, but a lot of companies in Tokyo are leveling trees in the area right now. Really awful stuff. Destroying entire ecosystems. Ruining the future of our society. Stuff like that. It's been making me angry. Just really angry. I've been losing my mind. I mean, this country used to care about nature, but some people only seem to care about money. Today, this one company took down half a forest."

Tadashi finished his beer and considered leaving, but the size of Itsuki was blocking his exit. His stringy legs widened their stance, and his shoulder span crowded over half the width of the narrow tachinomiya. Although his weight was most likely of an average man, his skinny limbs crept and filled the entire bar. Tadashi's annoyance ran red with claustrophobia. He felt trapped.

"I'm sorry," the lean giant laughed, "I'm talking way too much. I'm being rude. I apologize. This week has just been hard. Mimi, please pour another drink for my friend, Tadashi."

Before he could object, Itsuki laid money on the table, and Mimi placed another lager in Tadashi's hand. He bowed and took a long drink.

"I know you're just doing your job," Itsuki said.

Tadashi set the glass on the bar and considered what Itsuki said. How would he know? Tadashi had never mentioned what he did for work.

Then, everything went dark.

Itsuki grabbed the hair on the back of Tadashi's head and slammed his skull through his drink and against the bar, splashing fluid commotion into the air. Broken glass and alcohol danced through the lacerations around Tadashi's face as he reeled from the impact. He looked up, blood and beer streaming down his eyes and dampening the new edges of his flesh, and felt the towering, lanky man in dark rags slither his strong bony fingers around his throat.

"Remember that I'm the tree keeper," he whispered, "and next time, I will kill you."

Itsuki released his grip and silently walked out of the bar as Tadashi fell to the floor, petrified, coughing and overwhelmed with agony. He couldn't hear his footsteps. He was simply gone. Mimi brought him a towel and apologized.

The next day, Tadashi resigned from his position at the company. He sat at Mimi's Tachinomiya every night for weeks afterward, hoping to tell Itsuki, hoping to buy him a drink, but the tree keeper never returned.

The Yellow Screen

AMANDA AND LILY spoke on the phone together once per week, every week. Not always on the same day, but whenever they could. They had been close friends since childhood, and although they lived in different states, they still made time to stay in each other's lives. Sometimes, they only chatted for a few minutes, and other times, they traded secrets for hours. However, this evening, Amanda found herself very tired after coming home from work late and did not want to talk on the phone. But, of course, Lily called, and she answered.

"What up, babe?" Amanda said, radically altering her mood in response to the energizing and rejuvenating routine she shared with her friend.

"Hey, sorry, I know you had to work. We don't have to talk if you're too tired," Lily said.

"No, I'm good. How are you?"

The two women spoke of their weeks and checked in on threads from previous conversations. After a couple hours, the topics began to die down, and they focused on things happening around them.

Lily commented on the cute behavior of her cat, Seymour. The golden Domestic Shorthair had been chasing a fluttering bug throughout the room. He zoomed, hopped, and terrorized Lily's furniture through Amanda's phone speaker. When she heard what he was doing, she thought she could feel the bug on her leg. However, when she brushed at her prickly skin, she found none there. This phantom sensation was becoming a more frequent occurrence for her lately.

"Oh my god," Amanda said. "You know that feeling when it feels like something's crawling on you, but nothing is there?"

"One hundred percent," Lily said. "I hate it more than anything in the world. I just trust that my cat has killed most of the bugs in the house by now."

"So weird. What even makes that happen? My clothes aren't touching the spot where I thought I felt something. Like, is it my leg hair? Is my skin just being weird? Is it all in my mind?"

"It's probably a muscle spasm or something," Lily said in an overly confident voice that usually meant she was guessing. Her move was always to pivot into a joke in case her gap in knowledge was too obvious. She laughed. "Or maybe there are bugs under your skin."

"Ew, I just felt it again," Amanda said, brushing at her leg and again finding nothing but the bare mountaintops of her bumpy, clammy knees. "Whatever. I'm just hypersensitive because I'm exhausted."

"I use a massager when I feel like that, and it kind of helps."

Amber had not noticed that her phone was running low on battery until a notification appeared. She forgot to charge it the previous evening and didn't have time to charge it at work. Her battery was nearing the end of its total lifespan, and its ability to hold charge was decreasing after each fill-up. Charging it was becoming a more frequent practice, and it was concerning her that she would need to get a new phone. Now, she was too tired to get off her couch to grab the charger in her bedroom, and she worried that her phone would die, something she realized that she had never let happen before.

"Hey, my phone might die soon, just FYI," she said.

"Whoa, I don't think I've ever let my phone die before," Lily said, worried. "Is your charger broken?"

"No, it's in the other room, but I'm too tired to get it. I don't think I've ever let my phone die before either. I'm kind of curious to see what happens. Let's talk until it dies."

Amber waited for Lily to respond before realizing the phone was already dead. The screen showed a rotating gray arrow that evoked the feeling of powering down, and then it turned a light black. Backlit darkness. A soft glow pushed through the dingy screen, indicating that it had not completely lost power. It was losing consciousness. The backlighting slowly faded until the screen became a purely uniform onyx slab in her hand.

Then the yellow light appeared.

A harsh yellow screen shined brightly out of the pile of arranged metal, plastic, and glass in her palm. The entire screen turned a sick, sobbing yellow. The illumination seemed to be emitting many times greater than the phone's maximum brightness. It scorched Amanda's eyes and filled her with urgent dread. It pierced through and ricocheted off the walls. Tears ran freely down her cheeks as though her eyes were melting out of her head. Her senses had become completely jammed. She could only experience the phone's agony. Everything else around her dissolved into a nightmare.

She ran into her room and plugged it in, but nothing changed. The phone's display was still yelping its sick yellow cry. She unplugged it. It had to die fully at some point. It couldn't shimmer violence like that forever. Why had the manufacturer made it impossible to remove the battery without damaging the phone? She held the power button, but nothing happened. The phone sharply increased its body temperature and burned her fingers in its death throes.

Soon, the feeling of bugs crawling across Amanda's skin returned and intensified far beyond all previous feelings. It emerged as the leader of her discomfort, sending static shocks down her spine. It wasn't just one spot this time. It was all over her body. She felt like thousands of little thumbtacks were pushing her skin away from her skeleton with equal pressure, like she was wearing a wet suit full of vile little snarling, crawling creatures who all wanted out.

Tiny bubbles formed all over her. Her goosebumps grew, and each appeared to fill with a solid, dark fetus. She looked at her arms. Through the top few layers of her skin, she saw what appeared to be a small worm eating its way toward the surface. Finally all the bubbles burst open, and the hungry, chomping little mouths of thousands of gray worms came spilling out of her body.

A few worms broke free and plopped onto the floor. They writhed and rotated in small circles like arrows on the cold hardwood beneath her feet. Some slowly faded away and stopped rotating, while others maintained their hypnotic dance in a perpetual state of dying. Amanda screamed and threw the phone onto her coffee table. They slowly slithered around, looking fat and weak after filling up on her flesh and burrowing out of her. Small holes freckled her body, from which dangled chomping worms and thick strings of blood. Each occasionally plopped onto the ground with a wet slap.

Amanda ran into the bathroom and got in the shower. She ran hot water over herself. Over the holes. More worms continued wiggling their way out of her poor, wretched dermis and fell onto the bathtub floor. The water's current carried them all to the drain. She felt like she was boiling, exacerbated by the shower's heat, as if her entire body was about to pop.

Suddenly the rest of them, a wave of worms, gushed out of her body and splashed onto the floor in a heavy release.

Her arms, legs, and abdomen became riddled with gaping sores, all vomiting out the last of the gray infestations. They spilled into the bathtub like pounds of overcooked noodles slipping through a colander in a filthy kitchen sink. The pain of this massive release was mixed with equal parts relief, and the shift of weight combined with it to orchestrate a horde of sensations that was too much for Amanda as she passed out with her head resting just above the bathtub's edge. She lay there for a moment, powering down, life still vaguely glowing behind her dim eyes, while she felt the awful creatures wiggling around her exhausted legs and toes. Backlit darkness turned to total darkness.

***

The tub was overflowing when she awoke. A pulsing heap of the squirming organisms had clogged the drain. Her foot brushed over the slick, rippling dome made from their bodies. They were suctioned onto it. Amanda turned the shower off and stood up, splashing pink water onto the white tile bathroom floor.

After carefully walking into the living room, she saw her phone lying dark and lifeless on the table. She plugged it back in.

Some of the holes had stopped bleeding, but she felt a loud gnaw of pain rattle her brain with each movement. She could not escape pulling at her injuries and reopening them as she picked up the phone and plugged it into its charger. She stretched and ripped each temporarily healed gash with every movement. Moaning assumed the place of screaming due to her almost wholly depleted energy. Pleading grunts burst from deep within her core and lost momentum as they filtered through her raspy throat.

The phone would not turn back on. She sat for minutes, waiting for it to regain consciousness, but it remained unchanged. Amanda ran her fingers over the holes covering her arm and looked deeply into the dark caves that echoed just behind the fragile regenerative barrier that stopped her blood from pouring out. Many windows of multicolored glass stared into the putrid abyss. Most of them were still bleeding, or began bleeding again because of her movements. She felt dizzy. The few worms that had fallen out of her before she went to the bathroom were crawling around on the floor beside her. Once she noticed them, as though something deep within her DNA had been triggered, she knew what she must do.

Nothing other than pure instinct could cause a person to resort to such nauseating measures for survival. Her hands moved without her conscious command. Amanda picked up the fleshy tubes, all breathing differently in an unsettling, arrhythmic spectrum of life, held them up to the holes in her arms, and watched them crawl back inside of her, burrowing through the same tunnels they had used to leave. Each one closed the skin tightly behind it as it disappeared back into her body.

She entered the bathroom and reached into the overfilled bathtub, splashing more water onto the ground. She grabbed handfuls of worms and rubbed them on her arms and legs. They shook off and crawled back inside of her, closing the sores behind them as they faded back into her body. The tub drained faster and faster as she returned handful after handful of gray worms, each about an inch long, back into the oozing caverns that now consumed most of her skin. Her skin was a tattered mess of flesh that was hardly still connected in most places. Some areas had more holes than solid skin, and the groupings of holes made larger holes.

As she returned each worm, her body was slowly sewn back together. Each one nestled into its perfectly shaped pocket and disappeared behind a thin scar. Heaps of soggy gray tubes vanished back into the void, and the sensation of their presence dissipated. The wounds stopped bleeding. The holes were sealed. When the last one had been absorbed, she heard her phone turn back on in the other room.

Amanda picked up the phone and called Lily.

"Hey, did your phone die?" Lily asked.

"Yeah, sorry I lost you," she said.

"What happened?"

"It died, and I plugged it in."

"That makes sense," Lily laughed. "Thanks for finding that out so I never have to. I would probably puke all over the place if my phone died. That stresses me out. Oh my god, Seymour caught the bug. He was being so funny after we lost each other. You missed it."

Lily told Amanda about her cat capturing a bug with his paws and playing with it before eating it. They laughed and talked about cats until Amanda, drowsy and weak, fell asleep. Lily wished goodnight into her friend's resting ear, hung up, and connected her phone to its charger.

Wart Forest

COLIN HAD KNOWN Greg long enough to trust the perilous expression of gloom on his face when he emerged from the shadowy tree line. Greg had left the safe confines of their bonfire to relieve himself somewhere away from camp about fifteen minutes earlier, and the group was beginning to worry about him. They assumed whatever was keeping him must have been his own private business, and they dreaded the idea of checking in on him only to cause embarrassment for both parties. They thought at first that perhaps he was sick and he would inform them that he needed to go home. Instead, he instructed them to follow him back into the dark forest.

There were four of them. Greg, Colin, Macklin, and Dane. The men, all now in their middle years, had been friends since childhood, and although they had much different lives now, they still made time to go on a camping retreat together once a year. They tried to pick a new place to go each time. Most of the fun of the experience was hiking and surveying the new land and recapturing the wonder of exploration they felt back in their youths when such feelings were easier to come by. This year, they decided on a spring visit to a small patch of woods near Lake Michigan, somewhat close to the U.S. and Canadian border. The area existed in a strange, in-between place that felt oddly homeless and independent. It didn't feel like it belonged to either country. It was just there.

They had arrived later in the day than they anticipated and were deprived of that first chance to venture into the unknown before the necessity of shelter and warmth became paramount in their minds. They quickly unloaded their equipment and followed a short trail to the closest camping area to get as much assistance from the dying sun as it would allow before twilight turned its cold gaze to laugh at their unfinished camp.

They were using a single tent, large enough to comfortably house the four of them. The friends had learned to live together through the sleepovers of their childhood and various roommate living arrangements of their early adulthood. One big tent was all they needed, which made the construction process much more efficient. As soon as it was built and a fire was lit in the pit of charred remains of previous camping excursions, Greg announced that he needed to use the toilet and would be back soon.

"If I'm not back in fifteen minutes, come looking for me," he had said. "I don't have to poop, so it shouldn't take that long, but if I do end up having to poop and then you come looking for me, and that's what I'm doing, then I'm sorry, but better safe than sorry."

"Just go," said Colin.

"Yeah, stop talking," Macklin said.

"I'm not going to look for you," Dane laughed as he opened a beer.

Greg held a playful middle finger to the group and disappeared beyond the tree line. Then, fifteen minutes passed, and the men started to wonder. Was Greg kidding before? Was he playing a joke now? Did he want them to come looking for him?

Luckily, he showed his face before that feeling swelled up inside them and reached the point where they felt a need to discuss it. They all knew the others were feeling weird. What was Greg doing out there? A sigh of relief vented through their noses toward the ground and curved up into the sky once he appeared. But the tension was reinvigorated and evolved into a new collection of despair when they saw the look on his face.

"What's up? Are you okay?" Colin asked.

"We were about to come looking for you," Macklin said.

"I wasn't," said Dane, sipping his beer.

"You guys need to come with me," Greg said, his mouth barely moving. His eyes hung sourly in his dull face as his eyelids stretched toward the sky in an act of bodily surrender and panic. The muscles in his clammy visage were communicating emotions that seemed entirely burnt out in his mind. He held both of his hands in his front pockets as though he was a teacher about to ask a leading question that would carry him into a mind-altering lecture. The chemicals coursing through him were putting on a performance of normalcy that was wholly severed from his thoughts. He looked like he could barely feel any of it, and his body was taking over. "There's something I want to show you."

"No," Dane whined. "We just got the fire going and stuff. Let's chill."

"What is it?" Colin asked, concerned by the confusing mixture of emotions flowing from his friend's body language.

"I can't describe it," he said, muscles in his arms twitching as his hands balled into bulging fists in his pockets, "but I've never seen anything like it before."

"Is it next to where you peed?" Macklin asked. "Because maybe it can wait."

That's when the fire grew bright enough that Colin and Macklin were able to discern that Greg had urinated in his pants. A gasp of surprise and worry shook through them. His black jeans revealed a section of slightly blacker denim that soaked a vertical puddle through the material surrounding his groin. An energy of silence weighed down on the camp.

"It's not very far," Greg said before turning around and dissolving back into the twisting gateway of the crepuscule wooded kingdom before them. Colin walked after him, and Macklin followed. Dane finished his beer, opened another beer, grabbed his high-powered flashlight that he normally loved having an excuse to use, released an annoyed sigh, and ventured into the woods to find his friends.

Colin and Macklin held their phone flashlights up to light the path, but Greg led without one. His hands stayed in his pockets. He simply knew where to go. He dodged low branches and obstacles with memorized, conditioned precision. Everything appeared so calm and easy despite his tainted eyes looking back at his friends every few paces and his urine-soaked clothing telling a drastically different story. The other two tripped and stumbled along behind him as they quietly made their way. Any questions asked to Greg were met with a soft, "We're almost there."

Then a clearing opened itself to them, and the starry night sky waterfalled down onto their dusty heads. A brilliant rush of energizing visible light flooded the area as if the arena of distant worlds around them wished the men to see what was there. In the middle of the clearing was a small stub or stump, perhaps a collection of mushrooms, sitting about three feet tall and three feet wide. It was tan-pink, and the shedding of whatever comprised it littered the grass around it.

As they approached the specimen, Colin felt a hollow ache in his stomach, the type of empty bellyache that causes one to vomit whatever pathetic liquid is still contained in them in a misguided attempt to fix the problem. He worried he would be sick, but he couldn't easily find his way back to camp if he retreated. His breathing controlled and heart rate slowing, Colin continued following his friend's relentless, brisk pace toward the stump.

Once they reached it, they realized it wasn't a stump, or, at least, not one by appearance. Perhaps an invasive fungus of some kind had claimed a stump. Covered it. The grave of a tree suffocated beneath its new wormy overcoat. The dome of organic matter was a rough, callous blob of an unappealing texture reminiscent of cauliflower. Every few seconds or so, it would lightly shake as though a bubble had popped below its surface. It was alive, whatever it was.

Greg walked over to it, looked back at the men with a smile, and kicked it. A resounding thud rippled through it like a carnival strongman's abdomen after getting punched in the gut by an audience member. A small chunk of the fleshy tumor ripped off with the tip of Greg's shoe and landed next to them. Shortly afterward, the spot that had been ripped regenerated.

"I've been picking at this thing since I left camp. That's where all these other pieces of it came from," he said, gesturing to the mess around his feet. "But it just keeps regenerating. It's so gross. It hurts. I feel like it has to be hurting the forest. It hurts when I look at it, like, its existence hurts. Do you feel it?"

"I think we should leave it alone. I don't know what it is. I mean, it's cool, don't get me wrong, and thank you for showing it to us. But what if it's poisonous or something?" said Macklin.

"All the more reason we need to get rid of it," Greg said.

It pulsed again and shuddered under the stress of the damage it had withstood from Greg's shoe. Colin could feel it. Its presence was made of pain. Soreness. A tight, miserable tenderness that only more pain could destroy. He wanted desperately to rip it out of the Earth's poor body. It needed to be removed, whatever it was. Some deep instinct within him was screaming at him to do so.

"Isn't it just going to keep regenerating?" Macklin asked.

"It regenerates faster than I can pick at it, but if all of us are picking at it, then I think we can pick it all the way off before it has time to regenerate."

"That's a good idea," Colin said. Macklin looked at Colin in disbelief.

"I think you should do this in the morning," Macklin said.

"No," Greg said. He took his hands out of his pockets, and the others saw that they were covered in something. Gloves, maybe. It looked like hundreds of smaller versions of the bump in front of them coated the entirety of his hands up to his wrists. It was a sea of individual warts, rubbing through and against each other, creating a long, solid skin layer of rough growth.

Hard, wiggling, moaning warts were cracking around his palms and fingers and deconstructing his skin. His knuckles split open. His hands were falling apart as he reached down and grabbed two fistfuls of the excruciating lifeform. Soon, Colin found himself digging into the mixture as well. The hard shell of it broke open upon impact with his determined claws and released a terrible chutney of porous flesh underneath. It was an enormous wart, threatening the very woods it was attempting to call home.

A loud flashlight beam crashed through the cracks in the trees behind them as Dane emerged from the woods.

"What the hell is that thing?" he said.

"I don't know, but they want to pick it out of the ground," said Macklin.

"Oh my god, Greg, your hands are disgusting. What happened? Stop touching that."

Dane hurried over to the two men. The flashlight glared an aggressive wake-up call into Colin's eyes, and he was pulled from his daze. He backed away from the loathsome wart and threw up. He rubbed his arms and hands into the dirt to cleanse the disgusting material from his skin. Overwhelming fear obscured his consciousness, and he scratched his hands along the rocks and dry land until they were bloody and any infected layers had been removed.

"We did it," Greg said as he dropped the last handful of wart tissue on the ground. A crater sat staring up at them, surrounded by the dead remnants of its former body. Hard, sharp edges struggled to create new warts, rattled, and died. "Now we have to burn all this."

"We're not carrying that stuff back to camp," Dane said, "and we're definitely not starting a fire out here without someone from park services being present. We could burn the whole woods down."

"We have to," said Greg.

"Your hands are messed up, Greg, and you pissed yourself. Look at you," Dane said. "I'm taking you back to camp. Let's go."

Dane grabbed Greg's arm. Macklin blinked, and Dane was suddenly on his back with Greg on top of him, pinning his shoulders to the forest floor with his knees while a dropped beer bottle bled a fizzling ale beside them. Greg grabbed Dane's face with his bumpy, wart-coated hands. The warts on his fingertips found their way into Dane's mouth and scraped against his front teeth.

"We have to burn it."

Greg stood up, and Dane hopped to his feet, spitting.

"I'm getting a park ranger. You're being ridiculous, dude."

Dane and Macklin helped Colin stand, and they left.

***

At the lodge, the three men asked the lone ranger on duty for the evening if she had ever seen a growth that resembled their friend's obsession. She asked them if they had taken hallucinogenic drugs, then asked if they had taken drugs of any kind, then she shook her head and agreed to drive them back to camp.

When they returned, Colin was the first to start crying.

In that clearing where the stars had bestowed the power of their blessing lay a shriveled body next to a smoldering pile of ashes. The stench of burning flesh slowly venting from the area put the ranger in a fit as she covered her nose and gagged. She informed them that they weren't supposed to set fires anywhere except for the designated areas at camping sites before she called for a medical team. The men agreed and informed her that Greg wouldn't listen. He needed to burn it. She took a bottle of water from the glove compartment of her truck and doused the final fading memory of the fire, which released a vociferous exhale of smoke. A puff of ash choked out of the hollow wart crater. She stomped the smoldering out with her boot and covered it in soil.

Doctors later claimed that Greg died of smoke inhalation. They wouldn't say anything more beyond that, although they always looked like they wanted to. Greg's parents said they saw the X-rays of his lungs and thought they appeared riddled with tumors. Bumps. Warts. His lungs were saturated in warts.

The three men and the park ranger were given inhalers with a peculiar-tasting medication they were told was for smoke inhalation and kept overnight for observation. They bandaged Colin's hands and tended to the early signs of newly emerging warts around Dane's mouth. The night was eerily quiet. The doctors had never seen warts in lungs before. They didn't know how to tell them about it.

When Macklin returned with the park ranger to retrieve their camping gear the following day, they found the forest entrance blocked from public access. They ducked under the caution tape, walked a few yards, and stopped. Shaking, he removed his inhaler from his pocket and ran. The park ranger soon followed. Behind them, slowly fading into the past, all the trees, birds, animals, fish, bushes, flowers, grass, ponds, campsites, the ranger station, everything, all of it, all the wonders of that ravishing park, even the air, it was all covered in warts.

Red Swallow

THEO LISTENED TO only the sound of his engine while he drove, as he had many times before, into Red Swallow National Park to spend the day hiking. The leaves had changed colors under the influence of autumn's chill, and a silo of radiant oranges, yellows, and thick reds guided him deeper into the forest. It was a drive that Theo typically wanted to finish quickly so that he could begin his hike, but today, he dragged on slowly and savored each passing moment of the world around him. He would be making his own transition soon, and it was his last chance to be taken away by that mesmerizing display.

The car pulled into a small parking lot about a mile inside the park's entrance and came to a stop. He breathed calmly for the first time in days. Less than a week prior, Theo had killed a woman.

He didn't mean to do it. He hadn't planned on it happening. It just happened. They had been seeing each other for a while, and they started traveling together when, one night, they got into a fight. He told the few people he could trust that he didn't remember what happened. All he remembered was seeing her motionless body in his trunk and driving home.

His friends, who would join him in prison once he was caught, didn't ask questions. They helped Theo dispose of the body. They cut her into pieces, carefully snapping the bones and separating the limbs, and dropped each of them into different lakes and ponds around the region. Her heart had been buried in the curly, dense forest of Red Swallow. Her head was tossed into the deepest stretch of Red Swallow Lake. The woman was reported missing, and Theo was listed as a suspect.

The police, at first, didn't have many clues to go off besides speculation, but that was only a matter of time. They were eventually going to find evidence against Theo, and he would be arrested. If they didn't, the guilt would either cause him to turn himself in or commit suicide.

He opened the door, lost in the brisk, familiar air surrounding his body and filling his lungs. Theo felt cold at first, and then his body adapted. He let it in. It took over. He became the cold, and he was home.

A dazzling mixture of warm, glowing leaves covered the trail, creating a soft cushion between Theo's feet and the hard soil beneath them. His shoes sank into the leaves slightly and bounced off them, carrying more damp leaves with them after each step. One foot kicked a pile of them into the air. Soon, Theo was running like a child, laughing and kicking leaves.

When a carpet of foliage brightly litters the forest floor during the fall months, Red Swallow trails can become obscured and cause hikers to lose their way. The park is located on a massive host of land, which often causes mobile phones to experience a loss of reception. No bodies have ever been found in Red Swallow, but there have been hundreds of missing people reported. Some have made it out within a few hours, but some took days and emerged with a trauma they could not articulate. Others simply disappeared. It was as if the forest was swallowing these people whole.

It was dusk before Theo realized he had gotten off the beaten path. He was wandering miles away from a trail in an area of the park he had never seen. Beautiful, untouched, pristine forestry. Squirrels ran by him, plump and anxious for their upcoming hibernation. Deer picked through leaves for the last bits of living grass. The birds were gone. Sunburst rained down around him in a quiet dance as the day turned into night. The air turned gray, and Theo felt happy. He didn't care if he got lost. He wished to stay there forever, wandering an abyss that protected him from his past. As he turned around to head back, he kicked one more pile of leaves.

Then he saw it.

One of the leaves didn't fly into the air. Instead, it stayed on the ground as if it was being held in place. He kicked it again, but it held its position under his foot. He crouched to inspect it.

It was a red leaf, like any other red leaf, except upon closer inspection, it appeared to be synthetic. It was a convincing fake made of some kind of cloth mixture. It was fastened to the ground on one end, allowing it to rotate. Theo touched it and felt how genuinely fake it was upon tactile review. Vinyl grooves raked across his fingerprint. He rotated it on its fastened axis, revealing a hole hidden underneath it, roughly three inches in diameter.

Theo was shocked. Why would someone use a cleverly camouflaged fake leaf to cover up this hole? A person had to have done this. Had they done it just for him? Was it random? Was it for someone else? He could not ignore the feeling of pressing danger welling up inside him.

Voices, muffled and far beneath the ground's surface, came up through the thin void and echoed a gentle conversation against the leaf's underside. The gash led to people. There were people beneath him.

He jumped. They sounded like young women. He couldn't understand what they were saying, but there was no way anyone wanted to be where they were. They were buried alive. Theo set his face against the ground.

"Is anybody down there? Do you need help? Are you okay?" he called into the hole.

The talking stopped. The woods, even the wind through the trees and the leaves hitting the ground, were all silent for a moment. Soon, the screaming began.

The women, now sounding like a large group, pushed blood-curdling cries through the wet fissure that shook the ground around Theo. His legs wobbled. Their collective wail of terror filled the woods, and the wind of their screams whistled through the small opening before cutting into his ears and nearly bringing him to his knees. He could only make out one sentence amidst the chaos.

"Let us out."

"How did you get down there?" Theo asked, but they would not answer. They only continued screaming, bawling, and using those words. Those awful words.

"Let us out."

He looked around for a hidden staircase or hollowed-out tree that could lead him underground, but he couldn't find anything. An entrance had to be nearby. How large could this subterranean room be? Theo concluded that he would need to dig.

The dirt around the pit was cold and hard. Digging with his hands felt impossible. He had a shovel in his car, but he had no idea where his car was. Even if he did make it back, he wouldn't be able to find this place again, especially at night. They needed to be saved now.

Theo touched the rim and began pulling away at it, using it as a starting point. A thread to pull everything else apart. Dirt fell away from the rim easily under his fingers. As the break got larger and Theo got deeper, the voices got louder and closer. The sharp sorrowing shuddered the earth and sky harder with each new inch. The soil changed color with each passing layer. It went from black to tan to red. The red earth was fibrous, moist, and pulled apart like a rich grilled cheese sandwich.

After five feet, the tormenting yowl felt like it was right next to him. Urgency filled his muscles. He was tearing at the ground. His fingertips and palms were bloody, smoothly mixing in with the red soil. His fingernails chipped off in chunks. Two of his fingers broke, with the rest threatening to follow. Theo's hands were now simply tools to reach the voices and free them from whatever horrors had been brought upon them by any number of lunatics using this serene setting to carry out their disgusting fantasies. Theo pictured serial killers of all looks and sizes and felt anger. He could not accept that perhaps he shared a commonality with them. He was different. He would show himself and everyone trapped beneath him that he was different.

Once he reached six feet, the screaming stopped.

Again, the woods fell silent. The walls of the crater surrounding him, now taller than him, absorbed any extra sound in the air.

"Hello? Are you still there? Let me know you're okay," Theo called down the small gap beneath his feet where his work had momentarily ended. Every surface around him was dull with red. His voice disappeared once it left his mouth. No response.

A clump of dirt from the opening of the hole fell on his head, and he looked up. The hole was closing.

All the space around him began filling in with new ground. Long strands of roots and abysmal, bloody, nutrient-rich soil extended across the diameter of the area he had been expanding, now around four feet, and clasped onto each other to pull the hole shut. The earth was suturing itself around him.

He surrendered a high-pitched cry, but only for a moment. The earth pushed red clumps from every direction, quickly filling the breach and returning it to its previous size. From the surface, the dirt looked the way it had before he arrived. The nearest tree's last red leaf fell, and the roaring stopped just as it closed over the hole.

After his car was found and a search was carried out, investigators concluded that Theo had committed suicide in the forest. Enough of the woman's body was found to give her family closure, but Theo's body was never recovered. His friends were sentenced for assisting in the disposal of the body. They assumed he committed suicide as well. He had spoken about it, and Red Swallow was where it would have happened. Rumors spread that he was still alive, but no person living in the free world was searching for him. They knew he was suffering wherever he was, and that was good enough.

A Dead Entryway

SAM WAS ONLY in his hometown long enough to attend his friend's funeral and spend the night wherever he ended up after the celebration of life that would inevitably cause him to black out. He hadn't blacked out since college, but it was a nasty pattern that seductively consumed him anytime he tried to go out drinking in this town. Now in his late twenties, he found himself once again shooting awake in the passenger seat of a car he had no memory of, alone.

The previous evening, following the funeral, Sam had gone to a bar with a group of friends from high school to drink away their sorrows and trade stories. After a while, an old acquaintance named Ben invited him to stay at his new house out in the country. So, they smoked a joint in Ben's cream-colored '76 AMC Pacer as they rode the long stretches of desolate road out of town and into the neighboring farmlands. The road crumbled from solid concrete to gravel, and Sam's short-term memory soon faded into the darkness of the suffocatingly lightless fields around them, and he fell asleep.

He was drunk, really drunk, and high. Anxiety rattled his nerves when he awoke. Blood rushed out of his face and into his feet. Sheer panic overrode his motor functions. He should have reminded himself, like any sober person would have, that the foreboding, dark farmhouse beside the car that he had never seen before belonged to Ben, and he was, of course, allowed to come inside.

Ben had left Sam in the car to sleep after a few pathetic attempts to wake him. To his credit, Ben was also inebriated to the point where he should not have been driving. Neither one was thinking clearly, but only one of them would feel the consequences of those decisions while the other slept blissfully in his bed.

Sam leaned his head against the passenger window for a moment, weighing his options, watching the tall light pole above the car flicker and cast visions of horrific, foreign shadows lurking around the edges of the mysterious building beside him. He thought about knocking on the front door for help, but it was so lifeless and gloomy that it felt hostile. He couldn't see the front door, as if it was hidden. His manners and embarrassment over his staggering ability to communicate made the decision to simply walk inside the property feel impossible. Worry crept through his better judgment, making him feel like whoever lived in this house, forgetting entirely about Ben, would shoot him, or worse.

He thought about his mother's home and the fact that it was located in a similar area to this one. False confidence filled him with the sense that he knew where he was and that his mother's house was nearby. His body spilled onto the grass as he got out of the car to walk home.

Of course, his mother's home was thirty miles away, and he had no idea where he was going.

The car door slammed shut behind him, echoing out over the fields now bare in the time between harvests. Luckily it was a warm night, and the moon and stars were casting enough light for him to clearly see the gravel road as he walked alongside the ditch. It was quiet and peaceful, although he begged for a car to break that serenity. He didn't mind the walk until an hour passed, and his brain shivered at the realization that he hadn't recognized any of his surroundings since he fell asleep.

He stopped to urinate in the ditch where relatively tall overgrowth flourished, now hoping for any approaching vehicles to be slightly delayed. Once he finished, he felt a new burst of optimism that came after tending to one's bodily needs. No matter how far he had to walk, he would eventually get somewhere, and that somewhere would help him get home. However, turning around and heading back to that cold farmhouse never crossed his mind.

Sam buttoned his pants and saw the only other building for miles.

It was a grand Victorian home, three stories tall, that appeared old but more well-kept than the only other refuge he had seen that evening. Although its architecture was looming and almost condescending in its shape and size, and its color appeared monochromatic in the mellow moonlight, there was a warmth to it from the outside. It felt like whoever lived there would likely help and probably give him some kind of delicious food that was already sitting on their kitchen counter for guests out of an elevated sense of hosting duty. That was just the kind of people they were. They had to be.

A single yellow lamp glowed in the small entryway window beside the front door, shallowly illuminating the wide porch. He stepped into the gravel driveway, slipping slightly as the rocks rolled beneath his tired dress shoes, and looked at the sign lightly covered in sharp, curling brush. He could only read one of the words.

Manor

He was unable to read the rest of what was written, but the word "manor" was enough for him to trust its inhabitants. This was farm country, and if someone referred to their house as a manor, they were probably more sophisticated and less likely to shoot you. Sam didn't know that to be a fact, but the logic tracked in his drug-addled mind.

The pathway leading from the gravel driveway to the front door felt different. It leveled out his wobbly legs and seemed to breathe as he cautiously approached the front door. It warped in and out of his teetering vision. He had lost his balance and tripped a few times during his walk, roughing up his hands on the gravel road, but it was different here. It was as though the world was moving under him to catch him each time he stumbled too loosely to one side. It was moving with him to offset his ruined poise. The property cradled him into its company as their orbits increased the intensity of their attraction.

When he arrived at the frame of the enormous red oak door, he reached out a fist to knock but stopped. He couldn't simply knock on someone's door at God knows what hour. He felt the pull to continue down the road until he came across a gas station or late-night business of any kind. If he only had access to a phone, he could call his mother to pick him up. The embarrassment of that would have to be mentally dealt with another time. She would understand. He had lost someone, and he was grieving like people did. He wasn't the first drunk young man to get lost.

Suddenly, his hand, without his permission, finished its arc in the air and connected with the door. The knock cracked much louder than the force of its strike, and the big red oak door slowly creaked open.

Yellow lamplight spilled out onto the porch and enveloped him in a gummy, snuggly bubble that held his body. The air pressure shifted, and Sam found himself flushed inside the house, curiously closing the door behind him with his other hand.

Sam's spotty memory was skipping even while he was experiencing the event to be remembered. He did not remember crossing the threshold into the entryway even seconds after it happened. As if he was only just now opening his eyes from another long nap, he appeared in the house, wholly unsettled by the entryway's interior.

First, he noticed the area next to the door. Empty and hollow, the floor met the wall beside the wood frame and gave off very little personality or lived-in touch. It was a dead entryway. Drab. Although he needed assistance, Sam couldn't help but critique how surprisingly boring it was. He slowly turned his eyes to the rest of the room and gasped.

It felt impossible based on the way the building looked from the outside. The entryway was massive and cavernous. The tent of visible light that held him fizzled and ended before reaching the walls at the far end of the room, however far away they were. It looked like they could be miles away. He expected to see a grand staircase, but there was only endless empty space. There must have been something separating the various floors and rooms that must have existed in this house. *Could the building actually be completely hollow?* The ceiling stretched far into the shadows overhead and out ahead of him. He estimated that the visible light was reaching well above three floors, but the walls kept climbing until darkness took them. There was no ceiling that he could see, but there had to be. The only wall he was sure of was framing the front door behind him.

"Hello? Sorry," he timidly called out into the onyx vacuum. His voice barely reached the edge of the lamp's weak radiation. Sam was transfixed on the evaporating light at the edges of his bubble. The threads of luminescence coming apart in frayed strings at the border of his glow dazed his wet, confused eyes. Hardwood boards beneath his feet let out their winces as he shifted his precarious weight. Suddenly, it appeared.

At the very edge of the visible light field, in that gray area where the world went through a perpetual transitional existence, molting entropy, moving from chaotic to orderly in every corner of every second, a young woman's face slowly emerged. In the thin, distant air where photons either decayed or latched onto each other just enough to give the viewer a fragmented depiction of reality, the tip of a pale nose and the soft shimmer of long silver hair poked out of the darkness and floated into sight.

The tip of her nose and brim of her hair covering her forehead, clean and sparkling, moved slowly, slithering in and out of view. Her face was not necessarily getting easier to see, but there was a graceful, unnatural movement to her that brought her into focus. Murky, slow dancing. A hushed sway, mesmerizing in pace, moved her most protruding features in and out of sight like she was warming up the barrier before him. Her movement was music, crescendoing when she finally pushed her face fully through and into the light.

Her face sat surrounded in darkness like a swimmer floating on their back in deep water. Pale features warped and changed in the fractured light. Sam constructed hundreds of identities for her before admitting to himself that he still could not clearly see her. He could not see her body unless he slightly diverted his gaze and used his peripheral vision to increase his night vision. Each of the rods and cones in his eyes squirmed to locate traces of life. Maddeningly, this created a paradox where he was simultaneously seeing her better and worse. A shapeless dark mass made up her body, also shifting, melting, and reconstructing into hundreds of various body types. The shadows delighted in their tricks.

"I'm sorry, I just let myself in. That was rude. I'm sorry," Sam said. "I'm lost, and I need to use your phone. I've been walking for hours. I just came from a funeral, as you can see. My friend from high school died, and I'm in town. I don't live here, but I'm from here. I don't live here, though, anymore. God, I'm sorry."

Sam gestured to his funeral attire, which was miraculously still presentable enough to attend a funeral after his long night. In Sam's mind, a collared shirt and tie made up the outfit of a trustworthy man. He apologized again and continued doing the talking for both of them.

"This is a massive house. So gorgeous. Oh my god. I knew you could help me because anybody who lives in such a beautiful house like this one would surely be a good person and able to help. I'm sorry again for just coming in, too, but I think the door was unlatched. It just came open. Can I use your phone? Please? Then I'll be on my way. Or my mom will come get me. I can wait outside too, though, after the call."

The woman's face continued to undulate, expand and shrink, now gleaming like the metallic hue of an oil spot. One of her pale hands appeared at her side, reaching out of the darkness. Slowly, it crept forward as if it was working through thick, invisible mud. She strained like an interpretive ballet dancer trying to evoke the movement of suffering. Her hand, fingers wiggling, shook and pulled back.

Silence hushed over them. The gentle hum of a perfectly random assortment of noises caused by the world around them ceased, and a deafening fright chilled Sam's uneasy soul. A star died inside his chest. Panic welled up inside him just as it had back in the car, and he felt an overwhelming urge to flee. He desperately wanted to run back out into the night. It was brighter out there.

She stepped forward slowly. The movement of her body was only visible when Sam looked away, and even then, it was a hallucination of a body that felt impossible. Her face floated like she was lying in water that was rising toward him. Darkness' surface hugged her in its bath. Sam screamed.

"Hey," he called out. "Can you talk to me?"

Bulging raven eyes halted in their advancement. Her eyeholes were like reflections of shadows cast over charred craters. The face stopped. In a smooth, startlingly swift motion, it turned around, and her long hair, which he now saw ran to the floor, swung out into the light like a billowing silver dress. She disappeared back into the pitch-black of the enormous entryway's hidden splendor.

"Okay, thanks," Sam said. "Never mind. I'll get going. Sorry again."

As he turned his back, mirroring the strange woman, he reached for the door handle. But he couldn't leave yet, not after what he heard. He jumped when he heard it, and his hand drilled his hyperextended fingers into the handle, crunching their bones.

An agonizing, pounding series of thuds in quick succession hit the ground behind him, shocking him and the surrounding wood. A mist of syrupy liquid sprayed against the back of his neck and covered the back of his clothes. The sound of dripping and unfurling of thick meat mutedly pressed out from the vast entryway. He had to look. He didn't want to. He had to.

Behind him, on the floor, the body of his deceased friend, naked, had been sectioned into pieces. The pieces appeared fresh, and steam rose out of the open wounds that emptied the entirety of his blood and bile onto the floor in a massive puddle that stretched off into the haunting caliginosity. Bone shards rolled across the wood like dice. The visible entryway was entirely splattered in a red that broke through so vividly, making it the only discernible color in the room. His decapitated head was lying sideways when the eye pressed against the ground opened, appeared dazed, and then focused on Sam. The eyelids stretched wide in terror. His mouth fell agape. He was alive. But he couldn't have been. Sam had watched him be buried.

Sam fell backward, slipping on the blood now leaking through the hardwood floor. His shoes were soaked in the grotesque mess. He fumbled and reached, crying, mouth rotting with thick, white saliva. His nose clogged. In the unfathomable confusion, he found the doorknob. The woman's face floated again on the surface of the darkness across the room. Quietly, it fell to the floor, and she began licking the blood while his friend screamed.

***

The following morning, Sam was found by his mother curled up on the welcome mat outside her front door. His clothes were coated in dirt and gravel dust, and his shoes were damaged, but there were only small dots of his own blood included in the stains. He had curled himself into a ball so tightly that he was able to fit his body within the border of the welcome mat. It was a detail that made his mother's skin crawl.

"Sam," she cried, opening the door. "Are you okay? I didn't know you were coming home. What are you doing out here? Why didn't you come inside?"

"I don't know," he said, dazed, opening his eyes slightly, still soothed by the first few moments of waking up that veiled everything in a dream. "I blacked out. I'm sorry. I feel so embarrassed. I don't know what happened. I hate doing this. I haven't done this in so long."

"It's okay," his mother said, counting this lapse in behavior as a unique exception in his budding adulthood, brought on by the intensity of his visit. "You've been through a lot. Sometimes, grieving makes us act in ways we aren't proud of. It's perfectly understandable, honey. Nobody is upset with you. You're home now, and you're safe. How did you get home? Did you walk?"

Sam painfully stretched his horribly sore legs. They felt injured and exhausted. The fingers on his right hand were bruised and swollen. He felt cold and forgotten about, desperate in his self-loathing. At first, he thought his legs were sweaty, but he soon realized that he had urinated in his pants and groaned.

"I think I ran home," he said, two tears working their way down his cheeks as he began to cry. "I just wish I could remember why."

The Laughing Box

"YOU FELLAS BE nice to him. He's a laugh boy," Helen, the secretary, said as she patted James on the shoulder, closed the conference room door behind her, and walked back to her desk.

An oval of wooden chairs creaked under the weight of seven men in austere gray suits, waiting in a hazy brown conference room to hear what the peculiar metal box in front of them could do. James Ray had created his own laugh box, an instrument comprised of different recorded laughs that could be used to provide a laugh track to a television sitcom, and he was attempting to sell his services as a sweetener, or "laugh boy," to the only studio that would give him a meeting.

Charles Douglass had created the first laugh box, which worked quite beautifully, although nobody knew exactly how it operated. He was the trusted sweetener of the area. It was the early sixties, and canned laughter was a popular audience reaction control tool utilized by most studios for their sitcoms. Live studio audiences couldn't always be trusted to behave the way executives and producers thought audiences should, and Charles had invented a solution that changed television forever. But James was convinced that his was better, and he was trying desperately to convince others of that. He needed money, and laughs were paying.

"We already have a laugh guy. Can you do better than him?" one of the executives said, clearing his throat between sentences. The horizon of expressionless, shaved faces with cigarette smoke twirling into the air between their dull blue eyes applied miserable pressure onto the young man. He stood up straight and tapped the top of the box with his right hand.

"Oh sure, I've heard of Charles. Douglass, is it? Is that his last name? Haven't met the guy, but he seems like a nice enough fella. Does good work. Honestly, he's kind of a creep, though. I heard he's been running out of laughs to use, and he's hard to work with. That's why you agreed to meet with me, isn't it? He's probably a pain to deal with, what with being such a weirdo. And his machine only has, what was it, three hundred laughs or something?" asked James.

"Three hundred and twenty."

"Oh my. How primitive," James said, arching his eyebrows. He removed his hand from the top of the box and waved the back of it at them. "That used to be good enough, but pretty soon those laughs get all used up, and every laugh starts sounding the same, and then audiences at home, you know, they're not dumb. They'll get tired of it. It'll have the opposite effect you want it to have. My laugh box has over one thousand laughs from all different kinds of people. Different accents. Different ages. You get the full spectrum of human laughter. You'll never run out of reactions to use. It's a different audience for every show, doesn't matter how many episodes you shoot. There are gasps and oohs and aahs too. His machine can't do that. Mine doesn't break down either. I heard he's so secretive that he locks himself in the bathroom to fix it. Such a weird guy. Mine will never break down. I can promise you that."

"Will you show us what's inside? We'd like to know how it works."

The box was made of thick steel, muted with faded green paint, and it was padlocked shut. The stale color looked as though it would rub off onto your hand in a layer of dust. It stood about two feet tall and three feet wide. Inside was a typewriter that James had fashioned to be played like an organ, each of the keys corresponding to a different recorded tape loop that played many different kinds of laughs depending on its place on the tape. The keys were a glossy spectrum of orange and red, begging to be touched.

It was a copy of Charles Douglass' original design, but what made it different was that James had added a second keyboard and radically lengthened the tape loops assigned to each key, providing many more laugh choices. He also claimed that his craftsmanship was an improvement in the design. Charles had invented the idea, but James perfected it.

"That is one thing I agree with Charles on," James said, tensing his mouth. "A magician never reveals his secrets, and neither should a sweetener. Think of it as ensuring my job security."

"We'll have to see if you get a job first," another voice said, blowing out an enormous plume of cigarette smoke into the nicotine storm clouds forming above them. Two grunts and a throat clearing followed before the voice continued through a smile, "Let's hear it. Play us some laughs we've never heard before."

The room chuckled at this concept. The business of laughs. James unlocked the box and opened it toward himself. He showed them the typewriter keys.

"I can show you that it uses two complete sets of typewriter keys," he said. "Charles' only uses one. So, you know, that means mine has more.

Two is better than one, wouldn't you agree? Pretty simple idea. Now, would you like me to press one of the keys?"

"Yeah. That's what I asked you to do."

"Okay. Here goes. I'll just press the key, and you can hear the laughter. One second."

James' quivering finger came down softly on one of the keys, and the deep booming laughter of an old man, perhaps British, rumbled in a monotone voice out of the box.

The room was pleased that it worked, but not entirely convinced that it worked better than the machine Mr. Douglass had used in the studio's programming for years.

"Is that guy British?" one of the men asked.

"Yes," said James, puffing out his chest and trying not to sweat. "That's only a mild British laugh too. This thing can get really, really British. Some of these laughs, you can barely understand them because they're so British. Same goes for other nationalities too."

"Show us one with a really thick accent," another executive's raspy, office-worn voice choked out.

James' finger fell again on the key, this time much more confident that the following laugh on the tape loop would have a thicker accent. But, instead of a laugh, the sound that came out was a scream. A shattering, brain-frying scream. Smoke cleared out of the room, whirled into the vents by the highly pressurized aural assault of the invisible cry, desperate for space to escape the small office.

The men dropped the cigarettes from their mouths onto the table and lost what little color was left in their pale faces. Sweat poured out of their foreheads, and they clapped their hands over their ears, reeling in agony. The sound of screeching death throes from a mutilated older man entombed the hell of that meeting room.

"Turn it off!" they yelled.

He took his finger off the key, and the painful screaming ceased.

"What the hell was that?" one of the executives shouted, rubbing his ears. "Is this some kind of joke?"

"Uhm, I'm so sorry. I guess there was a scream on that one," said James, putting on a show of inspecting the machine. "Screaming is kind of like laughing. Some people scream because they're laughing so hard. Did you know that?"

"We don't want *screaming*. That was awful. People would think someone is being murdered!"

James dug his hands into the box with the lid facing the other men so they couldn't see what he was doing. After a moment, he took a deep breath and closed his eyes before snapping them open and clapping his hands together, smiling. His fingers were stained with a thick, dripping red substance that lightly splattered across his face.

"So, uhm. Whoops. Got some ink on my hands." James laughed, pulling a handkerchief out of his pocket to wipe his fingers. "I need to open this thing up really quick and just make sure that the next laugh isn't a scream. It isn't broken at all, not even a little bit, but I do need to get in there and double-check where we're at on the tape roll. Is there a place I can do that? I don't want the scream to go off again and upset you. This thing has so many reactions, you know, and not all of them will be pleasant to everyone. I don't mind, but I can see how some people might not like that particular one."

They stared blankly back at him before one of them pointed toward a door on the wall behind James.

"There's a bathroom through there," he said flatly.

"Right," James said, letting out another bit of nervous laughter. "That's perfect. I'll be just a second."

James closed the lid on the laugh box and picked it up. His arms fell taut, and his legs bowed under its extraordinary weight. He lugged it over to the door and propped it onto one knee against the wall while he turned the handle. Nobody stood to help him. Red stained the door handle, and after a few seconds of struggling, he closed the door behind him.

The executives traded disapproving glances and lit new cigarettes. Beyond the closed door, arrhythmic slamming and a commotion of curses punched at the wall. The men felt like they were listening to James and his machine having a private argument. They shook their heads, smirking. Why were all these laugh boys so damn weird about their little laughing boxes?

One executive poured himself a glass of brown liquor from a clear, diamond-shaped decanter neatly arranged on a drink tray in the corner. Another picked up the phone and told Helen, sitting at her desk far outside the conference room, that the meeting would be finished soon. He assured her not to be alarmed by any wild sounds coming from the room and that Mr. Ray would be leaving shortly.

They waited a minute more, softly making cynical remarks and snickering to themselves before James reentered.

"Okay," he said, "I think I got it now."

"Great."

James wobbled his creation back toward the table, supporting it with his knees. As he pushed through the door, he lost his footing and dropped the box on the floor.

The metal hinges split open with a harsh bang, and the dark insides fell out, exposed. A horrible chorus of screaming followed, flushing out of the opening and filling the room with sobbing phantoms. Oily shadows warped in and out of human shapes, throwing themselves around the room, laughing and crying hysterically. Blood and chunks of human bone flooded out of the opening, coating the brown carpet in a thick crimson liquid. A pool of rust rose to their ankles.

The executives stood up to leave, terrified, their shrieking lost in the air. James no longer had a choice. He picked up the glass decanter and shattered it over the closest executive's skull. He wrapped his hand in the stained handkerchief from his pocket, grabbed a couple sizable pieces of broken glass, and stood in front of the door.

"I can't let you tell anyone what's inside," he said.

One of the executives picked up the phone to call the secretary, but James kicked the table, pulling it out of his hands. He ripped the phone line out of the wall, and as each executive tried to power their way past him to the door, they were stabbed and gutted by the glass shards in his hands until enough of their blood had joined the growing pool on the floor that they fell face down in the muck. A few drowned before they bled out. One ran to the bathroom. Unfortunately for the trembling pile of pleas he melted into on the cold tile floor, the bathroom didn't have a lock on its door, and he soon joined the others in gruesome silence.

James carefully cut out the seven men's larynxes and meticulously worked them into the machine. His laugh box, now again brimming with mutilated tissue and blood, topped with tattered rags of gray cloth, quieted its heinous cry as James put his whole weight on top of it to force the lid shut.

Suddenly, a knock rapped on the door.

"Everything okay?" Helen asked. "I know you said not to worry about the sound, but it sounds absolutely horrid in there. And the phone wasn't working when I tried to call."

"Everything's fine, right, gentlemen?" James said breathlessly. He pushed a few keys on the typewriter, and the combined laughter of the executives roared out of the vile instrument.

"Well, pardon me all to hell." The secretary left the door, muttering.

James packed his things. He changed into clean clothes in the bathroom and washed his face before politely waving at Helen on his way out of the building. He would have to continue looking for work, but he had not left empty-handed. His machine had gained a few more laughs.

The Vanishing Gong

I HAVE LOST many things in my life, but the gong my mother gave me haunts me the most. Its sound. Warming it up. The crash. Like a storm on a cooking pan blasting toward Heaven.

Over time, I lost it in a move or something at some point. I'm not exactly sure when or where. I used to think about it every night before I fell asleep. I think about everything I've ever lost. They all burn inside of me and kill me with their memories. They all feel like a piece of my past that I will never retrieve, and they always end on the gong. Losing it panged like I had lost a part of my mother. Although people pass away, the items they leave behind are lucky enough to continue living for them. Its vibrations would feel like, for the duration of them, her ghost was physically in the room with me. I missed it so deeply. Until a few days ago, when, by chance, I found it again.

Walking the two blocks toward my favorite coffee shop, as I do most mornings, I passed a neighbor hosting a small yard sale on the patch of grass in front of her home. Regardless of being raised in Chicago and living here my entire life, I somehow still knew very little about the people around me. In her stack of old DVDs, bowls, and unremarkable furniture, it sat on top of a bookshelf and shined brightly in the morning sun. My gong.

It had to be the same one. The perfect dimples on its golden face. One large light blue circle was painted around the outer edge, with a smaller, lighter blue circle running around the inside. A pink string handle was attached on top. I have never seen another like it. Of course, to be sure, I needed to hear its crash.

"Hi," she said, putting down her book and leaning forward in her folding chair, smiling at me. "Got your eye on that gong?"

Her eyes were kind, and her flannel shirt was calming. The woman had no idea that this thing used to belong to me. There was no malice in her suggestion. She had simply seen my interest and wanted to know if she could make me happy. She probably would have just given it to me.

"I was wondering if I could strike it. You know, to see how it sounds," I said.

"Of course. The mallet is somewhere nearby. It should be over there. You know a lot about gongs?"

The smooth sand-colored wooden mallet was sitting in a pile of dirt beside the bookshelf. The carelessness of this arrangement made my blood boil. They did not deserve this gong. I grabbed the mallet, dusted it off, held the divine cymbal in front of my chest, and began to warm up a crash. A shiver of the great crescendo approaching washed over me as I was transported to the front row of an angelic band playing the notes of rain. Volcanos erupted. My entire life melted down my eyelids, and I never wanted to open them or see anything again. I wanted to live in this sound. I was reunited with that old friend that I so foolishly lost. It was mine again.

"I'll take this," I said, holding it up higher as if she didn't already know what I meant.

"I'm glad you like it. One of my daughter's boyfriends brought it over one time and left it here. Then she left it here when she went to college this year and won't text me back when I ask if she wants it, so I told her that I was going to sell it or donate it, and she still didn't respond. Kids."

"That sucks. How much is it?"

"Oh, I don't know. You seem like the expert. How much does a gong go for?"

"It's priceless."

"How's twenty bucks sound? You seem like you like it, and I'm happy to see that, even if I take a beating on the price."

As I produced the money from my pocket, another man approached our meeting. He was shorter than me and wearing a dirty green Adidas tracksuit. Pants and matching jacket. His hair was thinning, and a medical mask obscured his face. He had been lurking around, pretending to look at items. Once he saw that I was about to purchase the gong, he intervened.

"I believe that item is mine," he stammered.

"Sorry, pal, he beat you to it," the woman said.

"This same gong was stolen from me a long time ago. I lost hope that I would ever see it or hear it again. That is, until I heard this man strike it. I'm certain it is my stolen gong."

He approached me and reached out a hand to touch the hanging cymbal. I pulled it away.

"I'm sorry to hear about your loss, sir," I said, "but I'm sure there are many gongs that look like this. You can't be certain it's yours."

"I am certain," he said. "I beg your pardon, but please return my property."

"I don't know where my daughter's boyfriend got this thing, but I doubt he stole it from you. That would be weird as hell. I'm sure this is a misunderstanding. This young man was here first. He gets to buy the gong. That's it."

She grabbed the money out of my hand and nodded at me. The man tilted his head forward and looked up at me through dangling strands of what greasy, gnarled orange hair he still had left. I ran back to my apartment, completely forgetting about coffee or the day ahead of me. I had my gong back, and I couldn't let it out of my sight again.

I hung it above the fireplace in my living room. The perfect spot. The look of it. Its potential energy crooned the sound of its rise and fall in my mind without producing any actual noise. Each time I used it, my mother's ghost felt like it was in the living room with me for the duration of its fall. The fireplace only amplified this effect. Fire and metal, splashing together in a sea of emotion that held my entire life in its hands. I felt whole again. I felt like I had reclaimed a piece of my past. It was a second chance.

Then, in the middle of the night, I was awakened by a splitting crash.

I sprang from my bed and ran out into my living room to see the gong swinging above the fireplace. It had clearly been struck, but luckily, it had not been stolen. This sound was different. It did not invoke my mother's spirit. I felt a foreign presence fading away. I turned on the lights, but there was no intruder. I searched for hours. My apartment was empty.

I called the police, but they looked around and told me there was nothing they could do. Neighbors didn't see anything. One officer said they would schedule additional drive-by checks in the area and suggested buying a home security camera. Then they left.

The next night, it happened again.

Although I had been trying to stay awake in an effort to catch the returning culprit, at around 1 a.m., sleep consumed my trembling heart just before a loud crash jolted my home, and the sensitivity carved into my ears for that sound triggered harsh tremors throughout my body. Again, I ran around the apartment in search of no one. I was alone. Police would do nothing. I could only sit and think about the man from that day at my neighbor's yard sale until sunrise.

I considered going to the woman's house again and asking if she knew anything about him. It didn't seem as though they had met before, given their exchange. If nothing else, creating a stronger bond with my neighbors would help me feel safer. I wanted eyes around the community.

However, when I went to her home the following evening, she was gone. She had moved. That's why she was having the garage sale. The house was for sale. I laughed at how unobservant I had been. Then I was struck with terror. The gong was sitting in my apartment, wholly unprotected. Perhaps the intruder, that man, would return.

When I arrived back home, there was no evidence of a break-in. My treasure was safely hanging above the fireplace. I decided to take the gong into my room. I would not fall asleep this night. I put it in my closet. Locked away behind my clothes, facing the foot of my bed, anyone trying to touch it would have to pass me, and I would be ready.

I'm not exactly sure what time it happened, but as I sat and stared at the closet door, I slowly began to nod off. I don't remember ever falling asleep. I seamlessly moved from watching my room into a dream of watching my room. A loud crash from the gong swelled, rang out behind my closet door, and rattled its frame. It warmed up, coaxing me further into dreams, and broke my hypnosis upon the splatter of its release. I shrieked and jolted out of bed.

There was no way someone could have snuck into my closet. Impossible. I had been watching it the entire evening. I slowly stood up from my bed and cautiously approached the door. Once I plucked up enough courage to open it, I found something that shook me to my core.

Inside the closet, there was neither an intruder nor a gong. There was nothing. The gong was gone.

I searched the closet for hours. It was gone. It was nowhere. I searched the rest of my home. Perhaps I moved it in my sleep. But there was nothing. It had simply vanished.

The police held back laughter as I again reported mischief related to my gong. They assumed it was a friend of mine playing a prank. They said they would be on the lookout for it but didn't ask for a description. I asked if they wanted to dust for fingerprints, and they said it would be useless. My gong was gone again, and it would stay gone this time. The intruder, whoever it was, did not return.

Now, when I lie awake at night, I no longer think about the things I've lost. I believe that they are lost for a reason. I am not meant to have them back. They are no longer mine. Things must change, and one has no choice but to submit to that change to continue living. I don't longingly dream about the gong's beautiful noise. I fear it. I pray that terrible crash will not ring out again to taunt and torment me. The feeling of missing family and possessions had been replaced by crippling anxiety, like expecting a sneeze that never comes, waiting for that gong's cry. The absence of sound took on a heavier weight. The silence showed itself to be the next layer of Hell to peel away for me to gorge. Eventually, I found comfort in it and smiled.

You must enjoy things while you can. You will miss them when they're gone.

Sugar

I WAS RUNNING late for a job interview when I saw him screaming and throwing his briefcase at the wall outside my favorite coffee shop, Lynn's. I had stopped to get a surprisingly bitter pour-over, which sat warmly in my hand as I stepped outside. I didn't really care about the potential job, a construction gig that I was only trying out because I couldn't find work anywhere else, and his situation became vastly more alluring to me.

He was an older gentleman, short and hunched over with age, with long dyed-black hair, not his original color, wearing a tan dress coat, green corduroy pants, and brown leather shoes. The dye from his hair leaked down the back of his neck. He looked like he should be teaching young minds what to do with their lives and responsibly consuming THC gummies at night. Instead, he was yelling at people on the sidewalk and throwing his briefcase at the wall again and again, each time harder than before.

Soon, it broke open.

White sand burst out of it, and the man hollered. I couldn't tell if he was previously aware of its contents. He cried both like something was missing and as though he expected to find exactly what was there. Granulated shards evenly separated across the sidewalk. They expanded and spread apart like stars in the night sky. He lay down and licked some off the ground. It was sugar. He looked at me.

I froze.

The heat of the coffee intensified as a chill ran through my body. He stood up and walked toward me. His eyes appeared fully white. I know they weren't, but I could not remember their real color later. I could hardly remember them at all. There was no color.

He removed the lid of my coffee, spat in it, returned the lid, and walked away.

His briefcase sat broken on the ground, sugar rolling out of its pockets. I regained the ability to move once he was out of sight. I put my finger in one of the pockets, pulled the sweet sand up to my mouth, and licked it clean. I bathed my tongue in it. It tasted wonderful. I took a long sip of coffee, gorging on the sweet alabaster mud, and went back into Lynn's

Coffee Shop to sit down. That's when I threw up in the doorway and passed out.

When I awoke a few moments later, the employees were tending to my toxic state. One of them threw the coffee away and gave me water. Another one cleaned the mess outside. They assured me that everything would be fine, and I believed them. All while a *Help Wanted* sign swung gently in the window.

Williwaw Cockalorum

"COFFEE," SHE SAID.

"Coffee?" I asked.

"Coffee."

"Coffee?"

"Yeah, where is the coffee?"

That's when, I swear to god, I pointed to the coffee aisle and said, "Over there."

"What?" she asked, even though she could see my finger, "I mean like coffee in a bag." And then she mimed gagging with her finger. Her husband, who had already said her name twice, touched her back.

"I don't think they sell our brand anymore," he said.

"Oh no. It's my favorite coffee. Do you sell this brand anymore?"

She pushed a coupon toward me, but I don't sell anything. I went on break.

I walked into the employee lounge, where a small dog was eating coffee grounds off the floor. I don't know what kind of dog. A dog. The microwave dinged, and the stench of wilted, hot vegetables filled the air.

"She'll be nineteen tomorrow because of those grounds. Builds a strong foundation," said my manager, a slightly overweight, part-time yoga instructor with racist hair. He pulled his lunch out of the microwave. He owns the dog because of a handicap that doesn't exist, and he spends most of his shifts complaining about the weaknesses of others. He runs this grocery store.

"I don't care," I said.

"Whoa," he said in a mocking tone.

"Isn't it against health code for your dog to be here? You can't spill coffee everywhere for your dog to eat. Did you even buy that?"

"We don't have to pay for it, Willy. We're not selling this brand anymore."

"Why?"

"They got shut down. Poor labor conditions," he said before blowing his nose into a napkin.

"So our employee lounge is allowed to look disgusting with a dog eating garbage off the floor, and you get to act like you have a conscience?"

"She's cleaning." He smiled.

"This is your mess!" I yelled, and I shoved the employee microwave on the floor. He threw me, by my shirt, mouth-first into the grounds. I coughed, looking at his dog. There was nothing for me in her eyes as his breath filled my open ear.

"You are fired, and you will be escorted out of the store. Do you understand?" he said.

***

Williwaw Cockalorum is my name. I'm sixty-eight. Nineteen years ago, my son was shot in the stomach by a police officer because he looked suspicious inside his own coffee shop after store hours. The officer shot himself shortly afterward, and they both died before anyone could ease their deplorable journeys to the great beyond. I work across the street from the building, which has now been renovated into a wine bar, and I look at it every day. Every day.

My wife comes to see me at work, and I'm despicable toward her because I'm afraid of my coworkers. I know the teenagers make fun of me, although most of them have their own children, and they call me a joyless old bag. They say I hate music because I turn the radio off when I'm alone. I love music. I don't like their music. It hurts my ears.

***

A sliver of plastic fell from the microwave door and was ingested by his dog. There was blood and coffee swirling about a powerful vomit. Music. My boss inhaled his voice from my head, swept her up in his coat, and left. I picked up the mess, put it in a bag, and went back to work.

I gave the bag to that couple before I was escorted out of the store by police officers. My wife is on her way to bail me out now. We're going out for coffee. I can't wait to see her laugh.

Walking on Water

AS THEY FILED across the narrow footbridge onto the ship, wooden steps thudding and keeping time over the gentle waves, Geoff peeked over the railing and searched for signs of human feet. He had overheard his parents talking about a recent news story that reported a bizarre phenomenon of severed feet, still in their shoes, washing up on the shore. The coast guard was unable to identify who the feet belonged to or where they came from. But every couple weeks for the last few months, severed feet were found by traumatized beachgoers.

Geoff had never been on a cruise ship before. He nervously, excitedly told the woman greeting each guest at the entrance that he was eight years old and showed her the stuffed whale his parents had gotten him at an aquarium earlier that summer. She smiled at him before turning to his parents to answer their questions and give them directions to their cabin. His sister Katrina was thirteen, and her expression clearly communicated to the employees and other passengers that she was far less excited to be on a trip with her family.

"Have you seen any cut-off feet?" Geoff asked the woman helping his parents. His mother looked embarrassed, and his father laughed. The cruise line employee contorted her expression as though she didn't know what he was talking about, but he could see past her eyes that she was protecting a galaxy of memories.

"Cut-off feet? Somebody's been watching the news too much." She laughed with rehearsed precision. "Nobody on this ship has ever seen anything like that. The news makes things seem a lot scarier than they really are. Don't worry about that stuff. Just worry about having fun, okay? Hey, would you like a free sticker?"

His mother gasped with feigned excitement, and his father continued smiling, now eying the entrance to the restaurant across the room. The employee took a sticker out of her pocket and handed it to Geoff, who silently nodded to thank her for it. The sticker was a golden life preserver with a ship plowing through it, white waves welcoming its glide across the ocean, all of which glimmered in the sunlight shining through the door as he read the text above it.

Behemoth Cruises
Like walkin' on water.

"Hey," his father said to the rest of the family, "I'm getting pretty hungry. You guys hungry? What do you say we drop our stuff off in the room and hit up the restaurant?"

"I'm not hungry," Katrina said. Her mother rolled her eyes at this response, which had recently become the young woman's go-to reply whenever anyone asked if she wanted to eat.

"You're not going to just drink water, Katrina. I'm sure you'll find something on this boat that sounds good," her mother said. "Let's do it. Geoff, are you hungry?"

Geoff put the sticker in his pocket, unsure of where he would ever actually want to stick such a thing. He decided he would leave it unstuck and put it in the shoebox under his bed at home, where he kept all the knick-knacks and memorabilia that triggered emotions within his little heart. He nodded at his mother.

"Great," his father said. "Thank you, miss."

They asked Geoff to wave at the employee who had given him the sticker, and she smiled at him, her mouth unfalteringly pleasant as the family walked around the corner and to the room to drop off their luggage.

Behemoth Cruises prided itself on having extraordinarily large ships. They claimed to have vessels so enormous and stable that guests frequently forgot they were traveling across the ocean. They were so wrapped up in the quarter-mile worth of deck activities that the shimmering sea around them was often described as the least impressive part of the trip. The surrounding fields of crashing blue deep were at the back of everyone's mind while they gorged on extravagance.

After the family stowed their luggage in their cabin and the children decided which bunk they would occupy—Katrina choosing the bottom and Geoff delighted to have the top—they made their way to the restaurant. The entire ship would have to listen to a short presentation on safety before they took off, but there was still time to get a quick meal in beforehand.

The restaurant was relatively empty. It was one of many, and this particular version worked as a buffet. Most people were exploring the ship, still getting settled in their rooms or visiting bars. A couple families with small children were scattered among the long rows of tables. The buffet was only serving half its normal amount of food, but the parents of each family were pleased while their children ate small squares of pizza and chicken tenders.

"This is great, eh?" their father said as their mother smiled with a mouth full of barbeque ribs.

Katrina pushed a wet Caesar salad around her side plate and looked at her phone. Geoff was eating popcorn shrimp and drinking hot chocolate that his mother had helped him dispense from a machine he had never used before. He nodded at his father.

"It's yummy," he said.

Geoff looked past his father's face, which was devouring creamy pasta, and stared at an older woman wearing a green robe a few tables behind them.

Her face was overly made up with pale whites and harsh blushes, and her eyes were bright blue with chalky eyelid makeup to match. Her distraught expression dragged her face to the floor worse than the prolonged effects of gravity on aging skin ever could. Her hair was thin and gray, but she didn't appear to be quite old enough to merit it. There had been clear attempts to dye it dark red, which had been given up on long ago. Her mouth hung open, and she was staring out the window with distressingly sad eyes. On the table in front of her were a mug of coffee and a plate bearing the crumbled ghost of a chocolate chip cookie.

"I'm going to get more hot chocolate," Geoff said.

"Want me to help you?" his mother asked.

"No, I can do it. Thanks."

His parents were softly proud that their son was now grown enough to get his own hot chocolate. Geoff excused himself from the table and walked to the hot chocolate machine. On his way back to the table, he stopped next to the woman in the green robe.

"What are you looking at?" he asked, trying to look in the same direction out the window. "Are there any cut-off feet out there?"

The woman slowly turned her head toward him. An infinitesimal spark of warmth ignited and died behind her eyes as she focused on the young man's innocent face.

"Yes," she said in a low whisper. "I think I'll cut my feet off and throw them in as well."

Geoff's heart raced. He pressed his face to the window and looked all around the surface of the water, but he could not see any shoes or amputated limbs. She turned away from him, and his mother called.

"Hey, Geoff," she said in a shepherding tone. "Come back here, please. Don't bother her. Sorry." The woman continued staring out the window, and Geoff returned to his seat.

"She said she saw cut-off feet out there," he said to his parents.

"I'm sure she was just teasing you. People are on vacation, and they want to relax, Geoff. Please be respectful of their space."

Geoff nodded, and the family finished their meal. Katrina pushed her salad to the middle of the table, having only really eaten a few croutons, and stood up first. The ship's captain made an announcement regarding the safety presentation and where each cabin section was to report for it. They left the buffet, and Geoff looked back at the woman still sitting at her table, staring. He wanted to ask his parents why she wasn't going to the safety presentation, but he remembered what his mother had told him and respected her space.

The safety presentation was routine, explaining how to use lifejackets and lifeboats and where to go in the event of an emergency. Near the end of the instructions, the captain coughed and stammered. His changing cadence revealed that he was no longer regurgitating the prepared remarks he gave at the beginning of every voyage.

He told them that the wind tends to pick up at night and to be careful. Someone asked if they would blow away, and the crowd of passengers around them laughed. The captain earnestly assured them over the intercom, having not heard the comment, that they would not be blown overboard into the water, but to watch out for their belongings and remain inside during curfew, which ran from midnight to five in the morning. He ended with a deep exhale as if that part of the presentation had weighed heavily on him.

Picking up his mood, he finished by telling everyone to enjoy their stay and have fun. The crowd cheered, and they departed the dock to begin their cruise.

***

The first day of the cruise was wonderful. The family stayed together for most of it. They visited the pool, found the outdoor movie theater, played basketball and mini golf, and inhaled relaxing scents at an oxygen bar. The oxygen bar loosened Katrina's mood. She had been rigidly attempting to use her phone until she lost service and then switched to using apps she downloaded specifically to use once that happened. But now she put her phone away. She was starting to enjoy herself and even laugh.

Their parents scheduled a couple's massage for early evening before dinner, so they told Katrina to take Geoff to the arcade that was closest to the spa. The plan was to eat dinner afterward. They sustained themselves on snacks from the multitude of food stands throughout the day. Slices of pizza were never far from reach. Dinner would be a sit-down affair with full courses from a prepared menu. Katrina was ready for a proper meal.

In the arcade, Geoff walked straight to a shooter cabinet to decimate hordes of aliens with a red plastic handgun, and he could not have been happier to find his sister swiftly by his side with a blue handgun, providing backup against the invasion. They were having fun. It was already shaping into an excellent family trip.

"Starting to get windy out there," a man said behind them as he entered the arcade from the deck to talk to his wife, who was playing a pinball machine. "Should probably get the kids off the mini golf course and get ready for dinner." Distracted by the voice, Geoff looked away from the screen and lost his final life to the aliens. Katrina nudged him with her elbow.

"Dude," she said. "Pay attention. Do you need more quarters?"

"Are Mom and Dad going to come get us, or should we meet them at dinner? Should we go soon?" he said nervously.

"They'll come get us. Don't worry," she said.

"I want to go. I want to be with Mom and Dad," he said.

Katrina rolled her eyes and returned her gun controller to its holster, watching the aliens swarm on her character and drain her life.

"They're having their little romance time," she said, looking disgusted. "Do you really want to walk in on that? Remember when you walked in on them while they were boning?"

"They said they weren't mad at me," he said.

"Yeah, but you ruined it for them. Just let them have fun and do their gross adult stuff. They need it. Parents don't always want to be around their brats."

Luckily, a moment later, their parents appeared in the doorway of the arcade.

"Hey kids," their mother called, their father looking slightly miffed. "Let's get going. We need to clean up for dinner."

"That was a short massage," Katrina said.

"Yeah, people were talking about how it's starting to get windy outside, and we were nervous about getting to dinner and everything. We weren't there long, but it's okay. We're going to do a full one tomorrow."

The family returned to their room and freshened up before making their way through the ship's interior to the elegant restaurant on the floor above theirs. One of the beautiful aspects of the cruise was that guests could get anywhere without going outside if the weather was disagreeable. The restaurant was beautiful, the food was immaculate, and the parents delighted at the sight of their children wolfing down expensive plates of roasted duck and garlic-whipped mashed potatoes in the dim candlelight. But soon, a storm began to pick up speed outside.

After dinner, Geoff and Katrina were instructed to stay in the room with their parents. They were calling it an early night due to the storm. With the blinds drawn, they clicked around on the ship's available television and movie channels and explored the amenities of their room. Soon, the parents' rhythmic breathing and light snoring became concrete evidence that they were in a deep sleep. Katrina stood up and looked at Geoff on the top bunk, holding his stuffed whale tightly to his chest.

"I'm going exploring," she said.

"Mom and Dad said we aren't supposed to leave the room. It's almost midnight. We're supposed to go to bed."

"They said that because you're little. I'm a teenager. I can go wherever I want." Katrina flashed her room key, "You can come if you want or don't. It doesn't matter to me."

Geoff sat up on the top bunk, watching Katrina tiptoe across the room. Once she reached the door and quietly put on her shoes, he gestured for her to wait. With his stuffed whale in hand, he put on his shoes, and they silently closed the door behind them as they entered the hallway.

They walked to a door leading out to the deck. The storm had died down, and it was looking much calmer outside.

"Let's go outside. It's done storming. We could see if we can get into the basketball courts or something," Katrina said.

"It's windy, though," Geoff said, scared.

"It's fine," Katrina huffed as she opened the door.

The children walked out onto the deck and took in the mind-altering awe of the looming great beyond above them. They had never seen the sky like this before. A trench of stars as distant and vast as the ocean touching it on the horizon. The sky lit the deck and ocean's surface with a brilliance beyond what any light from the extravagant *Behemoth* could provide. They both involuntarily released various sounds of wonder and words of admiration. They crept toward the railing and looked over the edge.

Frigid sea waves lapped and crashed against the ship stories below them. The only contrast of the black water was the white edges of each wave crest, as glinting and peacefully temperamental as the stars above them. Geoff noticed that the water nearer to the ship appeared slightly darker than the hungry hell of the rest of the night ocean.

A colossal dark oval was outlining the water below the boat. Something big was beneath them. He clenched his stuffed whale tighter in his hands.

"I'm kind of freaked out," he said, holding back how truly freaked out he was. "I don't like being near the railing."

"We're fine," Katrina said. She walked closer to the railing and arched her neck over the edge to get a good look down. She pretended to lose her footing and quickly pulled back, laughing when Geoff yelped.

Then the wind began to pick up.

The fuzzy casing around the whale pushed through his fingers as he squeezed its smiling face. The wind was pulling it from his grasp. He saw the woman in the green robe from earlier in the afternoon walking out of her cabin on the other side of the deck. She looked at him with her hollow, agonizingly sad eyes, and his heart slid into his stomach as his body froze.

He dropped the stuffed whale, and the wind began to drag it across the deck toward the gap between the railing and the floor.

Geoff yelled, aghast. He dove for the whale and caught it in one hand before it rolled off the dock into the water. At that precise moment, the wind kicked up hard, and Geoff was lifted off the ground.

Hurricane winds suddenly entombed the ship, and Geoff was floating. He screamed, and Katrina grabbed his free hand to anchor him while she held onto the railing to keep herself from floating away. They both cried for help in breathless terror.

Shrill howling overwhelmed their hearing as they held on for dear life in the face of the devastating force suffocating their bodies. Harsh gusts filled Geoff's clothes and flooded his pockets with cyclones. The golden sticker in his pocket violently fluttered out and up into the air before diving straight down into the salty bath below. The wind was attacking them. It was as if something was creating the wind to throw them overboard. It didn't feel real. Although they had never been on the open ocean before, they couldn't believe that something like this could happen. And so quickly.

They pleaded with the woman in the green robe to help them, but she wouldn't look at them. Instead, she calmly walked to the ship's edge with her stomach resting against the railing. She held her arms out as if to give herself to the wind, held her chin high and closed her eyes. She started lifting off the ground, and Katrina screamed, hoping any of the thousands of people on the ship would come to their aid.

The woman fell.

A pile of green robes containing the woman clawed at the ship wall before shattering the water's surface. Geoff saw her feet as she fell, and the sight of her white New Balance shoes sticking out of the bursting waves before she disappeared burned into his mind. As soon as she hit the ocean, she sank beyond any visual depth with an unsettling swiftness, as if she never existed. Once she was gone, dissolved into the deep, wrapped in the full range of darkness that connected the sky to the sea, the wind died down.

Geoff's feet touched the ground, and he hugged his stuffed whale and sister as tightly as his little arms would allow. Katrina held him, apologizing as she dragged them inside. They ran back to their room and opened the door. Their father was putting on his shoes, and their mother was holding the room phone to her ear.

"Where did you go?" their father asked, angry but clearly thankful that they were safe. "I was just about to come looking for you. Your mother was about to alert the ship that you were missing."

"A woman fell overboard," Katrina said. "We have to help her. The wind was so crazy. I'm sorry. We just wanted to explore. The wind got so crazy. And the woman. The woman in the green robe that Geoff was talking to earlier. She fell over the railing. She's in the water."

"Oh my god." Their mother's mouth fell agape, shocked at the news. She straightened her face as someone on the other end of the line captured her attention, "Yes," she said. "I was going to report my kids missing, but they're not missing anymore. They're here. But they just told us that someone fell overboard. There is a person overboard. She's an older woman wearing a green robe. She just fell off the right side of the ship. Starboard, yeah."

The coast guard was called out to their location. They hadn't gotten far from shore. The sun was rising, and the waters had calmed, but the officials were still combing for her body. The cruise staff was ordered to return to shore and dock and inform the passengers of the tragedy. Passengers were told that they would be unable to continue the cruise. Everyone would be fully refunded and given a discount on future cruises for the inconvenience.

When asked if the woman's body was recovered, the cruise staff would not divulge any further. They didn't know how to explain what had happened after viewing the security footage. The wind had taken her, and she vanished into the water.

Once they docked and the footbridge connected them to shore, the disgruntled passengers filed out of the boat to return to their lives on land.

Some were deeply saddened by the news, while others were merely annoyed by the abrupt ending to their vacation. Irritated muttering mixed with echoes of "Oh my god, can you believe that?" crackled along the line of shuffling bodies.

"Guess we aren't going to get that full massage," their father said, half-joking.

"That poor woman," their mother said. "I'm just glad you two are okay. Don't scare us like that ever again."

Geoff was still gripping his stuffed whale in one hand and his sister's hand in the other when he got off the boat. He looked out at the calm sea water and combed the surface. He heard a light thudding drum against the dock below them.

He cautiously approached the edge of the dock with Katrina and his parents close behind and peered over it. He recoiled, sobbing as he hugged Katrina, and his parents alerted the ship employees of his discovery. Tapping on the deck's black slime and crustacean-coated support beams, a pair of white New Balance sneakers with a line of red still pooling out of the openings floated by.

Stargazing

I
THE FUEL DIVER

"HAVE YOU SEEN that cow walking around outside?" asked Leo. "Up the skinny path behind our building? She's got a baby with her. Scared the hell out of me last night."

"No, I haven't seen that," I said.

"I almost fell off the trail," he said. "Fell off once before, and I broke my wrist. I came out covered in spiders. Got a metal plate and fifteen screws put in it. I can't feel anything in this hand now." He flexed his hand to show me the full range of its movement. "It's a ghost hand. That cow and her baby were up high, though. I don't know where they came from. Nearest farm is about a half-hour drive. Do you hike much?"

"No."

"You have to go out at night."

"I work at night." I looked up from my desk.

"Oh, I, uh, I haven't seen the work schedule," he said, even though he's my boss and he created my work schedule. "You look out the window sometimes though, right?"

"Yes."

"This place is even more gorgeous at night."

"It sounds like it."

"Well, I won't keep you," he said before double-tapping his keys on the counter and bounding out the door.

I work at a hostel on the side of a small mountain overlooking the oldest fishing harbor on the northern island of New Zealand. It's the rainiest part of an otherwise sunny and beautiful island. The hostel is called the Fuel Diver.

We provide the only accommodation available for a few hundred kilometers. It's a cozy little luxury located in a town populated by less than one hundred people. Lush trees fill the spaces between modest seaside homes. Everyone here is wealthy, although you wouldn't know it by the look of the buildings. They only care about owning land and privacy. The nearest grocery store is a thirty-minute drive along the shoreline. Tomorrow marks my one-year anniversary of living here. I love it.

Some people get groceries from a bait shop that sits on the dock. A sign outside it simply reads *Bait Shop*. I got nauseous the first time I stepped in to buy warm milk. They have a few expired convenience items for folks who don't want to drive to the grocery store. They keep all of it next to live fish bait. It's allegedly the best bait on the island. However, this organization method creates a vortex of smells that I believe must only be enticing to fish.

They have a white Domestic Shorthair cat named Arthur who struts around the shop like a prince. The store is connected to a bar. Both businesses are owned by an older couple, Ron and Julia, who work every day. Arthur passes between them freely, never going more than a few hours without finding a full plate of fresh saltwater salmon waiting for him on a shelf somewhere.

Leopold owns the hostel and rarely stays for longer than a brief chat. He pretends to be interested in our lives, and sometimes he does such a sweet job of it that I'm actually convinced he loves us. I don't hate it. It's better than having a rude boss. He drives us into town on Saturdays so we can buy whatever we want. We have a small garden next to our boat shed where we grow fruit, vegetables, and spices. The ocean provides fish. The grocery store is for luxuries. I spend most of my budget on beer.

My coworkers and I sleep in a shared room. I like working at night because I can sleep alone during the day. It's slow enough overnight that one person can manage it. I rarely see the others who work here. I start at 11 p.m. and work until around 7 a.m. It's easy. I clean until midnight, and then I watch movies. The Wi-Fi works faster at night. Tonight, though, I'll be taking Leo up on his suggestion to go hiking. I want to find the path he was talking about.

***

My shift began, and I heard a customer pull up in the gravel entryway.

A woman with two boys asleep in her arms was standing in the doorway. She said her name was Lana. They hitchhiked here after their vehicle stalled in town and had to be towed. The driver left before I could see their car. Despite living in this country her entire life, Lana hadn't planned for the last several kilometers to be pitch-black and lifeless. She thought they would have found an open hostel hours ago, and she fumed with exhaustion. She's lucky. The road following the coast is dangerous at night. It's skinny and without the safety of railings or lamps. You could fall into the ocean and nobody would notice.

I showed them to their room and then returned to the lobby, which also serves as a kitchen, dining room, main socializing area, and office. It connects the employee quarters to the open accommodation rooms that can host up to six guests per room. Lana and her children are in one of the private rooms that can only be accessed from outside the building. There are three private rooms. We have a couple family-sized suites available around the property, but she said they would be leaving early in the morning, and they only needed one bed for a few hours.

When I asked where she was headed, she said, "It's a little outing we go on every year."

That didn't make sense to me because her actions told an entirely different story, but I didn't press her.

"Let me know if you need help with transportation," I said.

"Thank you," she said, and she closed the door.

*****

Back in the kitchen, I popped open a beer as Leopold burst through the door.

"Finchy," he said.

"Yes," I replied, even though my name is Mitch.

"Do you know anything about diving?"

"I mean, I know what it is, but I've nev—"

"Have you ever dived?" he asked. His face smoldered with an urgency I had never seen.

"No," I said.

"We're diving to a sunken ship at the bottom of the fishing harbor to strip it. We're trying to get parts and fuel and whatever else. We need an extra hand. Are you busy?"

"We just got guests."

"Oh, we did?" His tone softened. "Great. Yes. That's great. Where are they? Are they hungry?"

"It's a woman and her two sons. They're good," I said, showing Leo the guest log. "They're in one of the private rooms."

"That's awesome. Yes. Great," he said, remembering that he owned a business. "And they're all happy with everything in there? Right? Those rooms are clean? It can be easy to forget about a room, and then it's like, oh man, it got so nasty in here."

"They're happy. Everything is good," I said.

"Great. So, do you want to stay here?"

"No. I want to go with you."

"Wonderful! Does your phone work out here?"

"No."

"Perfect. Leave your phone number and a note saying you'll be back in an hour. Then slam that beer and put on some rubber boots and warm clothing. I'll be in the truck."

I did what he said. I left a note for Lana and any future guests which read:

> Dear Lana and Any Future Guests,
>
> It's 23:00 right now. I'll be back in an hour. So, I'll be back around midnight. Sorry for the inconvenience, but the boss man needs my help. ☺
>
> Feel free to call me if you have questions, or you can watch a movie and have a beer while you wait for accommodation. Thank you for your patience. Sorry again!
>
> Love,
> Mitch

I debated on whether the "love" part was inappropriate. I decided it was funny and got in the back of Leopold's truck.

***

Leopold is originally from New Zealand, but he moved to Japan in the Nineties to be part of a government team tasked with diving to and extracting fuel from sunken military ships. He made a dazzling sum of money in a couple years and moved back to New Zealand to open a seaside hostel and continue his life on the ocean. He's single and has two kids that he never talks about, besides the one time he told us he has two kids and then abruptly changed the subject.

***

"Comfy back there, Finchy?" he yelled. I was jostling around on the truck bed as we rode down the single-lane cliffside road to the docks. His passenger seat was full of fishing gear. I felt like the fishing gear could have gone in the truck bed so I could sit in the passenger seat, but I didn't want to be difficult.

"Yes," I said.

"We'll be there in just a second, alright, mate?"

"No worries."

We had to maneuver around two trucks, a few minutes apart, puttering up the hill. There are little areas every fifty meters or so along these single-lane cliffside roads where a car can pull to the side and let a car coming from the opposite direction pass. There isn't usually anyone on the road this time of night. I began to worry about business picking up at the Fuel Diver, but Leopold didn't seem to mind.

"No rain tonight! Stars are gorgeous!" He poked his head out his window and looked up at the sky.

"Do you usually dive at night?" I asked.

"When I can," he said. "It makes the water feel like you're in space. Makes our lights look like the stars. Have you seen that little island in the middle of the harbor? You should kayak to the little island at night sometime. Beautiful kayak ride. It's not far from shore. You've seen that island out there, right? Have you been out there yet?"

I looked up as the sound of his voice faded away from my attention. The bouncing truck was making me nauseous, and I regurgitated foam from my recently chugged beer, but I swallowed it and turned my eyes to the maw of our universe. I soaked in wonder at its holy demonstration of size and power and sat in silent awe of the looming great beyond. Then Leo slammed on the brakes.

"Jesus! Get the hell off the road!"

A cow and her calf were in front of our truck. I lurched forward and vomited sand-colored beer foam on the truck's rear windshield as Leopold brought us to a skidding halt. I wiped it with my hand before he noticed. We were both quick to react in our separate moments of panic.

"Is that the cow you were talking about?" I asked.

Leo growled as he inched the truck forward. The cow and calf stood still. He gently nudged the cow with the tip of his bumper and stopped. The cow didn't move. Leo slammed his door as his boots hit the gravel.

"Go away!" He flicked at them with the back of his hands, now standing in front of the truck.

"Get out of here!" I screamed from the truck. Nothing worked. Leopold walked behind the cow, the scene bathed in headlights. He pushed on the cow's rear, and then everything changed.

The cow kicked Leopold in the chest, and his heart stopped.

He died.

It just happened.

Leopold released a pained gasp and then fell limply to the ground. The cow sauntered with her calf off the road and into the darkness. I jumped off the truck and ran to Leopold's side. I checked his pulse and tried to wake him up. I pushed on his chest and breathed in his mouth. I didn't know what I was doing. Leo was dead, and we were both very far from home.

I moved all the fishing gear onto the truck bed and pulled him up onto the passenger seat, which was much more difficult than I thought it was going to be, and I sat in the driver's seat. I had never driven a vehicle in New Zealand before. The interiors of New Zealand's cars are situated mirror opposite from what I'm used to in the United States. Somehow, I found it to be an easy adjustment when sitting next to a dead body. I didn't notice until later that it was my first time driving in this country. The stress of the situation took away as many fears as it created.

Once we reached the harbor, I parked in front of the only boat with flood lights pouring out of it. The name *Fuel Diver* was proudly displayed on its back.

Six guys were quietly walking around on deck and doing chores. They didn't look like sailors. They were all skinny, younger guys. I got out of the truck and realized they were boys, much younger than me, probably in early high school.

"Hey! Do you guys know Leopold?" I asked.

They all looked at me. One boy dropped an armful of knotted rope that clanged inside an aluminum bucket.

"That's his truck," said the boy closest to me. He was handling something behind the boat's wooden railing that left his hands engrossed in red mucus. Snotty fish blood. Chum.

"Yeah, he's in here," I said.

"Why isn't he coming out?" asked the boy with pink hands.

"He's… He died," I said.

Each of the six boys procured a handgun from somewhere on his person and aimed it at me.

"How did that happen?" asked the kid who dropped the rope. He was a big kid with a fragile, airy voice that I found very surprising. Perhaps more surprising than his firearm. A smile escaped my terror for a second before I regained my composure.

"He was bringing me down here to help you guys. I work at the Fuel Diver." I pointed at the boat's name as if they might not have known what I was talking about. "I've worked for Leopold for a year. A cow walked in front of his truck and—"

"God damnit," the boy said.

"That damn cow," said a kid with a much lower voice. I couldn't see which boy it came from. I could only see guns.

"Right. He got out to shoo it off the road and it kicked him in the chest. It stopped his heart. I tried to resuscitate him, but I couldn't."

"Drive him to the hospital," said the boy closest to me.

"I don't know where that is," I said, using the most disarming tone I could muster.

"There's only one road. Follow it," he said.

"What about you guys? Are you alright?" I asked.

They stared back at me. The dark circles of their six barrels calmly stood in my vision like scars on my eyes. Some looked more confident than others.

"He shouldn't have brought you. Take him to the hospital," said the boy with the soft, airy voice.

"If one of you knows how to get there, it would be a lot easier for you to take him. I need to go back to the hostel. I don't even know what's going to happen to it now that Leo—"

"Time is crucial," said the airy-voiced boy. "Don't worry about the hostel. You need to stay with Leo so you can tell people at the hospital what happened. Just follow the road signs."

They showed no sign of holstering their weapons.

"Okay," I said. I got back in the truck and drove past the long lines of dark, lifeless boats, like floating ghosts, away from Leopold's child navy and along the coast toward town. I rounded a corner, out of sight of the boys, and pulled over.

I switched off the headlights. In front of my car was a three-meter drop into considerably deep water. I stared at the moon's reflection over black ocean waves and contemplated my options. I could dump his body in the water and leave. Get off this island. I barely had enough money for a plane ticket, but I had enough. It'd take the rest of this tank of gas to get to the airport, but it could be done. I think if I explained to them that I was an American who wanted to go home, then everything should be okay. I'd be gone before the body was even found.

Also, those kids shouldn't have guns. Absolutely not. I went hunting when I was around their age, but nobody ever gave me and all my friends nine millimeters and left us alone on a boat. That's different. The truly illegal stuff Leopold was doing with those kids would overshadow anything I could do. It wouldn't look any more suspicious if I dumped his body in the ocean and got out of town. I wasn't doing anything wrong.

Leopold's body slumped forward in the passenger seat.

No. I needed to take him to the hospital, or at least into town, so I could report his body. He had taken me in when I needed a home, and I had to return the favor. By which I mean avoid dumping his body in the ocean or anywhere except in front of the hospital. That's the plan. I'd take him to the hospital. I started the car and turned on its headlights.

Then, quite suddenly, the vehicle was struck from the rear by an enormous something that sent us crashing nose first into the infinite darkness below.

II
ERIKA

I felt my stomach lurch forward as we struck the water. Instead of vomit, my mouth was filled with a cold rush of broken glass and salt water that enveloped my body. I felt my clothes and skin tear and entwine until I could no longer discern between them. My consciousness caught up with the events taking place around me, and I screamed hot bubbles. Blood filled my eyes. I untied my seat belt and swam in the opposite direction of the sinking truck. My nose was broken, I couldn't see, but I knew which way was up.

I reached the surface and cried for help in between gulps of seawater. I felt around, but my hands only served in the battle against drowning. There was nothing to grab except water. The crash had left me blind, and I had no idea which direction held my salvation. I swam and cried until I finally grasped a chain. Had I reached the small island in the middle of the harbor? The one Leo asked about? There's no way I swam that far. The horror of swimming among the orca and various predatory marine life of these open waters at night was a vision from which I was happy to be excluded.

Then, two hands grasped under my armpits and pulled me onto a dock.

"It's okay. I got you. Can you hear me?" a woman said.

I spat seawater on the ground.

"My name is Erika. What is your name?" she continued.

I burped and spat more water on her face. I know I did because she sputtered and spat it back onto my face immediately afterward.

"I can't see," I gagged.

"I'm going to help you inside. We're going into the bait shop, okay?"

"Okay."

She helped me up. I could tell by the feeling of her body against mine that she was roughly a foot shorter than me and very strong. We hobbled across a threshold into a much warmer and calmer atmosphere. I got lightheaded as the smell of fish bait filled my nose, easily piercing through the blood, but I had never been so happy to feel this familiar sensation. For the first time, my gag reflex was suppressed. She sat me down.

"I saw your car go in the water, and I called an ambulance," she said, "but they won't be here for another hour probably. I'd take you to town myself, but my car is junk. I'm handing you a towel."

She put a towel in my hand. I held it to my face. I felt the warmth of my blood stick and mold to the dry fabric, and then I felt pain for the first time since we hit the water. The surge of adrenaline was beginning to fade. I wish I hadn't become cognizant of it because then it ended, and the pain was loud.

"I'm going to die," I whispered.

"It'll be okay. You're okay. Was anyone else in the car?"

"Leopold, my boss, but he was already dead. He died earlier. Oh my god. I'm going to die."

"What? Leopold? From the Fuel Diver?" she said.

"Yeah, and something hit our truck. Did you see it?" A wave of agony wiped over my brain.

"I didn't see anything. Your truck just kind of fell off the side of the road into the water. It looked like you released the brake or something."

"I swear to god, something big hit us and pushed us off."

"I didn't see that. I just saw you park over there. That's why I was watching," she said. "I asked myself what you were doing, and then you plunged into the water. I thought you were trying to kill yourself. You work at the Fuel Diver?"

"Yeah." My hands felt wet from the now blood-drenched cloth.

"Poor Leopold. My parents loved him. They'll be so sad. You probably know my parents. They run this bait shop. I'm visiting them for the week."

"Is something going on? It seems like there are a lot of people in town," I said, switching the hand holding the cloth to my face.

"There's always some celebration thing going on. Island people, you know. We love to party." She laughed. "Do you like tea?"

She put a hot mug in my other hand.

"Uh, sure," I said before the heat radiating off it engulfed my fingers in an inferno. "Take this back, please. Oh my god, it's burning my hand."

She didn't respond. A vast silence filled the room. It felt like she was never there.

"Hello? It's burning. I'm going to drop it," I exclaimed.

The moment I dropped the mug, she caught it.

"Sorry about that. Had a mouthful of tea. Forgot you can't see," she said through a smile.

"It's okay. Jesus," I said, blowing on my hand. "How long ago did you call the ambulance?"

"We've got a while."

"Can you call the Fuel Diver and hand me the phone, please? They need to know what happened."

"What did happen to Leopold?" she asked.

"A cow kicked him."

"A cow kicked him?" she repeated, astounded.

"In his chest. His heart stopped."

"There aren't any farms for kilometers. That's wild."

"Well, there was a cow on the road. One he was familiar with, apparently, because he got all pissed off when he saw it. Like they knew each other. He got out of the car to yell at it, and the thing kicked him. I put him back in the car, and we were on our way to the hospital when we went off the road."

I didn't feel it was necessary to tell her about Leopold's child navy yet. I didn't know what to say about it. I had no idea what was going on. I didn't even know her.

"Why did you pull over?" she asked.

"I was freaking out. I needed a second. Then, I swear to god, something pushed us off," I said.

"I didn't see anything."

"Do I look like someone who would try to kill himself?" I asked, even though I knew the answer.

"No," she said, "but you were freaked out. You probably weren't thinking. It's okay. You think a cow shoved your car off the road?"

"No! I don't know what happened."

I heard her move to the other side of the room.

"Where are you going?" I asked.

"Sit tight."

Based on our position relative to the entrance we used, I estimated that we were probably in the back of the store, somewhere near the cheap cowboy hats and license plate keychains with names written on them.

"What's going on?" I asked.

"I'm still here," she said. It sounded like she was in the next room.

"I can't see. Tell me what is going on."

"Open your hands," she said. She was suddenly standing right next to me.

"Is it more of that hot tea?"

"It's our phone. My parents have an old rotary phone. Sorry. When you get out in rural areas, people don't have much. Cell phones don't work great out here. Some of these people charge ten bucks per minute to use their Wi-Fi. This area is living in the past. I'll dial the number for you. My parents have it written down over here. Ready?"

"Yes."

The phone chimed and clacked its way through a phone number. It reminded me of my grandmother's house. I grew up with my grandmother. It was another stark reminder of how far away from home I was in time and space at that moment.

Erika handed me the receiver.

"Hello?" a sleepy woman answered. It was my coworker, Hanna. Hanna works the morning shift. She's a short German woman with blonde hair that reaches down to her knees, and she's an incredible pianist. She had shown me her skills on the hostel's communal piano the first day she arrived, and I knew I could trust her.

"Hey, Hanna." I coughed. "What's up?"

"Nothing," she said.

We were quiet for a moment.

"What's up with you?" she asked.

"I'm not at the hostel right now," I said.

"Okay."

"So, I'm sorry I'm not there because I should be working right now."

"Are you alright?" she asked.

"I'm at the bait shop. Leo's truck went into the water," I said.

"Oh my god," she said.

"Yeah."

"What, uh... What can I do?" she asked, "Are you okay? Is Leo still with you?"

"Leopold died in the accident," I said.

"Holy shit."

"Yeah."

"Fuck."

"Yeah."

We sat in silence, a half-kilometer apart, brought together by sharing the knowledge of this horrific development and thinking about what we could possibly do next.

"I'll tell everyone," she said. "Should we come get you?"

I heard a crash in the bait shop. Then I heard a crash through the speaker beside my ear, and the phone went dead.

"Oh my god," said Erika. "I'm sorry."

"What happened?" My heart dropped into my legs.

"Hold on," she said.

"What are you doing?" I asked.

"I got some bandages and cleaning supplies. I knocked the phone line out when I dropped them. I'm sorry. I'm an idiot. Here, let's get you cleaned up."

She took the phone out of my hand and hung it up. Then she pulled the towel away from my face. She gently took the remaining glass shards out of my cheek skin. She introduced a chemical to my slitted flesh that hurt worse than the accident.

"My coworker said she can come get me," I gasped through the sting.

"That isn't necessary. The ambulance will be here soon."

"How soon?" I asked, trying to show her as much of my bloody face as possible.

"I don't know, but they'll have to go slow on these roads. They're coming here, though, so it doesn't make sense for you to go to the hostel and make them chase you."

She added more mysterious, painful chemicals to my face. The fire beneath my skin roared.

"Why are you visiting your parents?" I asked, wincing.

"Do I need to have a reason?" she laughed.

"Where do you normally live?"

"The U.S. I moved there for college. I'm a damn Yank like you."

She must have gathered where I'm from by my accent.

"That's a long trip to see your parents for a week," I said.

"It's my dad's birthday."

"Where is he?"

"He's asleep," she said, clearly annoyed by my questioning.

"Why are you awake?" I asked.

"Because I'm awake. Thank goodness I was, or else you'd be dead."

She added a new chemical to my face. This one hurt far more. A searing, otherworldly pain shook my whole being. It scratched its way beneath my tissue and began reorganizing my wound. The pain of growth roared in my eyes.

"What's going on this week? A party, you said?" I asked, breathing heavily.

"Yeah," she said.

"What kind of party?"

"A party, party." Her voice became flat. Her chemicals scorched.

"For what?" I asked.

"I don't know. Otherwise, I'd probably be partying with them," she said.

Then a different phone rang. One that was in another room.

"I'll get it," she said.

She picked up the phone, listened for a moment, and hung it up.

"Who was that?" I asked.

"Okay, what was your name again?" she said.

"Mitch."

"Look, Mitch, the ambulance isn't coming."

We were quiet for a moment.

"Why not?" I asked.

"You want to know why so many people are in town this weekend?" she asked.

"Yeah, that's what I've been asking you."

"There's a cave in the mountain behind your hostel. There's a little path that leads up to it. I'm sure you've seen it, or someone told you about it."

"Okay," I said cautiously.

"A long time ago, a small group of people made the cave into a big room. Like, hundreds of years ago. The purpose of the room is to protect a giant clock. This clock is, like, an engineering miracle. It's supposed to last on its own for thousands of years because it's built into the mountain somehow. The mountain protects it from the weather and stuff."

"Okay."

"I know it sounds stupid," she laughed, "but it's there. Most people in this area stay away from it, but it's just a clock. It has an internal clock so it can conserve energy by not having to display the time all the time. It displays the last time someone was there, and then, if you can even find it, you have to crank a wheel for it to show you the current time. It's always correct. It never loses time."

"Sounds like a cool clock," I said.

"The reason they made it was to keep track of a very specific recurring event."

"And what is that?" I asked.

Silence.

"Erika?"

"There are monsters," she said.

"Monsters," I repeated and laughed. "Huh?"

"They live just below the seafloor in the harbor."

"The clock keeps track of Godzilla?" I asked.

"They're kind of like Godzilla in that way, yeah," she said, taking what I had just said very seriously. "They don't look like Godzilla, of course, not nearly as big, but they kind of work the same way. They're like cicadas that are buried underground underwater. They don't look like cicadas, though. I don't know what they look like. The New Zealand government has spent heaps of money keeping them a secret from the rest of the world."

"What the fuck are you talking about?"

"They emerge from the depths of the harbor every seventy-five years to mate. Before that, they're just kind of growing down there. Feeding and growing. Once they mature, they come up to the surface to feed some more before mating. They can live off some sea life, but they move through food pretty quickly and start eating animals on land. They used to surface to feed all the time. Then, once their eggs are laid and everything, people on the island usually slaughter them for a variety of uses. There are some of the monsters from the last harvest in these chemicals I'm using on your wounds. They have miraculous capabilities," she said, dabbing the horrific liquid on my face. "So the group put together the plans for this clock that sounds off every seventy-five years to alert people that the monsters are coming to the surface."

"Are they dangerous? Why are you calling them monsters?" I asked.

"That would make sense. I mean, everyone around here calls them monsters," she said.

"What do they look like?"

"I don't know. That's the reason I came back. I want to see them. There are old photographs, but only certain government employees are allowed to see them. A lot of guys out here work for the government in some capacity, either researching or tending to those things. I've only ever been told about them."

"So, it's not actually your dad's birthday?"

"I mean, it is, but that's just a nice coincidence." Erika laughed. "Yeah, I mainly came back to see the monsters."

"Why would you come back for that?" I asked.

"My parents are like everyone else who's in town tonight. They want to see the monsters too. They aren't afraid. They're excited for them."

"Why isn't the ambulance coming?" I asked.

"Anyone who would be driving that ambulance is already out here, waiting. They're probably on that little island in the middle of the harbor."

I contemplated this information and remembered to breathe. I took my first breath since she began speaking and exhaled slowly.

"When are the 'monsters' supposed to come out?" I quoted with my hands.

Then, deep within the mountain, a loud, low bell shuddered the earth.

III
HOME

I grew up in Chicago, where I lived with my grandmother Elaine. My dad didn't want to be a dad, and my mom wasn't fit to be a mom, so I moved in with her when I was a few months old. My grandpa passed away before I was born. She and I were the only family either of us had left.

When I turned eighteen, and it was time for me to go to college, my grandmother got lonely. She started looking for love on dating websites. She got catfished, and over the next four years, she lost all her money by giving it to a man she had fallen in love with who didn't exist. She was never able to find the person responsible for tricking her into giving away her money, and she never got over the heartbreak and shame she felt for falling for it.

On the day I graduated college, my grandmother took her own life.

People close to her told me that she did it because she didn't want to make me feel responsible for taking care of her. She felt too old to go back to work. I know that we could have made it work, but she never told me the truth about how she felt during our phone calls. She wasn't thinking clearly. It crushed her.

I took what little money I had, and I moved to New Zealand. She had told me about traveling there when she was about my age. She said it was the happiest time of her life. After hearing her romantically reminisce about its natural beauty, I settled. I needed to get away from Chicago. I needed to figure out what I wanted out of life.

My degree in business administration felt as if it never happened. I couldn't squander everything my grandmother had given me. When I came across the Fuel Diver's information listed in a backpacker's guide my grandmother had given me, I never thought I would end up staying there for a year, or that it would need me to so terribly.

As I write this, looking back on what occurred, I am reminded of something that she would tell me when I got quietly upset around my birthday or any other day when a child normally spends time with their parents. She would say, "There's an entire world inside of you, and I can't wait to see it."

It would make me feel better, not only in those moments but throughout my life. I like being alone because, in my mind, I can't get bored. I no longer feel lonely, not in any destructive way at least. Every emotion I felt about my past is in the past. The only thing that matters is the future that I carve for myself by exploring the world within me. I'm grateful to my grandmother for taking care of me, and I wish she would have felt the way she made me feel.

***

Unfortunately, however, during my time working at the Fuel Diver, I found out who catfished Elaine, and I became consumed with taking back every stolen dollar.

IV
OBJECTS IN THE WATER

Erika pulled on my wrist to make me stand up. The walls of the bait shop shook as if an earthquake had begun, and the sickening echo of a low bell bellowed deep within the mountain where I left the Fuel Diver not one hour before.

"We need to go outside," she said, her voice shaking like the walls of her parents' shop that were now dropping snacks and dry bait on our heads.

"Is there an earthquake?" I asked stupidly.

"Kind of," she said.

When we crossed the doorway threshold out of the bait shop, I felt the cold air outside. It felt different. The air was wet, but it wasn't raining. There was a thick mist. It felt like the ocean was rising into the air.

I changed into one of the t-shirts for sale in the shop, and Erika gave me a pair of her dad's old board shorts. My free hand was covering my eyes with a towel. I was dry and relatively safe, but I felt exactly the way I felt when I was drowning in that truck.

"Where are we going?" I asked Erika.

She stopped walking. It felt like we were standing at the edge of the dock right outside the bait shop.

"Oh no," she said.

"What is it?" I asked, drained of patience.

"You should consider yourself lucky you aren't seeing this," she said.

The ground rumbled with another thunderous bell toll. A piece of the bait shop's roof fell and hit the dock behind us with a loud bang. I jumped. Erika didn't move.

"Tell me what it is," I said.

"Lower the towel and see for yourself," she said.

I lowered the towel. The cool breeze slapped against my hastily healing wounds and bounced off the heated blanket of moisture surrounding us. I strained my eyes to open them. The swelling had softened. The chemicals worked. The burning in my hand had dissipated as well. I grabbed my eyelids and pulled them open. Color and light faintly pushed through my eyelashes to reveal the vision in front of us.

Scattered over the surface of the ocean as far I could see were hundreds of similarly-shaped objects bobbing in and out of the water. They weren't living creatures. They were objects, slightly varying in size but all relatively the same shape. I looked to my right and saw the beach was covered in them.

I knelt down to get a better look over the side of the dock, blinking the remaining blurriness from my pupils, and I reached out to grab one of the objects. My eyes began to focus. As it touched my hand, I recognized its shape.

"They're feet," Erika said.

A severed, male, adult-sized foot was dripping thick crimson salt water out of my hand. I dropped it and gasped as it plopped back into the water. I looked out over an ocean of severed feet, all in varying phases of decay. A lot of them were still inside their shoes. The bell stopped tolling, and the ground stopped vibrating. Gusts of wind and the gentle thud of several hundred severed feet bumping against wood and rocks in the ocean below us filled the air. Erika grabbed my shoulders to keep me from falling into the water. I sat at the dock's edge.

"We don't have more dry clothes, so don't go in the water again," she said.

"Where did all these severed feet come from? What the hell is going on?" I was breathing heavily. My head was spinning. The sight of them, bobbing in and out of the water, resting on the beach, as if they were learning to swim, stomped on my soul.

"They don't like feet. It's weird," Erika said.

"Who doesn't?" I asked.

"The monsters."

I looked up at Erika, my eyes now able to keep themselves open through the sheer strength of my confused expression.

"Sea monsters cut off everyone's feet?" I spat in disbelief. "Did they kill everyone on the whole god damn island?"

"What do you think Leopold does for a living?" she asked me.

"He owns the Fuel Diver hostel," I said.

"Oh, come on, you know he doesn't care about that place," Erika snapped. "What do you think he actually does?"

"He dives to sunken ships and strips them of useful stuff?" I said, unsure of myself.

"He watches over them," she said, lowering her voice.

I stood up.

"Watches over what? What are they?" I yelled.

Erika walked inside the bait shop and closed the door behind her. I stood at the edge of the dock, afraid to look back at the water. I stared at the front door of the bait shop, pleading in my mind for her to come back. The door was the only place I could safely stare and not be met by pools of rotting severed feet. I heard splashing behind me. It differed from typical ocean noise. Something sounded like it was coming toward me.

I quickly walked to the bait shop's door without a glance behind me. I couldn't. I didn't want to know what I was hearing. I just wanted to be inside. The splashing got louder and turned into crashing waves. It was coming toward me. Faster and faster. The moment I put my hand on the doorknob, Erika opened it.

"Sorry, I wanted to grab my tea." Erika smiled, showing me her mug.

"Go inside!"

"Hey," she said, putting down her mug and grabbing my shoulders again. She looked deep into my eyes, and for the first time, I trusted her. "It's okay."

I looked behind me at the calm water. The only things I saw splashing around were severed feet, now a normal sight by which I was somehow relieved.

"I thought there was a monster swimming up behind me," I said.

"Dang, I wish I would have seen it if there was," she said, looking out at the water over my shoulder. "You're having a crazy night."

Erika laughed and reached just out of sight behind the door frame to reveal what I assumed was my teacup from earlier. I was seeing it for the first time, but it looked like how I remembered it feeling. She offered it to me.

"Thanks," I said.

"Of course." She smiled. "Want to drink inside together? I think the bell is done tolling. We just need to keep our eyes peeled now. That earthquake it caused was pretty annoying, huh?"

We went inside and sat on either side of the check-out counter next to the cash register. Erika brought a bag of wafer cookies out from behind the counter and opened them for us. We ate for a moment in silence and enjoyed the luxury of tea and cookies. The sound of soft chewing calmed me down.

Arthur was astonishingly napping on a shelf above our heads, oblivious to everything that had just happened. He purred happily, his full belly moving with his breath next to what once was a heaping plate of fresh, boneless fish. I watched him lick his lips, and then I turned to Erika.

"So Leopold feeds people to the monsters?" I asked her.

Erika stopped chewing. She looked at me and laughed, spitting wafer cookie bits on my bait shop t-shirt.

"I'm sorry," she said, wiping away the soggy crumbs. "It just sounds so stupid when you say it like that, but yeah, that's what he was doing."

The color left my face, and my heart raced. My head spun.

I fainted.

***

When I woke up, I was in a bed in one of the private rooms at the Fuel Diver. On the tails of a dream, I wanted to believe everything that just happened would be wiped clean from my consciousness. I wanted so badly to believe that Leopold was alive and that everything was normal. Of course, I knew it wasn't, because I was wearing the same clothes I put on in the shop, and my body ached. But I enjoyed what time I had to rest in that reality.

I looked out the window and up at the stars. I lay there, wondering about everything happening in the universe all at once, about my grandmother, about Leopold, and I thought about Erika until someone knocked on the door.

"Mitch?" Hanna said through the door. "I came to check on you. Are you awake?"

I stood up and opened the door.

"Hanna." I hugged her much tighter than it felt like she wanted to be hugged.

"Hey, Mitch," she said, laughing nervously. "You're feeling better?"

"I feel insane, to be honest," I said, releasing her, "but how's it going here? What's up? How long was I out? How did I get here?"

"I feel insane too, yeah," she said in her dry German accent, straightening her shirt. "It's going fine here. Well, not really. Leopold is dead, but you already know that. That bell went off, and it really shook this place, my god. Did you feel that?"

I looked over her shoulder to see the area surrounding the building was littered with fallen branches and debris.

"The building withstood the shaking for the most part," she continued. "Some stuff inside got messed up, but nothing big. You were passed out for maybe one-half hour to forty-five minutes. Erika brought you here in her car."

"She said her car didn't work," I whispered.

"Okay, well, she drove it here, so maybe it's working now," Hanna said. "She said that you passed out while you guys were talking."

Then I remembered.

"Where is Erika?" I asked.

"The dock, I think," Hanna said, looking over her shoulder. "She took all the other employees down to the water because they asked her for a ride. I've been alone with you since then. Someone needed to be here to watch you and the hostel."

"Thank you," I said.

"Yeah, no problem," she said.

"Do we still have guests?"

"I assume we do. I haven't, like, looked in their room or anything. I found your note, by the way. It was funny."

I walked past Hanna and made my way to Lana's room, just two doors away. I banged on the door three times, much harder than I intended.

"Mitch," Hanna said. "Chill."

Nobody answered.

"Lana!" I yelled, banging on the door three more times. I checked the doorknob, and it was unlocked. I opened it.

"Oh no. It smells so gross," Hanna said, covering her face with her shirt. The sweet stench of freshly rotting flesh poured out of Lana's room. I covered my face. My nose was still full of blood, but I could taste the smell.

I turned on the light and saw two bloody bundles, each wrapped in a bedsheet, sitting in the middle of the bed. My brain ruptured with fear, and my vision went wavy, causing the bundles to appear as though they were moving. I knew they weren't moving, but still, I was watching them move.

Hanna walked into the room behind me. She unwrapped one of the bundles.

"*Scheiße*," she said.

I unwrapped the second bundle. Inside was a pair of recently severed child's feet.

"Why the fuck did she have to do it here?" I yelled, tears streaming down my face. "Why couldn't you have cut your kids' feet off on the side of the road? People have to clean these rooms. What is the matter with these fucking people? What the fuck is even fucking going on?"

Hanna ran out of the room and threw up on the grass in front of the door.

"Why would she do this?" Hanna said through gobs of partially digested salmon. I followed her outside.

"I don't know. The monsters don't like feet or something. That's what Erika said. The beach is covered with them. Feet, I mean," I said.

"The...what?" she asked.

I told her all about the bell and the clock inside the mountain. She appeared to be more interested in the engineering accomplishment than the fact that it was one big alarm clock keeping track of an appalling deadline, which calmed me. To the best of my memory, I explained why people were in town and why the bell had gone off. She asked me what the monsters were, but I could not answer her. I could only show her what I had seen.

"Have you seen the water?" I asked.

"I've been here all night," she said. "I haven't seen the water since yesterday, if that's what you mean."

I grabbed Hanna's hand and guided her to a clearing next to the main building of the Fuel Diver. Typically, this vantage point provides a gorgeous view of the ocean that gets used in most of the ads for the business. At this moment, it was looking toward a horizon now filled with all those bobbing severed human feet, cleanly sliced at the ankles.

Hanna collapsed. She cried. She dry-heaved. She retched and puked up what little bile she had left in her gut and blew her nose on the grass. I crouched next to her and put my hand on her back. She looked up at me.

"What is going on?" she asked.

"I don't know," I said, "but I think we need to go down to the dock."

"I need to lie down," she said. Hanna lay down on the grass and gave her attention to the stars, and I lay down beside her. "Erika said the ambulance was coming here to get you, but I don't think it's coming."

"It's not coming," I said.

We watched the twinkling sky. Any lingering pain I had been feeling fell into the background of my consciousness. A shooting star flew by, trailing dust and sparkling carnage behind it, and Hanna sighed. We didn't speak for what felt like hours.

***

"Okay," she finally said, "I'm ready."

I sat up. The meditative state I was experiencing slid off my body and into the rich soil beneath me. I shook off the remnants of peace I was still feeling and got to my feet.

"I guess we'll have to walk down there," I said. The moment I finished speaking, Hanna grabbed my wrist.

"Stop talking," she whispered. She pointed ahead of us. Deep in the brush, near a path that led farther up the mountain, a person's face peered out at us from behind a tree. I couldn't tell if it was a man or a woman. I didn't care.

"Can we help you, motherfucker?" I snarled. After everything I had gone through this evening, I was not in the mood for a spooky face to be watching me from the woods. "Do you need a fucking bullet in your head? I can help you with that."

The face turned away from us and disappeared into the dark brush and up the mountain path.

"Was that Lana?" Hanna asked.

"I don't know who it was, but I'm not in the fucking mood," I said.

Hanna walked toward the area where the face had appeared, stopped, and looked at the ground. She picked something up, brushed it off, and walked back to me.

"Do you recognize this?" she asked, opening her hand to reveal a folded blue pocketknife. One that would have trouble amputating limbs.

"I bet that belongs to one of Leo's boys," I said.

"Like, his kids?" Hanna asked.

"Leo had this group of high school kids that was helping him on his dives. They all had guns when I met them, so I bet they all had pocketknives too."

"Wow." She laughed. "We'll hold onto it for him, then."

"Can I hold it?" I asked. Hanna handed me the knife.

I felt its weight in my hand. It was a great little knife. I flicked open the blade and waved it around. It felt like it was made for my hand. I closed it and flicked it open again.

"Bet you can't stick it in that tree from here," Hanna said, pointing to a tree on the side of the road about four meters away.

"Check this out," I said confidently, throwing the knife at the tree without looking.

"You missed," she laughed. We walked over to where it landed, and Hanna shined her keychain flashlight.

The knife was sticking straight up out of the ground. The blade's tip shallowly dug into the dirt. Cast in a mixture of shimmering moonlight and flashlight beam, I saw what was etched in small cursive letters on the blade.

My grandmother's name.

V
MONSTERS

Hanna and I crept down the narrow mountain road toward the dock. I did not mention that my grandmother's name was written on the blade. I didn't know what to say about it. It was possible that someone else had the name Elaine Donovan. Right?

In addition to feeling sick and tired, we remained quiet because there was no telling what horror would be waiting for us near the dock. The anticipation clamped around our ears and mouths. Whatever it was, we did not want it to notice us before we noticed it. We took our time inching side by side down the mountain for half a kilometer.

Once we got to the dock, where waves the colors of a bleak dawn lapped exposed ankle bones against its wooden pillars, I looked in the direction where I had met Leo's teenage diving assistants earlier that evening. The space where Leo's boat had once been docked was now empty. All the other boats swayed lifelessly in the breeze.

"Where is everyone?" Hanna said.

"Maybe they went into the bait shop," I said.

We looked in the direction of the bait shop and saw a dim, warm light coming through its green flannel window shades. We walked toward it, drawn to it. I don't remember making the conscious decision to do it. We were suddenly just standing outside its front door. Hanna knocked as loudly as I had knocked on Lana's door.

"Erika!"

No sound came from within the bait shop. No movement at all. Hanna knocked three more times, each with enough force to rock the whole building.

She stopped, but the world kept moving. The dock under our feet vibrated. A low rumble swayed the waves around us, disrupting their natural waltz on the water's surface. I got the same feeling I had when I thought a monster was behind me. I felt an ancient anxiety deep in my stomach. I closed my eyes. Paralyzed. I did not want to turn around.

"Oh my god." Hanna grabbed my shoulders and turned me around. I opened my eyes.

It's difficult to describe exactly what we saw, because neither of us saw exactly the same thing. The only thing we agreed on was that hovering inches above the surface of the water, one of the monsters was watching us.

To me, it appeared to be a ten-foot-tall jellyfish-looking abomination, glowing, tentacles hanging, somehow causing waves to be suspended in the air around it as it hovered slightly above the water. Its transparent and bulbous inkblot body undulated with the ocean as electricity coursed through it. I could see its organs dancing beneath its translucent skin. I saw a whole world appear through the liquid barrier. Its innards, dark masses floating in the bright pink ether like stars in the night sky. Like divers. They formed into images that fell apart and formed into new images. It glowed even brighter as a harsh rumble concussed its milky frame from within. Then I saw my grandmother's face reflect off the surface of it. My grandmother's face stared back at me out of the monster's body as I held my mouth open to scream.

***

When I later told Hanna what I saw, the expression left her face. She whispered to me, "That isn't what I saw," and softly asked to discuss something else.

***

The door to the bait shop swung open, and we were pulled inside. Erika sat next to the cash register, sipping a mug of tea big enough to require both hands. Two of the teenage boys I had met earlier let go after pulling us inside. They slammed and sealed the door shut behind us.

"Hey, guys. Want some tea?" Erika asked, smiling.

"One of those things is outside," I yelled. The energy in the room was at ease. I cautiously pulled the flannel shades open and peeked through the window of the bait shop, but I could no longer see the monster. A circle of disrupted water pulsated where the sea creature once hovered. I sat down across from Erika.

"What is that thing?" Hanna whispered, still watching the circle of upset water slowly smooth and conform back into its normal wave pattern.

"Didn't Mitch tell you about them? That was one of the monsters," Erika said. "They're beautiful, aren't they?"

"It's a big jellyfish," I said.

"Huh? You ever seen a jellyfish look like that?" Erika laughed. "Maybe they're distantly related to jellyfish, maybe, very distantly, but these guys have a little more 'umph' to them."

"Why are there feet all over the place?" Hanna asked after finally pulling herself away from the window and sitting next to me.

Erika took a sip of her tea. One of the teenage boys left the room and walked into the bar area. The other boy locked eyes with me.

"Thought Mitch would have told you about that too. They were given," Erika said. "Like I said, the chemicals coursing through these creatures have unique capabilities that are crucial to the way of life people enjoy around here. After they're fully grown and come to the surface to mate, they're harvested, but until then, they need to be fed."

"Human sacrifices?" I said. "What kind of stupid superstitious bullshit is that? Is this a cult?"

"They're not just sacrifices for the sake of being sacrifices. That would be stupid. That's a stupid word too. Sacrifices," Erika said, irritated. "They *need* to eat people. It's their diet. They'll eat people even if we don't provide bodies for them. Back in the day, they would come to the surface to feed as well. They killed thousands of people before fishermen almost made the creatures go extinct. That was until people realized their abilities. Now this harbor holds the last of their population. It's controlled. Leo and a few other people were tasked with keeping them contained under the surface by providing bodies for them until it's time for them to mate. They only use as many bodies as they need to. The government aims to protect the small population and continue harvesting them. Once they mate, we kill the adults and maintain the population. They usually just use people who are already dead."

Erika took another sip of her tea and placed the mug down on the table in front of her. Next to the mug was a small notebook that proudly displayed Leopold's name in gold lettering across its cover. She picked it up and threw it at me. It hit me in the chest and fell to the ground. I picked it up and opened it to the front page, which showed a crude sketch of something similar to an inkblot, drawn by Leopold's shaky hand. Underneath the drawing, Leopold had written:

"If they don't kill me, the next person I take down there will."

"Leo didn't realize how much killing would be involved in it, I guess. Again, they prefer to use people who are already dead, but if they can't, they would kill backpackers, travelers, people from other countries, whatever. Homeless people, if they can find them. Plenty of parents have given their children to make sure that the monsters grow. I mean, it's super fucked up," she laughed, "but it's important. Are you guys hungry? I'll get you some cookies or something."

Erika clapped her hands on her knees and stood up.

"Why are there so many feet?" Hanna said, unable to focus on anything else.

"Because they don't like feet," Erika shouted, finished with her questions. She walked out of the room and into the bar area. The teenage boy still in the room with us continued to stare at me. He was a big kid.

"I never made it to the hospital with Leo," I said to him.

"I know," he said. I recognized his voice as the one from earlier. The bulky kid with the soft, airy voice.

"I think the monster knocked our truck into the water," I said.

"No, it didn't. We did," he said.

"You did what?"

"Leo said you were supposed to be given to the monsters," he said. "That's the whole reason he brought you down there. But we didn't know what to do when Leo died. We honestly thought you should go to the hospital, but after you left, Erika said you were stopped next to the water and that we should knock you over the edge with her car."

"You tried to kill me?" I stood up and walked toward the boy.

"I mean, she said—"

Erika poked her head into the room and crunched a wafer cookie in her mouth.

"Everything okay in here?" she asked.

"You told them to drown me in Leo's truck earlier?" I asked.

"Oh," Erika said as she pulled her head back into the other room and disappeared again.

I grabbed the teenage boy sitting across from me. No adult wants to wrestle a teenager, but I knew he had a gun. I had to eliminate the closest threat to me. He reached for it, and without thinking, I pulled out the knife, flipped it open to see my grandmother's name, and stabbed it into the boy's temple until only the *"onovan"* part was showing.

Hanna's mouth hung open in disbelief as I removed the handgun from his waistband and let his body slump over in the chair. Goopy blood from his head dripped down the knife handle and splattered in blots on the bait shop floor. His eyes fluttered and twitched like hummingbirds trapped in a strobe light. I put my foot against his head and pulled the blade out of his skull.

"He tried to kill me, Hanna," I said, "and he would have killed you too."

The boy fell out of the chair and sprawled out on the ground following a tremendous thud.

"I'm keeping the gun," she said.

"What?" I said, turning around and looking at her with red freckles covering my face. I realized later that I must have been quite a sight.

"You are apparently comfortable killing people, teenagers, with a knife, and I don't want to do that," she said, her eyes now completely sober of emotion. "I would rather shoot people. You don't need to have two weapons, so give me the gun."

I gave her the gun.

We walked into the bar. I didn't notice him at first, but within a blink, Hanna raised her handgun and released two shots into the chest of the armed teenage boy standing in front of the exit to our left. He fell to the ground and amassed a pool of blood twice the size of his body, flooding through the artery Hanna had precisely targeted. There was an open bag of wafer cookies sitting on the counter. I ate a cookie. It was stale, but it was the best cookie I had ever eaten in my entire life. Hanna poured two beers from the tap and handed me one.

"*Prost*," she said.

"Cheers. *Prost*. Yes. Uhm. Salute," I said.

We clinked our glasses together and chugged our beers. Hanna finished before me and placed her glass on the table. Once I finished drinking, she held out her hand, and I gave her my glass. She cleaned them both and returned them to their spots on the shelf.

"Thank you," I said.

"There is no reason to be rude and leave dirty glasses," she said. "I'm sure we'll be using them again soon."

A loud noise cut through the walls of the building. At first, it sounded like it could have been one of those monsters. That deep, low cry. Then it sounded like the bell tolling from within that mountain. Then it was clear. A boat horn. I looked outside through the window and saw Leo's boat docked in front of the bait shop.

VI
LEAVING

The ship appeared empty at first. It quietly swayed in the water as if it had been docked for hours. Leo's entire life, untouched.

Erika sprinted out from behind the building. The sudden appearance of a woman running for her life startled me as she frantically made her way down the dock and jumped onto the boat. She vanished below its guard rail, and the vessel drifted back into open water. Hanna opened the front door.

"Hey!" she yelled. A single gunshot rang out as a bullet found its way into the *Bait Shop* sign next to Hanna's raised hand. I ducked beneath the window. She hurried back inside and closed the door.

"Shoot at them!" I yelled.

"I don't know what to shoot at! I don't know where that came from. I can't see anyone."

I peeked out the window.

The boat was far enough away from the dock to turn around. It began picking up speed toward deeper ocean. Fog slowly materialized over the water in a spectral ballet of water rising into the air. Within a few moments, the ship was lost in a cloud connecting the sea to the sky.

"Okay, well, cool," I said.

"Erika's car," Hanna said.

We exited the opposite side of the building and walked to Erika's car. It was damaged but drivable. Unfortunately, each of the tires had been slashed.

"She probably did this after she ran from us," I said.

"Do you think there are any spares?" she asked.

"There's got to be."

We looked all around the building. We looked in Erika's trunk and the utility closet. We searched up and down each dock. Nothing.

"Do you think we could just drive it like it is?" Hanna asked, gesturing toward the car's completely deflated tires.

"On rims, during a foggy night down a narrow coastal road with no guard rail? I don't know. We might be better off walking," I said. "Plus, Erika took the keys. I don't know how to hotwire a car. Do you?"

"I bet I could watch a video about it on my phone and figure it out," she said.

"Does this place have Wi-Fi?"

"I have a hotspot."

Hanna took a small device out of her pocket and turned it on.

"I always have this with me," she said. "It was free with my phone plan. It's great out here where people want to charge you like ten bucks to use their Wi-Fi."

"Can you contact the police?"

"I tried that a while ago, but they didn't answer. Like you said about the ambulance. They're probably already out here. I don't think anybody is going to help us."

Hanna quickly found a video online explaining how to hotwire this specific car model. She watched it while I continued looking for spare tires. Then, underneath a tarp next to a lawnmower, it appeared.

"I found one!" I pulled it out from under the tarp and rolled it over to Hanna.

"Nice, we just need three more," she said flatly, keeping her focus on her phone.

"Yeah, I guess, yeah, that's true," I said, now feeling as deflated as the tires on Erika's car. "We'll need to look up a video on how to change a tire too."

"I already know how to do that. I can do it."

"Cool. I'll just keep looking for tires."

Hanna put her phone in her pocket, got a tire jack out of the trunk of Erika's car, and started changing the front left tire. She finished a few minutes later and began hotwiring the car with her phone propped on the center console. I returned to confirm that I couldn't find any more tires.

"There aren't any more tires," I said. "There aren't even any cars around. There were a ton of people in town earlier tonight. Did they really all go to that little island? Where did they put their cars?"

I tried to peer through the fog toward the small island that normally sits directly in the middle of the fishing harbor, a little less than a kilometer offshore, but I could only see the stale haze of a wall of moisture and smoke.

"I think I've got this figur—" Hanna was cut off by the roar of Erika's engine.

"Hell yeah." I jumped in the passenger seat. "Let's go."

"We only have one good tire. It's going to be weird."

We fastened our seatbelts.

"Let's try it."

We began moving. The car felt off-balance in a wholly dangerous way. Every slight turn felt like we were sliding off a cliff. We had made the ride more reckless than it was without any good tires. Nevertheless, Hanna cautiously navigated us out of our little dirt parking spot by the bait shop and onto the road.

The car squealed, clunked, and slowly dragged its metal body down the narrow coastal road toward town. The damage from its earlier collision with Leo's truck only added more distressing nuance to the car's overwhelming steering issues.

"This bitch is veering toward the water," Hanna grunted while she pulled on the steering wheel. The car was very slowly veering toward the ocean side of the road.

"Stop," I said.

We continued moving.

"Stop."

"I can't," Hanna yelled. "I let go of the gas, but the brake is messed up. It's not doing anything."

We slowly coasted for a hundred meters, Hanna's knuckles clenching the steering wheel so hard they went from pink to white to dark red.

"We're going to go in the water," I said. "Let's get out of this car. This isn't worth it."

Hanna silently kept her eyes on the road.

"Turn the car off," I said.

"I don't know how," she said. "I didn't get that far in the video."

"Just undo whatever you did." I took my seatbelt off.

"Put your seatbelt back on," she said.

"I'm going to get ou—" The thump of our car coming to a sudden stop crunched our knees as I lurched forward and caught myself on the dashboard. Hanna had hit a tree.

"Sorry," she said.

"No worries," I laughed.

"We need more tires."

We got out of the car. Worry flooded through me, as deep and cold as the ocean that sat a few meters below our feet. I looked out at the black water in front of us; light from the moon and stars bounced like static electricity off its waves, and I happened to see the slightest glint of something beneath its surface. Fishing equipment.

"Leo's truck is right there," I said, pointing at the water. "That's where we got pushed in."

"Wow," she said. "Do you think we could get the tires off his truck?"

Chaos washed over me as I imagined reentering the hell where I left Leo earlier that night. Why did Erika rescue me? Why didn't she leave me to scream and wander until the monsters devoured me? Why was I alive? Why was Leo dead?

"Yeah," I said. "I'll get them."

VII
THE DIVE

The bait shop had a few spare oxygen tanks lying around. Diving excursions happened so frequently that it was not uncommon to trip over oxygen tanks when doing yard work or whatever else. Luckily, Erika had one stowed in her trunk, and Hanna brought the proper tools to change a tire.

"I'll shine a light down there so you can see," Hanna said, holding up a flashlight. "Obviously, I'll keep the car headlights on. There's a little light attached to the strap on your oxygen tank too. If anything weird happens, surface immediately, and I'll help you out of the water."

"Oh, I definitely will," I said, gazing into the devastating abyss below us. "Luckily, it's not as deep as I thought. I can still see Leo's bumper."

Leo's truck was a few meters beneath the surface of the water. Scattered traces of light from Hanna's flashlight gleamed off the chrome finish around its license plate. I pulled the oxygen tank out of Erika's trunk and slung it on my back.

"Your levels look good," Hanna said, checking the tank gauges. "Feel good?"

"Yeah," I said.

"Have you ever dived before?"

"No."

Hanna switched on the small light attached to my shoulder strap and patted me twice on the shoulder.

"You got this," she said as she handed me the tire iron. "It'll be over so quickly. I'll be watching the whole time. All you have to do is breathe."

"Thanks." I smiled.

I looked out at the horizon. The line between the ocean and the night sky blurred and made one long stretch of lonely darkness leading all the way up. I put the breathing apparatus in my mouth and inhaled deeply. My heart was racing, but my mind was calm. I sat in sweat until the vibrations of my heart and mind compromised and matched each other. I put on a pair of cheap goggles I found hanging from Erika's rearview mirror and plunged into the water.

Swimming with an oxygen tank on my back was surprisingly difficult at first. Everyone I'd seen do it made it look so effortless. As I moved in suspended animation, my consciousness returned to the objective at hand. I looked up to the surface and saw the headlight beams cast over the water's surface. Hanna's searchlight pierced through the dreamy galaxy around me and stopped on Leo's truck. The vehicle was positioned vertically with its nose stuck in the sand and tail end sticking up toward the surface, stabilized by a few surrounding rocks. Hanna aimed her light at the back left tire.

I swam to it and started working on loosening the tire. I got halfway through, desperately trying to replicate what Hanna had done earlier from memory, when I noticed something strange. I looked in the cab, expecting to see Leo's body still trapped, but it was empty. He must have floated out after I escaped. Maybe one of those monsters already came by and dismembered him. This thought did not put me at ease as I removed the final lug nut holding the tire in place. My left hand began to shake, reminding me of Leo's "ghost hand" story. I became distracted, my grip slipped, and I dropped the tire iron.

Releasing a storm cloud of air bubbles in terror thick as a school of fish as it fell to the ocean floor, next to the nose of the truck, I looked up at the shattered windshield. I swam to the surface and took the breather out of my mouth.

"I dropped the tire iron," I yelled at Hanna between gulps of water.

"God damnit," she said.

"I'm going to get it. It's okay," I said. "I just wanted to let you know. Can you shine the light here?" I pointed to the general area where the tire iron fell. She moved her light. It wasn't illuminating much, but I managed to notice a faint flicker shooting out of the depths.

"Good?" she asked.

"Perfect. Be right back." I popped the breather in my mouth, sank out of sight and down to the bottom.

Shining my light around to find the tire iron and get a larger sense of my surroundings, I finally reached the bottom and found it. I gripped it in my hand and looked up at Leo's truck in front of me.

Two bodies were now sitting in the cab. Their hair floated in a shocked expression. They were dark blobs, inkblots, moving with the water inside the warmth of a familiar structure. I swam closer to the driver's side door and kept my light shining on the window. The light reflected at me, and I was unable to see inside. I opened the door.

The cab was empty.

Leo's body must have been taken by one of those things by now. My mind had been playing tricks. Swallowed in the belly of the beast, I was fed visions of terrors that lurked deep within me. I returned to the tire, finished my work, and brought it to the surface.

"Nice," Hanna shouted. "I was starting to worry."

Hanna pulled the tire up onto the road next to her using a metal bar from a discarded road sign that was at one point used to warn motorists of the dangerous driving conditions.

"I'll start on the next one," I said.

I dove down and extracted the second rear tire in remarkably less time than the first. I brought it to the surface, and Hanna dragged it onto land. We only needed one more, and it would need to come from the front of Leo's truck.

After landing on the ocean floor, I kicked a cloud of dust into the air. My vision was obscured by the floating sediment, but I knew I was about a meter from the driver's side front tire. I moved toward the vehicle, my free hand feeling around in the cloud of wet dust, and soon found a door handle.

I grabbed the latch and used it to pull myself down toward the wheel. As I swept by the cab, I didn't attempt to look inside. My only concern was retrieving the fourth replacement.

The closer I got to releasing the tire, the more my body shook with anticipation. It felt like the closer I got to completing my task, the more likely it became that I would be murdered by one of those monsters, or encounter a ghost that would bury me in this shallow grave.

I released the final lug nut after an eternity wrapped in seconds, and I turned to swim toward the surface. The door opened hard, hitting me in the face, knocking off my goggles and stopping my ascent. I screamed. Hot bubbles.

The breather fell out of my mouth as escaping oxygen rushed by my cheeks, both from the breather and my muffled cries. I couldn't see, but I still had the tire, and I knew which way was up. I kicked my legs and raced toward the surface.

"I need to get out!" I yelled. Hanna was already lifting the tire out of the water.

"What's going on?" she asked.

"Something kicked the truck door open! Get me out of here!" I frantically swam toward the short cliff wall and began pulling myself out of the water. However, my oxygen tank wouldn't leave the water, as if it was bound to the sea.

I took the straps off and let go of the tank. It immediately left my side and disappeared. I looked up at Hanna to see her face turn white. The water beneath me began to glow, brighter and brighter, and a loud hiss like a boiling teapot filled the air around us.

I pulled myself up on the cliffside and scurried up onto the road. Hanna stood beside the tires, soaked in awe of the spectacle behind me. I ran to one of the flat tires and began changing it. Under the stress of the situation, the puzzle of replacing a tire became clear. The light grew so bright around us that I could no longer see the job in front of me. Then, the light vanished, and the world became darker than it had ever been.

My eyes took a moment to adjust to the sudden dramatic change, and I was finally able to make out the faint outline of Hanna standing on the cliff's edge. She was looking down at the spot in the water where I had appeared.

"Mitch," she said.

I dropped the tire iron and walked over to Hanna. I looked down at the water. About fifty feet in diameter, an enormous white circle of rushing water was pulsing and bubbling below us. It looked as though something massive had recently submerged. Leo's truck was gone.

"This isn't like the other monster," she said.

"Was it even a monster?" I asked. Hanna stared at the water.

"Let's go," she said.

We started the car, and again, my left hand began to shake.

VIII
ON THE ROAD

Hanna drove and I gazed out the window as the lucid nightmare we had just endured dissolved behind us. Neither of us noticed the divergence in the road, and suddenly we were no longer on the two-lane street toward town. People say there's only one road, but we must have veered off it somehow because we soon found ourselves on yet another single-lane road moving into deeper and darker woods. We were lost.

"Where are we?" Hanna said. I snapped out of my waking dream.

"I don't know," I said. "I don't think I've been out here before."

"Let's turn around," Hanna said. The road had become so skinny that turning around felt impossible. Hanna stopped the car and weighed our options. She threw the car into reverse and started slowly backing out. I rolled my window down and stuck my head out to hopefully help guide the car.

"You're good," I said four or five times before considering the fact that Hanna probably had it under control without my help. Still, I needed to occupy my brain with a task. I was scared. I think Hanna appreciated it, not because I was keeping us on the road, but because I was assuring her that she was safe and that whatever had been in the water a moment ago was not in the woods with us now.

We backed up to a dead end.

There was no way we could have backed up to a dead end. It felt unreal. At some point, we must have gotten on this road from the main road. The transition was so seamless that neither Hanna nor I noticed. It didn't make sense. She stopped the car.

"Okay," she exhaled, throwing the car into drive, and blasting gravel behind us. Hanna didn't seem interested in thinking about it. She just wanted to keep moving.

The road started moving upward and gently curved. It stretched on for kilometers with nothing to see but a fence of dark woods on either side. The forest was thick, and we could no longer hear the ocean. Overhead, canopies blocked the stars. The farther we drove, the more the light dimmed.

Then everything opened up.

The left shoulder of the road quickly dropped away, and we realized we were driving along a cliff edge, up a modestly sized mountainside. The mountain behind our hostel. The view to our left was a flat rock wall, and our right side looked out over a lush forest, about twenty meters below the cliff's edge.

I looked up to see how tall the mountain actually was, but from my viewpoint, I couldn't get a good estimation. The wall jetted upward at an angle that made it difficult to see more than a couple meters above us. The car stopped.

"Okay," Hanna said again. Her tone told me that she was overwhelmed and exhausted by trying to make sense of everything around us. I looked forward and saw, just a few meters away, a cow and her calf were standing in the middle of the road.

I couldn't be totally sure if it was the same cow from earlier that night, but it had to be. My heart told me it had to be. It felt like they were waiting for us. Like the mother was guarding something other than her calf. Like they weren't even really cows. It felt as though they were only visions, a mirage appearing to stand in our way. I told myself it had to be true because one of them had kicked Leo and killed him. That moment was real.

My left hand was shaking out of control at this point, but Hanna had gone perfectly still. She rolled down the window and slowly leaned her head out.

"Move," she shouted while she pressed on the horn for a few seconds. The cows stood unmoving and stared at us with our headlights reflecting off their eyes. Hanna honked again. Nothing. She moved her hand to open the door, and I extended my shaking hand to stop her. I pulled it away, scared.

"Don't get out of the car," I hissed. "The big cow killed Leo."

Hanna relaxed in her chair and left the door closed. The calf yawned and sneezed. It was cute, despite the situation, and both Hanna and I acknowledged it.

"That was cute," Hanna said. "I don't feel comfortable reversing down this narrow mountainside road, but now I don't want to get out of the car."

"We could try nudging them with the car," I said, even though that plan hadn't worked last time.

"I don't want to hurt it. Plus, if I hit them, they'll mess up this car."

"You don't have to hit them. Just nudge them. Scare them off the road."

"Okay."

Hanna took the car out of park and gently pressed on the gas. We slowly crept toward the cow and her calf. The calf second-guessed its footing for a moment before quickly recovering and standing straight up like it was summoning bravery for its mother. The mother did not stagger. Hanna stopped about one meter from the calf.

"I don't want to hit them," she said.

"I know," I said.

The cows' eyes appeared strangely wise. I felt like whatever the reason was for their presence here, right now, I supported them. Soon, I felt like we were intruders in someone else's home. It felt like we should leave. Hanna pressed on the gas a little more and stopped a few inches away from them.

"They aren't going to move," she said.

"I know."

We sat staring at each other for a moment. Then, slowly, the two cows turned around and started walking up the road. They got a few meters from the car, stopped, and looked back at us, gesturing with their noses for us to follow them. Then they continued walking.

"Thank god," Hanna said.

She was relieved that they had moved without having to resort to any kind of violence, but I had become more nervous than ever. The cows were waiting for us to follow them. At that moment, I realized that killing Leo had not been a mistake. It sounds insane, but I think they were waiting for Leo. They were waiting for us. Now, they were taking Hanna and me somewhere, like we were animals to slaughter, and the amount of control they had over the situation made my instinct to flee swell.

"They're trying to take us somewhere," I said.

"I mean, maybe," she said. "There isn't really anywhere else to go. We're in their way just as much as they're in ours. Someone needs to backtrack."

"I don't think we should follow them," I said.

"There's nowhere else to go, Mitch."

The cows walked a little farther and then stopped and looked back at us. They waited.

"They're waiting for us."

"They're cows," she said. Hanna lightly pressed on the gas as the cows turned around and started walking again. They led us for about a quarter-kilometer around the mountainside. I had assumed I would be able to see the ocean once the trail curved around to the other side of the mountain, but we continued to be surrounded by lush, dark forest. Then, once we had nearly reached the top, we could make out sea waves far over the canopies. We were further off course than I had imagined, but as long as I could see the water, I knew we could get back to the Fuel Diver.

The car stopped again, and Hanna took my gaze from the ocean and focused it on the door ahead of us. The road ended in a small oval area big enough to turn the car around. It was a small parking lot, similar to the one at the Fuel Diver, roughly big enough to fit four or five cars. There was a cave entrance that appeared to be manmade. We drove into the oval area and stopped in front of it. The cows sauntered around us, down the road again, back toward the bottom, tails swishing.

"We can turn around now, and I think we should," I said. "I can see the ocean. If we hit a dead end, we can just get out and walk. It doesn't look that far."

"Don't you know where we are?" she said. Her face was bright with excitement.

"A parking lot?"

"Mitch." She laughed before putting the car in park, taking off her seatbelt and opening her door. "It's the clock."

IX
THE CLOCK

I stayed in the car. I had no intention of going into that cave. I had heard the clock's bell and understood its significance. That was enough for me. I didn't need to know what it looked, smelled, felt, or tasted like. Hanna, however, needed more.

"I'm going to get up in this thing," she yelled from the edge of the doorway. "You can stay here if you want. I'll be back."

Hanna disappeared beyond the door, and I was left in aching silence. The only other sound I heard beyond my breathing was the gentle hum of the car engine. Hanna didn't want to turn off the car in case we were unable to turn it back on, so it provided the soundtrack to my panic. I sank into the echoes of my anxiety until they became unbearable.

"Hey, I'm coming with you." I got out of the car and jogged toward the doorway.

It opened to a vast, tall room, roughly thirty meters in diameter. The ceiling reached higher than I could see. It was very dimly lit. In front of me, a few meters off the ground, was an enormous clock displaying a time that felt too early. It wasn't the current time, but it was from earlier that evening. It had to have been the moment when the bell tolled.

Darkness suspended softly above our heads. The cave walls were red with dust and laughing with shadows. In what I can only describe as the corner of a circular room, Hanna experimented with a relatively well-maintained, polished hand crank.

"I think I'm pushing it the right way," Hanna said as she fell forward. The crank had given way to her pursuit, and the massive numbers in front of me shifted to what I assumed was the current time.

03:42

I ran over and helped Hanna to her feet. The clock showed a host of other information. Date, temperature, atmospheric readings, time in other cities, but they all faded away eventually, leaving only a receipt of the last time the hand crank was used. It appeared the main reason for the clock's existence was not necessarily to be a clock, but a demonstration to prove that someone could build a clock that could last thousands of years.

"Cool clock," I said.

Hanna walked around with a hand pressed against her chin in wonder. She felt around underneath the clock with her other hand and eventually felt her way a few meters to the right of it. She was touching the wall as if a specific sensation was guiding her hand. I couldn't see it, whatever it was. She stopped.

"Here's something," she said.

Hanna flipped a switch on the wall that I had not seen and could not see even after she pointed it out. I heard a depressed click within the mountain. The clock suddenly jumped the amount of time that had passed since Hanna used the hand crank and started counting down.

03:02

03:01

03:00

We had three minutes to figure out what was about to happen.

"What did you do?"

"I bet it will just ring again or something," she said, looking closely at the clock.

"Do you think being inside this cave is really the best idea if it goes off again?" I asked.

Hanna looked at me with a smile. She looked back at the clock.

"Why did you come here?" she asked.

"You drove me here."

"No, I mean, why did you come here, to this country, from the U.S.?"

"I wanted a vacation," I said, annoyed by the question. "Why did you come here?"

"Because I shot my mom and killed her," she said.

I stood still, unsure if she was joking, and concluded that it would be safer to assume she was serious. I stood quietly and waited for her to continue.

"She tried to kill me," she said. "I came over one day, and she just picked up a knife and tried to kill me. We were sitting in the kitchen. I was eating mac and cheese, and the next thing I knew, she was holding it and stabbing it into my stomach. It was a short knife, kind of like that pocketknife."

Hanna raised her shirt and showed me the scar on her stomach.

"Oh my god," I said. "That's horrible. I'm sorry."

"It hurt so bad," she said. "I had gotten my license to carry a handgun not too long before that. People in Germany don't really like guns the same way Americans do, but I had a few too many run-ins that scared me, so I took shooting lessons and started carrying a gun in my purse. Didn't think the first person I would use it on would be my mom."

She put her shirt back down and looked at the clock again.

"Do you know why?" I asked, trailing off at the end, unsure of myself. She shook her head.

"No, but when I saw what Lana did, I felt it. I could feel it again."

"I was raised by my grandma, but she killed herself because she got catfished and gave all her money away," I said. "That's why I came here."

Hanna looked back at me.

"Family," she smiled. She walked away from the clock.

2:01

2:00

1:59

It ticked away.

"Can you make that countdown stop?"

Hanna flipped the switch back and forth, but nothing happened. The numbers kept moving. Slowly creeping forward.

"Use the hand crank again," I said.

Hanna walked over to the hand crank and touched it. It spun without any resistance. It ran its useless circle while we watched, powerless. Nothing happened. The countdown persisted.

"Let's leave," Hanna said.

"Yeah," I agreed.

1:00

0:59

0:58

We walked to the door where we had entered, but we could not push our way through. It was stuck. Hanna kicked the door. I ran at the door and hit it with my shoulder. We could see our car through the cracks. I reached my fingers through the gaps and tried to pull it toward us, but it would not budge.

Then I saw a pair of eyes in what I can only describe as the opposite corner of this circular room. They were the same pair of eyes from the woods earlier. I knew they were. They were crouched in the shadows beyond our field of vision, dead and cold, but they were reflecting the little light in the room back at me. They had been watching us. I touched Hanna's shoulder. She drew her weapon.

"Hey," she shouted. "Who are you?"

The figure slowly stepped out of the shadows. I pulled out the knife.

0:04

0:03

0:02

X

LANA

Lana's face emerged from the darkness just before the clock struck zero. She hit a switch along the wall, and it stopped. The room stood still.

"It's just a timer," Lana said. "Don't worry about it."

She limped over to the clock and readjusted it to show the current time. There was blood on her pants and a makeshift bandage wrapped around her thigh.

02:46

"A timer for what?" Hanna asked.

"For the monsters," Lana said.

"We heard the bell toll earlier. The timer already went off," I said.

"That was for the first wave. This one is for the second wave. I didn't want it to be super loud again, so I stopped it before it went off. Like a microwave, you know, before it dings. I hate when microwaves ding. The next group will rise whether that awful sound happens or not. Everybody already knows about it."

Lana limped over to the door and hit a specific part on the corner of it to make it pop open. I lowered my weapon.

"This stuff is so old," Lana laughed. "You've got to hit everything just right. I don't think they did as good of a job on this place as they thought they did."

"Did you kill your kids?" I blurted out.

Lana stopped and looked at me very seriously.

"We found them…in your room," Hanna said.

"They were taken from me."

Lana walked outside and stood next to the car. We followed her out.

"By whom?" Hanna asked.

"I heard you two talking about why you came here," Lana said. "I came here because I thought the medicinal properties of the monsters could help me. I'm sick. I brought my kids with me because I couldn't leave them alone or with anyone else. A bunch of young guys, teenage boys, children with guns came into our room in the middle of the night and took them."

Lana began crying. Hanna hugged her.

"I'm so sorry," Hanna said.

"They held me down, shot me in the leg, and cut their feet off in front of me. They killed my babies in front of me."

"Who did?" I asked.

"A group of boys. I couldn't see their faces."

Leo's boys.

"Motherfuckers," I said.

"I got loose and ran into the woods. They left. I wrapped the wound with my clothes. When you saw me, I wasn't sure if you were one of them or not. That's why I ran away. I stumbled upon this place and took shelter. I knew nobody would be here. They're having their celebration out on the water."

"We have to take you to the hospital," Hanna said.

"I think you and I both know the hospital is nearly impossible to get to right now," Lana said. "This area is different now. The bell has tolled."

"Yeah, we noticed that," Hanna replied. "We were trying to drive into town, but the road led us here."

"Even the roads changed?" Lana wondered.

"I'm sorry. This is horrible," I said. "I have to ask, though: Why did you have this knife? It has my grandmother's name on it."

Lana opened the rear passenger side door of our car and sat in the back seat with her legs sticking out. It did seem like standing up caused her a great deal of pain, although it confused me that Leo's boys would want to kill her children in front of her. Why wouldn't they have killed her too?

What's the point of shooting her in the leg and making her watch? Did the monsters particularly like children? Did they not like Lana for some reason? They were killers, but were they sadistic maniacs? It was an impossible story to challenge but an even tougher one to believe.

"I didn't see a name on it, but that knife you're holding does look like the one I dropped in the woods," she said.

"How did you get it?" I asked again.

"I found it in the Fuel Diver. I took it in case I needed to defend myself."

"Where in the Fuel Diver?"

"The common room area where the kitchen is. I found it in the kitchen."

I gazed deeply into her still eyes. Finally, she looked from my face to the sky.

"How could a knife with your grandma's name on it, that you've never seen before, be in the kitchen?" Hanna asked.

The engraving on the blade comforted my fingertips as I rubbed it. I took turns rubbing it between my thumb and each of the fingers on my hand. I felt its weight perfectly combine with my own and considered what I had learned. The knife flicked shut, and I put it in my pocket.

"Welp, no use sitting here," I said. "Let's see if we can drive back now and find that hospital."

"We can try," Lana whispered.

"Let's hurry before this tank burns. We should try to find more gas too," Hanna said.

Hanna resumed her position in the driver's seat, and I sat in the passenger seat. Lana lay down in the back. We began driving slowly down the trail, away from the clock.

"Did you see those cows on your way up here?" I asked. Lana sat up.

"What cows?"

"The big cows that were up here. On the trail. You must have seen them."

"I didn't see any cows."

"It must have been such a terrible walk to get up here with a bullet wound in your leg," Hanna said sympathetically.

"It was awful, but adrenaline can get you through a lot."

"Know the feeling," I said.

Before I finished speaking, I grabbed Lana by her hair, pulled her head up to the front of the car between Hanna and me, slammed her face nose-first against the center console, then took the knife back out of my pocket, flicked it open, and held the blade to her throat.

"Oh my god," Hanna yelled. "What are you doing, Mitch?"

"Keep driving," I said. "I don't want her to get out before she answers some questions."

XI
THE DESCENT

Hanna stopped the car.

"Hey," she said, "I'm not going to keep driving if you're thrashing around with a knife. Do whatever you have to do, but I don't want to go off the side of the road."

The parking brake pulled, Hanna sat back and observed the scene now filling the car. She grabbed Lana's hands to keep them from resisting, trusting my instincts. Lana growled and squirmed, but we had her. I had her. Lana's injured leg lay across the length of the backseat while she bent sideways, and I connected her left ear to the center console. The dash light turned on, and its reflection shot from the knife through the windshield and into the nightly heavens.

"I know you killed those kids. I checked you in. I need you to admit that first."

"I didn't."

"I'm not stupid," I said, and pushed the knife against her throat with enough depth to feel the excited rush of her blood. A small amount of friction, just enough to slit the skin only a little, enough to hurt, but not enough to do any real damage. The right amount for blood. "So just admit it, and we can move on."

"They weren't my kids. And they were already dead."

"Whose kids are they?" Hanna asked, astonished.

"I don't know. Look, I work in a morgue on the southern island. I'm like, really, really southern. Way south. Almost nobody knows anything about any of this where I'm from. I heard about it from one of my coworkers when I got sick. They said the things were coming out of the water, and there was a local festival or whatever, and they could help me. So, I drove, drove, mind you, all the way here. Getting here from the south is tough. I had to take ferries and everything, but I couldn't fly with a couple dead bodies, you know. I had to do it. I had to drive. No choice. It was awful, but they're preserved. It's not like they're getting overly gross or anything. They were obviously decomposing, though. I was surprised you didn't notice. One of the most surprising moments I've ever had in my life was me standing in the front door of that hostel with these two dead kids in my arms, and you just took me to my room like we were all good. I started laughing when you closed the door.

"I wasn't sure if you were part of it, but it felt like you weren't. Then I was sure you weren't when I heard you enter my room. I wanted to offer the bodies as a gift to whoever was doing the thing or getting the fish out or whatever. I heard that's what I should do. Offer a sacrifice. Or, at least, it would help me get preferential treatment. I don't know. My coworker made it seem like it would sweeten the deal. He said it would save me from being used as food myself. I'm pissed because I had to hide them in the woods when I ran from you. Who knows if they're still there. But anyway, yeah, I just took the kids from the morgue. They were already dead."

Hanna was lost watching Lana's eyes widen like a fish about to be struck by a rock and gutted.

"Nobody at…the morgue? You said you work at a morgue?" I began.

"Yeah."

"Nobody there said anything to you about taking two bodies? Don't they check that? How do you not know whose kids they are?"

"Everybody does it. I mean, my coworkers, like, they don't care. Not everybody, but if you need a body for some reason, and one is being cremated, then it's fine. The kids were supposed to be cremated, so I just cremated some stuff that looked like a person, like enough for a kid's body. It's easier with kids because they're smaller, even though, mind you, I took two kids. I was greedy, but we didn't have a ton of choices. Like, we aren't flooded with dead bodies that need to be cremated all the time. We had two kids, and I was excited to bring them. What a haul. I thought two would be better because showing up with only one kid would look like I did the least amount of work possible. Then, I just set the other ashes aside to be given to the family. I don't deal with any of that stuff, so I don't know if they noticed or whatever, but I'm sure they didn't. It's really convincing stuff."

"The dead kid-looking stuff you burn instead?" I said.

"Yeah."

"Is it just other animals?" Hanna asked.

"Yeah, it's just, yeah, it's pigs and cow parts and stuff. Yeah," Lana said. "Pretty easy."

"I'm sure it's easy," I said, chilled by the comfort with which she recounted her tale, "but you can't do that. That's insane. You dismembered somebody's children."

"That's pretty much my job anyway. So I don't see why it's suddenly a big deal when I'm not at work. They're dead. I'm alive. Why can't I use their bodies to help me?"

Lana struggled with her hands and nearly broke free by taking advantage of Hanna's brief daze. The clinical nature of Lana's description sickened Hanna to her core. Her unabashed callousness toward the deaths of these children. Hanna couldn't help but return to looking out the window for a moment to let her soul recover. She desperately wanted to be among the nature below them and rid of it all. She wanted to go over the cliff, but she returned to the situation at hand and tightened her grip.

I wasn't sure what to believe. Could I believe this story? Lana told it with such ease and detail that to call her on it somehow felt even more difficult than her previous cover. Although, of course, if one were to murder children, their story would need to be good. I kept the knife to her throat.

"What are you sick with?"

"It's a kidney thing."

"What kind of kidney thing?"

"What are you, a doctor? You won't know, and I don't need to explain it to you."

"Where did you get a knife with my grandma's name on it?"

"I told you, I found it on the floor."

"Don't lie."

I cut her again. Blood ran down the knife more freely than the first incision. Twin streams, one more fed than the other, intertwined down the handle and became a single red river running into my soaking palm. The pained screech that wretched from Lana's throat, only centimeters from the knife's edge, filled me with infinite strength. She would answer. I would make her.

"I'm telling you the truth, you idiot," she spat. "I found it on the ground, and I thought it looked cool. After I saw all the feet in the water, I was like, oh, I guess I have to cut off their feet. Their tissue is soft, so I could manage it with that little thing. You have it back now, so why are you freaking out? You need to look around. Maybe start with someone you live with, huh? Like her."

Lana gestured toward Hanna with her eyes. I looked at Hanna and saw her gazing out the window again. She was lost in the green stretching out before her. I said her name, but she wouldn't move. I repeated her name, and she turned. Our eyes met, but I couldn't see her. She simply wasn't there.

"Are you okay?" I asked.

"If you're going to slit her throat, you should just do it," she said. "I don't see how else we'll be able to leave this situation. It doesn't matter, right? You can keep thinking she catfished your grandma, and then you get to feel like you solved it."

"I need to hear her say she did it."

"Dickhead, I didn't do it. I don't even know your grandma. I don't care about any of this," Lana grunted. "Hanna is starting to sound guilty to me, to be honest."

Hanna couldn't have done it. That wouldn't make any sense. Why would the knife show up on the night that Lana arrived at the hostel? What were the odds of that? It couldn't be Hanna. I tried to communicate all of this to her with my eyes, but she continued to stare as though her eyes had been turned off.

"I don't want to be in this car anymore," Hanna said. "Mitch, can you hold Lana? I need to use my hands."

I held the knife to her throat a bit longer. I didn't want to give her an edge. Her eyes had shifted from frantically searching to the cold stillness of an experienced shark. A massive predatory presence filled the space around her pupils. She was anticipating my movements further ahead than I was. I waited for her to blink, and then I shut the knife and grabbed her hands.

Hanna placed her hands on the steering wheel, put the car into drive, and began accelerating down the cliffside single-lane road toward the bottom of the mountain.

"I'm going to drive us to the bottom, and we can figure out what we want to do, but I don't want to be on this road anymore," she said.

"Me neither," said Lana.

We were moving faster than we should have been. Faster than I've ever seen anyone travel on these kinds of roads. I had visions of the cow and her calf stepping out in front of us. The car would be totaled. We would all be thrown through the windshield or impaled on the dash. It would be a slaughter.

However, my instinct to support my only ally held firm. I couldn't ask Hanna to slow down. We couldn't show dissent or contradict each other in front of Lana. Could we? We couldn't show weakness in front of these people. They'd take advantage of us. I decided it would be better if I relaxed and let her drive.

"Hey, maybe you should slow down," Lana said.

Hanna revved the engine, and we flew down the road toward the densely wooded pathway at the bottom. The swollen mouth of the forest's entrance began to suffocate me as I considered the focus that would be required to pass through it unscathed. I held my breath. When we were about a quarter of a kilometer away from the base, still well over ten meters off the ground over the cliff's edge, it happened.

A lapse in consciousness fell over me for a window of time just large enough for Lana to escape my hold. I remember looking at Hanna and wondering if she was already planning it. Of course, there was no way she could have known how it would exactly come to pass, but our future was secured regardless of the route taken to arrive at it. Every path led to the same end. There was only one road.

I remember looking out over the tops of the canopies as they came closer to greet us. I thought about what it would be like to make it back to the hostel and change my clothes. My stomach yearned for food, and my eyes were heavy with sleep. Although the world around me was rushing by and the action before me was urgent and fierce, I grew tired. Blissfully tired. The idea of a warm bed filled me with such sorrowful hope and happiness, wrapped in a divine comforter so soft it made me cry. I felt, for the first time, perfectly comfortable in my chair. Warmth rushed over the whole of my skin. My eyes closed, and it happened.

Lana's hand slipped out of mine. Although the moment had taken me by surprise, she had seen it. She had been waiting for it since we left the cave. She pulled a handgun out of her pocket and immediately, most likely by accident, shot a hole through her seat and into the right rear tire.

"Shit," Lana said, attempting to regain control of the firearm whose recoil had dislodged it from her loose grip during the misfire.

Even while these events took place around me, I remember being at peace with them. I wanted it all to continue without me while I slept. I was drifting, and the tether was not yet ready to pull me back. The slack was still unraveling behind me, and I was flying.

A blast.

The sound of a firearm combined with the explosion of air from the tire and that dreaded compromised balance finally penetrated my subconscious, shaking me awake and rattling Hanna's composure. Lana regained control of the gun and excitedly fired another round. It tunneled through the air between Hanna and me and pierced the windshield without shattering it. A jagged hole accommodated the bullet as it carved a path ahead of our vehicle.

Hanna's hand strayed only briefly. Just enough. We swerved and met no resistance as we veered off the road, cleanly careening over the cliff's edge and into the sea of trees below us.

XII
FALLING

We couldn't have been in the air long. Maybe a couple seconds. However, within that usually untraceable amount of time, I slept a deeply pure, revitalizing, and dreamless sleep. An entire moonless evening passed before my eyes. For a moment, my world was atramentous, and my body was given new life. Then the car stopped.

A tree, perhaps eight meters high, was holding the vehicle's weight in its branches. We had been caught by the strength of this remarkable giant. We were saved. The odds of it. We were saved.

The moment we collided with the tree, everyone was rocked forward and forced to catch themselves without the aid of seatbelts. The seatbelts were available, but none of us had thought to use them, except for Hanna.

Hanna held her grip on the steering wheel as her seatbelt caught her. I dropped the knife on the floor in front of me and caught myself on the dash, slamming my hands against it and bending my arms like dry noodles. I would learn later that I broke my left wrist, but I was unable to feel it in the moment. All pain signals were faint calls from a reality no longer hosting my world. It had lost its sensitivity. It had become, like Leo said, a ghost hand.

Lana, who was lying in the back and unable to use any of the seatbelts, caught herself by slamming her body into the back of our chairs. As she desperately held herself from being thrown any farther, she lost her grip on the pistol again, and it rotated its way through the air between Hanna and me, barreling through the hole left behind by its most recent discharge, shattering the windshield, and falling to the forest floor below.

Unable to move my left wrist without combating screeching resistance and unaware of the damage done to it, I grabbed Lana's hair with my right hand. I cupped my left hand as much as it would allow and scooped the knife into it. The phantom sensation of its weight on my fingers skipped through my brain and squeezed the remaining tears from my eyes. Hanna grabbed Lana's hands.

"The car is going to fall," Lana said. "We need to get out of here."

"You better hope it falls, because I'm not letting you out of this car until you admit what you did," I said.

"I guess whoever you stole that gun from is the person who shot your leg," Hanna said.

"No, I shot myself on accident. I barely ever use guns."

The car teetered forward in the tree. Loud creaks and splitting wood drove blows through each of our ears. We were scared. Hanna and I locked eyes. Everyone clinging desperately to acting tough for each other.

"Just admit to whatever it is you did, and we can figure out a way to get down from here," Hanna snapped.

"Are you out of your mind? I didn't do anything to his god damn grandma. I don't give a shit about your grandma. I have nothing to admit to. This is ridiculous. You want me to admit to something I didn't do so you can feel good about murdering me? Yeah, that sounds awesome."

"You've come clean about everything else," I said. "I think. So why not come clean about this too? Do yourself a favor."

"Listen to me, you psycho," Lana said, rotating her head as much as her neck would allow. Her eye exhausted its peripheral, straining to catch a look in my own. She was trying to take my trust from me. "I don't know your grandma."

"Bullshit." I slammed my broken hand on the center console. I felt nothing as my fingers weakly flopped, and the knife fell from my hand to hit the floor again. I bent over to pick it up.

"Your hand looks broken," Lana said.

"It's fine."

"It doesn't hurt at all?"

"It's fine."

"Hanna, weigh in here. Doesn't his hand look broken?"

Hanna quietly stared back at Lana. She had no further desire to speak. My hand, mangled and unpredictable in its movement, meekly convulsed and dropped the knife again.

"You can't even hold that thing anymore," Lana laughed. "Look at you."

The rocking of my weight released another pained moan from the tree beneath our seats. The massive wooden guardian buckled under the gravity of our presence like Atlas holding an overpopulated Earth. It faltered.

I immediately leaned back. Perhaps if I had let go of Lana and pushed her farther back in the car, I could have kept it from happening. There is a reality where we're still up in that tree, and Lana is telling me everything I want to hear.

We fell.

Just before the weight distribution in our car truly submitted to the way of the world, during the final moments of our control over the situation, Hanna let go of Lana. She had hoped I would do the same but soon realized how lost I had become to my cause. My madness. She leaned over and fastened my seatbelt.

We struck the ground.

Lana was thrown from the car's backseat and brushed her way between Hanna and me. Her body folded to the narrow passage that allowed her limbs ample space to jettison through the open windshield and brutalize the ground below us with enough impact to echo a horrific thud. She didn't utter a scream. She was just gone.

Her body, wrecked and mangled roughly one meter away from our faces, relaxed as the car's nose dug into the ground and held the rear of the vehicle against the tree's trunk. We were a mirror image of Leo's truck in its sunken tomb. Blood slowly drained out from underneath her. Her spine uncurled, and she naturally rolled toward the right side of the car. As this occurred, the car finished falling over in the same direction, crushing her body against the driver's side door and propping the floor of the passenger side against the tree.

Hanna screamed. Blood, glass, skin, and skull fragments showered her like wedding rice. Lana's bones rocketed out of their assigned places in her body and generated chaos throughout the vehicle. I opened my door, released my seatbelt, climbed out, and reached for her hand. Hanna threw up on the remains of Lana's face, now a mess of human matter, metal, and glass, and released her seatbelt. She grabbed my hand and climbed out.

We stood next to the car, still propped against the tree, blood soaking through it and leaking from it as Lana's legs peeked out from underneath it. We stood quietly for a moment.

"She looks like the Wicked Witch of the East," I said, laughing nervously. "Do you know what I mean? Do they have *Wizard of Oz* in Germany? She's the witch that dies in the beginning. Like, I feel like her legs are going to curl up and—"

"I know what *The Wizard of Oz* is," Hanna said sharply. "She didn't have to die like that. She didn't have to die at all. We should have helped her. We could have put her seatbelt on."

"Don't feel too bad for her. I mean, she cut those kids up."

Hanna hugged me, and I hugged her back. She buried her face into my chest and my face into her hair. She cried, but I had no more tears to give. It was the only thing we could do. We needed something warm to keep us from going cold and losing all hope of regaining our humanity. Both of us needed to grieve over everything. After a moment, I lifted my head.

"I know she's the one who catfished my grandmother. Thank you for helping me."

The distrust that filled Hanna's eyes more with each look at me was beginning to become a concern, but I let it pass. She only glanced up at me, but our eyes connected long enough to understand that she was worried about me.

She pulled away from our embrace and briskly walked into the shadows of the dense collection of trees ahead of us. I bent down to retrieve the pistol that Lana had thrown from our vehicle and secured it in my waistband.

"Hey, now we both have one," I said. "Okay, let's figure out which way to go."

"It doesn't matter," she said as she dissolved into the tree line.

I ran after her under those dark canopies and into the thick heated humidity of the forest, and as the moon disappeared behind me, so, too, did the desires of my past.

XIII
THE SLAUGHTER

Although morning would soon cast its grace upon that evening, and a new horror of reckoning would replace the old, the forest was as dark as it had ever been. Black. No light at all. It was darker than the ocean had appeared the first time I tried my hand at surviving a car wreck. I worried that I might run out of luck by morning. If it came.

I could no longer run. I couldn't chase Hanna. After running a short distance, I slowed to a shoegazing sneak. This change of pace had partly come from both a shift in mood and the amount of viewable light that now surrounded me. Soon, the only phosphorescence I could see was cast behind me by the moon and facing the wreckage of my past. As blindness retook hold, I breathed deeply and remembered the water. I didn't know exactly where I was, but I knew which way to go. I turned ahead, extended my good hand, and pushed forward into the night.

I called Hanna's name three times, losing more of my voice with every attempt, but she did not respond. However, I doubt she would have reacted even if she was right beside me. There was no reason to worry about her.

I tripped over exposed roots and broke through many spiderwebs, the occupants of which clung to my clothing and dug in with skin-crawling persistence. My shirt had become moist from sweat, fog, other people, and whatever else. I shook and wiped myself with my dead hand after each gentle silk screen broke across my blind face. At least the absence of feeling in that hand would protect me from the sensation of having to make further contact with these foul creatures.

The hand I used to probe the air in front of me, unfortunately, took the brunt of deflecting unwanted interactions with spiderwebs along with a torture tunnel of sharp branches and jagged edges to a wall at one point that seemed to form around me. I think I passed through a short stone tunnel, free of obstacles, somehow, ideally during my walk. I'll never be certain if that happened. I shudder to imagine my despair had my face been met by a cold rock wall during my wandering.

Shadows played their games with me. Monsters and murderers lurked around every corner that I constructed in my mind's eye. I felt spirits approach me and leave my side. My urge to push forward was only kept aflame by a spark of a feeling just barely strong enough to know now when it was most needed. Something kept me moving when I could have just as easily curled up into a ball on the ground and cried as beings of the dark consumed my pathetic body. What a joke to be killed by the bedtime horrors of the forest floor when such hellish creatures were emerging from the depths of the sea and monsters were making themselves known.

It must be similar to the feeling a swimmer has when they're lost at sea. That drive to keep swimming for great distances when they otherwise couldn't. A pulse that grows not only in rhythm and intensity, but depth. It's a fuller, highly detailed pulse capable of so much more. It's proof that living things are programmed to stay alive.

At various points throughout the walk, every member of my family appeared before me and jabbed my progress with startling anguish. Short yelps escaped my belly upon each sighting. However, an immense testament to the human mind's ability to protect itself from trauma, I had grown so used to terrible visions by this point, and the waking nightmares were becoming familiar. The sight of my grandmother's ghost no longer filled me with ill displeasure. Although I had not gotten her money back, I had found the person responsible for her pain and taken back her power. There were times, though, when I saw Lana's face swirling around me in the darkness, smiling. And then I saw the kids' bodies, and I was afraid.

After what felt like several kilometers of slowly creeping through the forest and fending off startling sensations, a welcomed sound pierced the dome of infinite obscurity imprisoning me, and it filled me with hope. The unsteadiness of my future was the most pressing fear, and it was partially relieved when that beautiful noise greeted me with its whispering crash. I could hear the waves of the ocean.

I started to pick up my pace. I wasn't running, but I was going as fast as the darkness would safely allow. To fall on my wrist and injure it further would be devastating. The longer the shadows held me, though, the more I felt like I was back in that water, drowning and screaming for salvation. I ran faster. My heart drove fear and movement throughout my body. Finally, I saw a small glimmer of light through the trees ahead, and the shadows gradually peeled away.

As I pressed forward, the sliver of light became many slivers. Like lightning flashing deep within a cave or claws tearing through black construction paper, the wall of lightless woods was falling apart before my eyes. Soon, I was close enough for it to touch me. I stopped to feel it. I reveled in it.

The sun was rising, and the fog was falling away. As I pushed through the final few trees, I squinted and saw the road with the coast beyond it. The waves crashed against the cliff's edge and misted the air above the rocks. Then I saw her.

Hanna was standing on the side of the road and staring out at the water.

I called her name, but she did not respond. So I softly approached her and touched her shoulder. She didn't turn. She continued to gaze out at the water. I turned my head, and the terror against which I had counted myself blinded revealed itself to me.

At first, I noticed that the air had cleared immensely since dawn. The thick mist that once hung in the air was gone. As if it clung to and dissolved with it any air pollution in the area before its arrival, the air was cleaner than I had seen it over the last year. I felt like there was no limit to the distance of my sight, and it proved to be a very unlucky day to possess and explore such capabilities.

Across the small temples of ocean waves moving with and through each other like dimples passing beneath luscious hair, splashing crystals into the air that glittered and glinted at me from afar, there was the small island in the middle of the harbor. It's visible sometimes, but it's usually the first to become obscured on foggy days. Last night, I couldn't see it at all. We could only imagine what was taking place there. But this morning, I could see it as if we were sharing the same patch of land. It felt like it was right next to us, and I so desperately wanted to be as far away from the scene taking place there as possible.

A cluster of ships was rocking with the waves next to the small patch of beach facing us on the island's coast. To call it an island was being generous. It was more of a skerry, although larger than most, touching the water with the bottom of a shallow cliff's edge that was most likely submerged at one point in the recent past. The mouth of this small beach edge exhaled an event that my memory continues begging my mind to repress.

One monster, sea creature, whatever they were, enormous titans of the deep that fit two to a vessel with tendrils and fleshy strings hanging off the side, was held in the air by a crane reaching out from land. It dragged the colossal beast's wretched body against the wind and toward the island. Next to it sat a large machine. From where we were, it appeared to be a big metal box with an opening on top. The crane strained under the weight of the monster as it took position.

The air between us cracked as the crane dropped the creature into the box, and a squelching, choked gargle splat and sputtered and ricocheted off the edges of it. Harsh metal grinding and death cries rippled across the water's surface, and a pulse wave of sound punched both Hanna and me in our lungs. The blood-curdling, sea-boiling screech of that otherworldly haunt. It rattles through my mind as clearly today as it did when it happened. They were being slaughtered.

We then realized how many were on board the surrounding ships. When that noise bellowed from the machine now breaking down and processing the creature's blood and organs into usable material, movement awakened above the water.

Two beasts were on the deck of every ship. There were at least twenty boats that I could see. They thrashed, squelched, and four of them broke free. The newly freed monsters rolled into the water and immediately took advantage. One ship capsized. The crew on deck swam to shore, although most did not emerge from the water. The others picked up weapons that must have been stowed on land already for this exact reason and began firing into the ocean. Every ship began firing on the monsters in the water and those still restrained. They were firing weapons I had never seen before, tools designed explicitly for this purpose. These things.

The seawater did not turn pink or red, but a moaning wicked purple as a cloud of blood maneuvered its way through the wreckage, growing with each being—both human and sea beast—thrashing in the water. There were hundreds of people scattered about the boats, land, and water. Some were burning holes in the creatures and sedating them. Many of the creatures had already passed. Some were alive, and the humans nearby had their limbs removed from their bodies and discarded into the water as the beasts tore through them. Bloody waste discolored the entire harbor. They were wasting it, whatever it was. Those precious life juices. I felt a loss for humanity as the prized resource returned to the sea.

"Oh my god," I said. Hanna watched, unblinking.

Each scream worked together to form a visible obstruction in the air. The sum of all noise formed an unbelievable mass. The air shook and fell apart. The leviathan of sound seemed to be degrading the air from the inside out. Flakes of sky fell, twisted, and rotted. The surface of the water vibrated, and droplets danced above the waves. The area glowed brighter as the fighting got louder. Ships began to pull away. The crane dropped a few more monsters into the slaughtering box before the water beneath them suddenly emitted a harsh and blinding light. The circumference of the circle of light looked to be about the same as the one that had appeared beneath me during our mission to retrieve the tires. I grabbed Hanna's hand.

"Let's go," I said.

We turned to our right and started walking with hurried, instinctual purpose. Then, a sudden explosion pushed us into the street and away from the water. It was not a fiery explosion, but pure sound, like a sonic boom. It was physical pieces of air clacking into one another at incredible speed. It was the fabric of our physical world tearing and splitting apart.

Shielding our eyes as light stretched out of the water, blinding even the sun that had come to greet the new day, we were careful not to look back at the unfolding events as we made our way along the coastline. Soon, I knew where we were. We were near the bait shop. The Fuel Diver was in sight. We were near home.

"We're almost there," I said.

I started running, pulling Hanna along with me with my good hand. If we could just get home. Home to the Fuel Diver. If we could barricade ourselves inside, then we could ride out this ugly ordeal. It would be better once we got inside. We just needed to be inside of something safe.

Unfortunately, my excitement caused me to trip and attempt to catch myself with my broken wrist.

The bone broke apart further and pierced through my skin. It was not necessarily a gory mess, although there were now bits of bone exposed to the sea air and squeezing blood out of the tight breaks in skin and along their grooves. There wasn't as much blood as I thought there should have been after thinking about it.

This sight was enough to entirely pull Hanna out of her daze, and she started tending to the wound. Bringing her back was crucial because I was no longer myself.

"You should take off your shirt and wrap it around the wound," Hanna said. "I can help."

Removing my shirt felt like it would only make me cold, which would greatly shock my already compromised immune system, and it would increase the likelihood of further injuring my hand. However, she was right that I would need to cover the bleeding for now, and I wasn't going to suggest using her shirt.

Clumsily, Hanna helped me pull my shirt over my head and pass my arms through the sleeves without pulling my bones any farther out of my body. She reacted a couple times as though she had accidentally done something that should have caused me considerable pain, but my shirt was over my eyes for those moments. I still couldn't feel anything. With the cloth now fastened safely to my arm, we continued.

"There's fish medicine somewhere in the bait shop," I said. "Erika used it on me earlier. We'll find that, and it'll be okay."

"Will it be able to mend shattered bone? This break is really bad, Mitch."

"It'll make things better. It'll be an improvement, at least."

Muted and mangled, my dark purple and bloody flesh looked back at me with as much disbelief as I looked at it. The wicked purples. I got lost in the world of color produced by my injury as I took in the total destruction that my body had endured. My brain was simply attached to a machine breaking down under my control. Temporarily faulty wiring was the only thing protecting me from colossal pain and contributing to the cloud of screams that were still echoing behind us. Before that useful misfortune subsided, I needed to make it to the bait shop.

The light shined brightly, dimmed, waned, glared brilliantly, and then a goliath flushing shot crisp moisture into the air. Neither one of us strayed. Instead, we stared down the road toward our goal, blocking our eyes from the dreadful radiance across the water. I could taste the seawater in the air, and it was rancid.

When we rounded the next corner, the bait shop greeted us with a warm glow from behind its flannel curtains. Arthur, the white cat, sat looking out at us from the windowsill. He slowly blinked at us as we approached. The sharp edges of his pupils narrowed and expanded. Then he jumped down and skipped into another part of the shop.

"Do you remember where it is?" Hanna asked.

"No. I was also blind when she was using it on me, so…"

Hanna opened the door, and we went inside.

The once offensive odor of the bait shop was again a welcomed old friend compared to the sensory carnage outside. Our energy calmed slightly. We searched behind the counter, in the back, in the supply closet, but none of the items appeared to have miracle healing properties. Hanna went into the connecting bar and searched. Nothing.

"Want another drink?" Hanna asked, smiling. It was the first smile I had seen on her face in hours.

"Yeah."

She walked behind the counter and grabbed the two glasses we had used earlier in the evening. We both drank a full glass of water, per her instruction, which I respected and was grateful for, and then she poured us both a beer.

As I took my first sip, Arthur sat and watched us. He looked at me with a loving, eager expression and slowly blinked. I scratched his head with my good hand, and the little cat began to purr. Then he turned and looked back at me as though he wanted me to follow him. I trusted him. Setting my beer down, I rose to follow. I thought he wanted to take me to the medicine until that smell filled my nostrils and ruined our brief respite.

Arthur had not brought me to the medicine. Instead, he had led me to the corpse of the teenage boy that Hanna had shot earlier that evening. The little white cat, still so clean, had eaten a piece of his face. A hole sat where there was once a nose, exposing a volcano of human tissue and decaying blood. Arthur licked a small drop of red off his back leg and looked up at me with pure delight, as though he had found exactly what we were looking for and answered all our prayers.

I thought about the boy I had stabbed. I hadn't been able to smell them until I saw him, but they soon became the only odor. It poisoned my mind. The stench of it. I walked back outside, and Hanna followed.

"Are you sure she left it here? Maybe she took her first aid stuff with her. I can't find anything useful."

"Let's go to the Fuel Diver," I said. "It's not here."

The sky returned to normal brightness, and the sun was again alone in its duty to illuminate the world. The air was calm. Screams were no longer cracking and fracturing the air around us. We stoically made our way up the road to the Fuel Diver, making sure to look away from the water. I did not want to see anything but the road. At this moment, here in this field of vision, everything felt manageable. It was as though nothing had happened, and Hanna and I were sharing a typical morning. On an average day, we would soon be changing shifts.

We got back to the hostel and found that it was still empty. The door to Lana's room stood wide open. Hanna closed it while I went inside the main building to shower.

After standing in the shower and crying for five or ten minutes, and then carefully cleaning my wound while desperately trying to keep myself from unblocking the barrier in my brain for pain in that area of my body, I walked into my room. I put on a fresh set of my own clothes. We had a basic first aid kit, which Hanna had found and set outside the bathroom for me. I bandaged myself with warm, clean bandages and returned to the main living area.

Hanna was sitting in the kitchen, eating potato chips.

"There's fish in the fridge, but I didn't want any," she said.

"Yeah," I said.

"Good shower?"

"Amazing."

"Can I help you with your bandages?"

"All good." I showed her my wrist. "Thank you."

She popped a chip in her mouth, dusted off her hands, and faced the chip bag toward me.

"I think I'm going to grab a shower too," she said as she walked to the bathroom.

I sat at the table and ate a couple chips. My mind wandered, and I floated in the feeling of being safe, even if we weren't. I thought about watching a movie and walked over to the computer to find one. That's when I saw it. A wallet.

It was a dark, waterproof wallet. It looked familiar. I opened it to reveal Leo's driver's license.

"Hey, I found Leo's wallet," I called to Hanna through the wall.

"Oh yeah, he was dropping stuff all over the place when he came in last night. He was nervous and being weird. I see why now. Poor guy. It's nice that we still have that, I guess."

I leafed through the stacks of various business cards, discount cards, punch cards, credit cards, family member photographs, and everything else. I took in a snapshot of his life and thought about his smile and the night he died in front of me. Then I saw her.

Inside Leo's wallet, lightly hidden behind everything else, was a photograph of my grandmother.

XIV
A NEW DAY

Hanna emerged from the bathroom wearing a fresh outfit from her luggage with her hair wrapped in a thick blue towel. The past few hours were wiped from her shimmering eyes, and she inhaled meditatively before releasing a restful sigh. She leisurely walked to the computer and perused movie titles before turning to smile at me, noticing the wallet still sitting in my hands.

"Oh," she said abruptly, "I almost forgot. God, that shower was wonderful. What did you see in Leo's wallet?"

I produced the photograph of my grandmother before realizing that Hanna had never seen her and would have no idea what she looked like. She gazed at the photo and back at me with a puzzled expression.

"Who is that?"

"It's my grandmother Elaine," I said. "He had a picture of her in his wallet."

Hanna took a pause to contemplate the best way to proceed with me. I was clearly very emotional, and I had made a tremendous mistake, sentencing Lana to death over a crime she did not commit. I gave her time, and she gave me mine.

"So the knife was his," she said.

"Yeah," I said.

"Did they know each other?"

"I didn't know about it if they did."

"You think he was the catfish?"

"I don't know."

She closed the gap between us and sat next to me, gently collecting the photograph from my hands to examine it. Then she flipped it over to reveal the writing on the back.

Dear Leo,

Even when we're a world apart,

I'm still in your pocket.

Love,

Elaine

"Maybe they were in love," Hanna said. "I mean, like, why would he keep it if he was only using her for money? And why would he use his real name?"

I took the photo back and stood up. Visions of burning the cursed image ran wildly through my mind. It would be a service to her to incinerate this photo and any evidence of her momentary lapse in judgment with this man who must have lied to her.

Why did he use his real name? I'll admit, it did make me consider the possibility that they were mutually benefitting long-distance lovers at some point and that I just didn't know about it. Elaine had her own life going on. She never really opened up to me entirely about her relationship issues. Probably for the best that she didn't. No grandmother wants to burden their grandchildren with the affairs of lovesick elders, and I didn't really want to hear about it. Still, the odds of it. Wouldn't she have told him about me? Maybe she did.

Soon, the gas stovetop was lit, and I was holding the photo to it, watching the corner curl. Hanna appeared at my side and turned the gas off, but the image was still burning in my hand. Elaine's smile warped, and her hair turned to ash. The photo was knocked from my grip into the sink and extinguished before further damage could be done.

"I want to burn it so that there isn't any evidence of her mistake," I said.

"It doesn't make the world any better to have one less photograph of your grandmother. If you want to preserve her memory, then don't remove pieces of it. Just take it back. It's yours now. Enjoy it," she said.

Owning a burnt photograph that my grandmother had given to a man who drained her of her financial and emotional wealth until she committed suicide didn't feel like a win by any means, but Hanna was right. I would eventually feel glad that I still had the photo. In fact, I would later regret burning it as much as I did. There would even be times when I felt angry at Hanna for not stopping me sooner, and I would laugh at how silly such thoughts were.

She took the photo from the sink and gently dried it off with a towel. I walked into the employee quarters, where all our bunks sat empty, while she laid it on the counter. Sitting on my bed, I was soon overtaken by exhaustion. I curled into a ball and stared out at the wall in front of me.

Hanna entered the room and sat on the bed next to mine.

"You probably haven't slept in a while. You'd normally be done with your shift by now," she said.

"Yeah," I said.

"I'm probably not going to work today," she laughed. "I think I'm going to sleep in. I know I'm the one who is supposed to relieve you. Sorry."

I smiled weakly in an effort to keep the lighthearted mood that Hanna had so graciously brought into the room aloft between us. Our little den filled with warmth. She stood up, grabbed a blanket off one of the other beds, and draped it over my fetal posture. Then she lay on her own bed.

"Thanks," I whispered.

"Do you want to try to walk back into town? We need to get to the hospital if we can't find any monster stuff. We'll probably need a hospital even with it. I don't know how magical it actually is. I guess I'm not sure what we should do to proceed. Everything got so strange."

"Let's try again," I whispered. "I just need to sleep a little bit."

"Fair."

As we lay in the quiet comfort and protection of our room, I fell asleep before Hanna did. I'm sure, because the last memory I had before drifting away into a dreamless rest was hearing Hanna lock the door. The ease I felt with the click of that lock was the final push I needed to finally lose consciousness.

***

I'm not sure how long we were asleep, but it couldn't have been very long because the daylight outside felt the same. The feeling in my hand had returned, and pure searing pain overwhelmed any relief I had received from that much-needed nap. I winced hard, shutting my eyes as tightly as I could to release the horrendous pressure coursing through my body. Tears streamed down my face as I looked over to see Hanna sitting up awake.

"Did you hear that too?" she asked.

Thinking I had woken up on my own out of agony, I shook my head. I had no idea that the reason I was awake was due to the rumbling commotion of footsteps in the kitchen. Hanna stood up, and I followed her. Luckily, we had brought our weapons into the bedroom with us. She held her handgun, and I held Lana's.

"Who's out there?" I said quieter than I wanted, with my broken wrist overriding most of my attention. The movement stopped, and there was no reply.

"You'd better answer," Hanna shouted through the door.

Still, there was nothing. Hanna set her hand on the door handle and looked at me. I nodded, and she turned the knob.

The door swung open, and we stood on either side of the door frame as an evasive maneuver in case any violent dangers were triggered by the first sign of movement. Stillness. I poked my head around the corner to see a room that looked largely empty. Hanna and I stepped out and were soon greeted by Erika sitting at the kitchen table, reaching in the chip bag and pulling a handful of crispy potato skins to her mouth. She wiped her hands together and spilled crumbs onto the table in front of her.

"Hey," she said. "You two are finally up. The door was locked, so I didn't want to intrude. Thought maybe you were fucking. I haven't been here long. Come on, come sit with me."

We continued standing.

"Where is everyone?" Hanna asked.

"The harvest was insane," Erika laughed, "but it went really well, thanks for asking. Super powerful batch too. A lot of people said it was one of the best ones ever. It's never perfect, they were saying, which makes sense, but we had a lot of tools they didn't have last time. So it was easier than it could have been. I mean, damn, last time was seventy-five years ago. I bet it was a bloodbath. I can't imagine doing it without the tools we had. I don't even know how they did it."

"Where is everyone?" I asked.

"Who are you talking about?" she asked.

"Our coworkers," Hanna said.

"Oh, I don't know. I don't work here. I came up because I wanted to see if you guys were here. I saw some of your stuff. I found the note you wrote to the guests, Mitch. Cute."

I looked at the spot where the picture of my grandmother had been placed by Hanna and saw that it was missing.

"Where did the picture that was sitting there go?" I asked.

Erika looked at the counter and back at me with a confused expression. She shrugged and focused her attention back on the chips in front of her. After a few more crunches, she cleared her throat and dusted off her hands again.

"Listen, you guys, there are men outside that have guns and knives and whatever else you have too, okay? If you want to be tough, they'll be tough, but I don't want to do that with you. I'm not here to hurt you. So please, put that stuff away and sit with me."

Outside stood four men that I had never seen before. They appeared to be fishermen, but I couldn't be sure they weren't simply dressed like that because of the current situation. Erika motioned a hand toward the seats in front of her, and Hanna and I followed her example.

"Mitch, your hand looks terrible," she said. "Holy shit. I bet the feeling has returned to it at this point. It must hurt so bad, oh my god."

She crunched another handful of chips in her mouth, splitting their bodies into millions of shattered fragments and spilling their entrails on the table in front of her.

"Yes," I said.

"I don't know why I keep dusting my hands off if I'm just going to eat more chips," she laughed. "When I used the fish medicine stuff on you before, it has, like, a numbing effect on any pain you experience for a while after you use it. But there's no way you're still enjoying those effects at this point. Oh my god, wow, the bone is sticking out. Yeah, that's really bad."

"Do you have any of that stuff?" I asked.

"Not on me, but there's some in the car outside. Tell you what, listen to what I have to say, and I'll get it for you."

"Just go get it now," Hanna said. "He needs it."

"Oh, he needs it?" Erika sneered sarcastically. "It's not going to kill you to feel the pain a little longer. Take solace in the fact that instant relief is on its way. I don't know if the stuff will be able to fix a break that bad. I mean, wow, a doctor would need to do, like, serious surgery on this thing, but we can try. Maybe it will. It'll at least take the pain away, you know. It'll do something."

"Say what you came to say," I snapped, the miserable pulse of my discomfort pounding in my mind. Erika ate one more chip and dusted off her hands for the last time.

"One of those guys outside will drive you both back into town. They'll take you to a hospital, and then you can get to the airport from there. Obviously, this place is no longer in need of employees. We're going to have to figure out something to do with it. Get your stuff together, and let's get you home. You probably don't even want to be here anymore, I bet."

"How do we know you aren't going to kill us?" Hanna asked.

"There's no reason to. It's over. I'm not a psycho. We'll just give you a couple drops for the pain and send you on your way."

"Why didn't you kill me before? In the water," I asked.

"You were so pathetic and flailing around. You kept screaming. It made me sad. Like I said, I'm not a psycho."

"What if we tell someone about all this?"

"Go ahead. Got any more questions?" Erika asked in an eager and confident voice. She smiled and pointed at my arm. "I know you probably want to get that wrist taken care of."

Hanna and I looked at each other, and she could tell what I was thinking.

"Can I have the picture back, please?" I turned my head to face Erika.

"What picture?" she asked.

"The one in your pocket."

Erika smiled and pulled the photograph of my grandmother out of her pocket.

"Oh, you mean this. I thought this was trash," she said. "I was going to throw it away."

"Do you know who that is?" I asked.

"I think it's one of Leo's old girlfriends. Poor guy."

"Did he ever take money from her?" I asked, breathing heavily.

"I don't know," she said.

"Did you ever pretend to be Leo to take money from her?" I asked, now shaking.

Erika laughed and shook her head, but she didn't speak. Her face contorted in a performance of honesty, and she closed her eyes. She faltered. She was lying. While she choked on her words, I held up the pistol, but my arm was heavy, which caused the rest of my body to move slowly under painful duress. She drew her gun, but Hanna drew hers faster. Fire.

The four men from outside entered the room, and soon, a red cloud draped over our shoulders and laid to rest on the ground beneath our feet. The spiritual energy shifted, and an immense weight was lifted. I took the photograph from Erika's pocket and placed it in my own. Hanna and I gathered our belongings and walked outside to a parked yellow pickup truck with the engine still running.

XV
HOME AGAIN

As Hanna drove us down the short cliffside and we passed the rows of filthy boats anchored near the dock, I applied an enormous helping of the extraordinarily painful chemicals to my wound, dumping almost the entire bottle. The bone twisted, gnarled, and cracked back into place. A loud *tick* pronounced the fusion of my bone back into its original form. My exposed skeleton and perverted flesh cooed, stretched, and burned as it tidied and folded itself back together. The door to my arm shut, and only a faded scar remained.

I couldn't feel it, and it didn't move very well, but those lingering issues would be resolved soon. In the truck's bed, under a blue tarp, sat hundreds of glass containers full of that enchanting liquid.

The shore continued to volley small groupings of severed feet back and forth from the shoreline. Mauve seawater ushered them along their journey as it transitioned from light purple to dark and back to light. Most of them had either been cleaned up, sunk, or eaten by the slowly reemerging sea life. The few that strung along the shoreline would be cleaned, the ocean's color would drift back to blue, and the world would move on in short order soon enough.

Passing the bait shop, I peeked in through the flannel curtains at the warm glow of the merriment inside. Both the bait shop and bar were lit up and full of fishermen. The bar owners, Ron and Julia, were serving drinks. They all appeared to be toasting to a day well caught. It didn't seem that anyone was grieving. I coul'd not see if the bodies of those two boys were still inside, but the general atmosphere did not presume the presence of decomposing teenagers.

Before the shop window was far enough behind our vehicle to obstruct my ability to see through it, I saw their white cat, Arthur, jump up on the windowsill as if to see us off. He licked his paw and groomed his little fuzzy face, and then he disappeared.

Of course, we were worried that following this road again would perhaps feed us back onto another road that made little sense, and we would return to having visions of horrible creatures. The call of the mountain to pull us back to its core shook my newly numbed body, but miraculously we continued on the road as normal into town.

"Do you still need a hospital?" Hanna asked.

"No," I said, flexing my hand as much as it would allow, its cramped tightness loosening with each movement. "I think we can just go."

"What should we do with all of it?" She gestured to the truck bed as the sound of hundreds of clinking glass containers danced around her words.

"Let's send half of it to your place back home and half of it to mine. We'll just say it's alcohol or something. I want to keep my half, at least. It'll probably come in handy," I laughed.

Hanna nodded, and we headed to a post office to arrange for our packages to be delivered to our respective home countries, the price of which was staggering. I had enough for a plane ticket, but Hanna had to lend me money for the postage. I promised that I would pay her back, and she eased my insecurity with her eyes. It was simply what friends did for each other.

***

We found our way to the nearest airport and parked the car in the long-term parking area. I worried about the car's eventual tow and impoundment once we abandoned it. I felt sad for it. It had helped us. I laid my warmer hand, full of touch, on its hood and said goodbye.

I asked Hanna if she wanted to continue traveling together, but she politely declined. She wanted to see her friends and return to her life in Germany.

"I am done traveling for a little while after this," she said.

"For sure," I said.

I didn't feel ready to return home, but I understood her position. Similarly, I could not stay on this island any longer, but I did feel a need to prolong this feeling. Not knowing what else to do, I bought a ticket to return home to Chicago. Once I regrouped, I would find a new place to travel. Maybe I would visit Hanna.

Beer filled our bellies and relaxed our tongues as we sat at the bar after buying our tickets and getting through the light security. Hanna and I reminisced about times we had throughout our stay at the Fuel Diver before the clock struck and the world turned. We talked of silly days and mundane annoyances we harbored toward the other employees. We looked back with admiration at all that we had seen of this beautiful country. The events of a small group of hours near the end did not have to commandeer and ruin the trip as a whole, no matter how significant those events were.

We drank until we could no longer afford drinks, or Hanna decided she no longer wanted to pay for mine. Her flight began boarding, and she gave me her contact information along with one last hug before running to her gate and tripping over her bag in front of the forty other people waiting in line.

She laughed, shot back up, and waved at me. As long as we were within sight of each other, it didn't matter what the people around us thought. They had no idea. We were the only two who understood each other.

Then she disappeared beyond the gate, and she was gone.

I sat in a chair and looked out the window as I waited for my plane to begin boarding. The flight was later in the evening, and the crowd turned over as the sun lowered on the horizon. The most distant stars were again granted passage to shine brightly through the darkened atmosphere, drenching our side of the planet. No longer a drink in my hand, I drank in the night sky. I consumed the stars above me.

I watched them twinkle and adjust themselves. The glittering bulbs repositioned and realigned, and I gasped as they organized the story of the sky. They moved around like words on a page, but each word contained an entire saga of its own. Billions of abbreviated fantasies flickered and postured before my dewy eyes, compressed in my window of vision. The more distant stars felt like ancient folk tales that were losing permanence in the minds of storytellers. I considered the fact that their glow dulled from where I sat, but if they were brought closer, they would shine so brightly that the night would turn to day, and whether for better or worse, the world would be changed.

The galaxies above my head filled me with a pleasant calm. I reflected on the speed of forgotten life and how light can only preserve so much before it's lost to radiation beyond our control. Every single star was a moment in time that desperately screamed its history to the closest eyes that could still grasp its brilliance. All this light and so few eyes to remember it.

I did not want that moment that defined me in so many ways to be lost to time. I wished the star of this moment would continue shining as a reminder of our adventure long after I am unable to recount it. Above all else, I wanted the memory of my grandmother to be preserved as the reliable beacon to lost travelers in the night sky that I knew her to be. So I asked for a pen and paper from the airport staff.

After a couple distasteful looks that would surely be recorded in my cataloging of events, they found me an airport notepad and a pen, and I began writing. My writing hand was, of course, the hand I had injured, but the chemicals were almost complete with their work. Rebelling against the minor stiffness I felt, I wrote throughout the entire plane ride and continued writing once I arrived home in the United States. Each night, gazing up at the stars, I thought about the back of Leo's truck, and I wondered if he knew who I was. I wondered if he had put it together or if it was put together for him. Did he know what Erika had done to the woman he loved? I wondered if death could be so wise.

A small, dimly lit star shined its brightest before disappearing, and I lowered my head to sleep, taking comfort in the fact that my past was nothing more than distant, dazzling light.

Acknowledgments

THANK YOU TO Grace Ehlinger, Nathan Miller, Ansel Arnold, Ryan Sparks, Collin Hegemeyer, and Evan Clark for helping me figure out a lot of these stories. They wouldn't be the same without your careful eyes. Thank you as well to everyone at Trepidatio Publishing for publishing this book. And thank you to my family for being my family.

About the Author

AUSTIN MOONEY is a writer and editor based in Chicago. Initially interested in comedy, horror soon became his focus, and the two forces mix throughout his work. His stories have been featured in the Black Hare Press horror anthology, Horror Tree's "Trembling With Fear," *Allegory* magazine, and the horror podcast *What If It's True*. Blurring the line between real and imaginary, he loves to create exciting worlds where anything can happen and characters laugh in the face of terror.

www.ingramcontent.com/pod-product-compliance
Lightning Source LLC
Chambersburg PA
CBHW030254270626
47156CB00022B/2727